Something Beyond A Dream

a novel

JO COTE

ISBN: 979-8-218-63628-9

For my daughter, Bellamy

Something Beyond A Dream

When life offers you something beyond a dream, it's not unreasonable to grieve when it's come to an end

Chapter One

The sun cut through the marine layer and a cool summer breeze lofted through the town as people strolled the streets above the dock chatting and laughing with each other. You could hear the old familiar coos of the seagulls, and watch as sailboats came in to dock. Nathan loved days like these, the true essence of summer. He had just finished up his last year at the academy and started working for the marina again. This wasn't where he planned on working forever, but until he was placed on active duty for Sitka's finest, this is where he loved to be. Working at the marina had always been a place he called home. He had been working there every summer since he was eleven—every summer since things at home had become too much to handle.

"Hey Tommy, wanna grab a bite? I'm just about finished up over here."

"Yeah man, let's go to the Spar. I could use a nice cool down; it's hot today." Tommy said as he dipped his hand in the water and wiped it along his forehead.

Nathan finished tying the sloop up to the dock and playfully smacked his friend on the back as he made his way up the ramp.

"Hi, uh—two please. And can we sit near the back window by any chance?" Nathan asked the hostess politely.

Tommy shook his head in pity as they made their way to the back of the dining room. "You know she's never gonna notice you." His voice tainted in mirth as they took their seats.

"Maybe not yet, but one day she will." He smiled as he watched her walking towards them.

Tess wore a pale-yellow blouse with white shorts, her skin was subtly sun-kissed from working on the deck and her wild, reddish-brown curls framed her face in a way that made her green eyes even more striking. She walked towards them with a small spring in her step and a smile that made his heart stop.

Tess had moved to Sitka three months ago from North Carolina. When she moved she told everyone back home it was because she was offered a great job and after everything with Bobby, she felt like she needed to take this chance. The truth was there was never a job waiting for her in Alaska, only the prayer of a new beginning.

She never really fit in back home, she always knew she was meant to be somewhere else, maybe even *be* someone else. She just needed a change of scenery and a chance to start fresh, somewhere where no one knew her name. Sitka seemed to be the perfect place.

She fell in love with the small town after a trip with her girlfriends a few years back. When she arrived she barely had enough to rent a little cabin, but she didn't mind the small space, she didn't need much. A new start was more than she could hope for. Within a few days of arriving she got a job at a local diner on the waterfront. The Spar's owner seemed to take pity on her after listening to her explain her financial situation, or maybe people here were just willing to help someone in need. He hired her right on the spot.

She loved working there, she was always near the water and the people were genuinely kinder than necessary. After a few weeks of working she could spot who was from the town, who was passing through, and who ordered what if they were regulars. In such a short time she had already grown attached to the small town. Nothing had ever felt like home before, but she finally felt at peace, like just maybe she would find her place here.

"Hi boys, warm out there huh?" She smirked to herself. It was incredible to her that sixty degrees made everyone in Alaska act like they were melting. The natives here just really don't understand what actual "heat" is.

"Very warm. Enjoy today, mid-summer is here, and I'll bet by tomorrow this place will be crawling." Nathan spoke as he studied her face.

Her mouth would curl into a small, delicate smile as she spoke, and when she would need to concentrate she would tuck a loose strand of hair behind her ear and gently clasp her bottom lip with her teeth.

"I guess we'll see if your predictions are right tomorrow." She gave a soft wink.

"Girl is that all you do? Is work?" Tommy huffed out with a laugh.

She shot a venomous look at him that made Nathan almost spit out his sip of water in laughter.

"I'll have you know I do have a life outside of this place mister." She chided with conviction.

"Don't mind Tommy, sometimes he doesn't think before he speaks."

Nathan glared over at him when Tess wasn't looking. Tommy lifted his shoulders apologetically.

"No worries, besides you're harmless anyway aren't you Tommy?" She teased playfully touching his shoulder.

"Yeah, yeah. So then, Tess, what *do* you do for fun?" Tommy poked.

"Well lots—not that I can think of anything at the moment—" She blushed; a little embarrassed that in all honesty, she couldn't remember the last time she did anything fun or just for herself.

"Leave the poor girl alone Tommy. We'll have our usual. Thanks Tess."

She gave him a silent thank you for saving her from having to answer, and a warm smile before she left for the kitchen.

"Nathan, man, you gotta make a move—*do* something." Tommy urged as they made their way back down to the marina.

"I know, but I don't wanna scare her off. I have it under control." Nathan said as he climbed onto the sailboat.

"Yeah, right." Tommy murmured under his breath.

Nathan shot Tommy a scowl even though he couldn't see it.

"Look all I'm saying is, Tess is a catch, and if you don't make a move soon, someone else will."

"Like who? You?" Nathan retorted knowing Tommy would never do something like that, not when Nathan had so plainly been interested in her.

"No, I'm just saying—"

"Yeah, I got it."

Tommy lifted his shoulders and let them down with a heavy sigh before he went back to work. Nathan shook his head at his friend, but deep down he knew Tommy was right. Tess was not only gorgeous, she was one of the sweetest persons he had ever met. She ensnared the attention of everyone in her presence. Any guy would be crazy not to want her. He tried to shake the thought from his mind as he focused back on work.

He loved the feel of the sea breeze caressing his face, or the sound of the water lapping up at the edges of the wooden beauty. He had been working on MARTHA II for a few weeks now, preparing it for the captain. It was his favorite, the true wooden beauty of an old sloop, with its classy, black stripe that accented the white and tan of the wood. Its massive sail post loomed high overhead; he couldn't wait to get her out into the water.

"You takin' her out there today?" Tommy hollered over to Nathan as he watched Nathan staring at the boat in admiration.

"Yeah, I'm gonna check the sails today, make sure everything's workin' properly." Nathan said with exuberance.

Tommy laughed at his friend, that man couldn't resist the call of the ocean.

Nathan heaved at the main halyard, tugging the sails down into place, and watched as the great, white sails descended and expanded into giant wings. A gentle current was guiding the boat out of the marina and with the help of the sea breeze; MARTHA II was well on her way out to sea. As soon as she had passed the daybreak and was sea bound, Nathan looked up at the sails taking off in a rush of wind and whooped in excitement. There was nothing better than a summer day out there, with the sun shining down on you, and a cool mist drawing up from the bough. Out there, on the water, he always had the space just to think—to be himself. Maybe that's why he found himself out there almost every day of summer, and on occasion he would work some of the fishing boats during winter. Anytime he needed to get away, he would escape to the sea.

------●◦●◦◦------

"Tess, one of your regulars is asking for you. He's a cute one for sure." A fellow waitress commented as she walked by Tess and pointed back at the bar.

Tess craned her neck to see who was sitting at the bar waiting for her. A small smile spread across her face when she saw Nathan sitting there shaking his leg like crazy and running his hand through his soft, brown hair more than necessary. She wondered why he was back; usually Tommy was always with him. As she walked towards him, she could see the muscles through his soft, short-sleeve, grey, linen shirt, and his hair shined in the dimming light coming from the windows. She had always thought he was an attractive man, and although she never fit in back home, he did remind her of a southern gentleman and found it oddly comforting. Try as she might, she would find herself missing North Carolina, and to have a reminder of home was something she cherished more than she realized, perhaps even more than she wanted.

"Well looks like that sun did get to you today, back again huh?" She bantered playfully as she approached him.

"Yes and no, aha— Well you see, I actually came to see you." His voice shook softly.

She noticed the way his normally deep and gruff voice had softened. She stepped forward to tentatively place her hand on his exposed arm and furrowed her brows in concern.

"Are you okay?"

He glanced down at her hand that was sending sparks straight through him like an electric current. He looked back up into her eyes, a small smile tugging at the corners of his mouth. "Yeah, I'm fine. I just wanted to ask you if tomorrow I could show you that Sitka is fun—" His voice started to trail off when he saw the expression of shock cross her face.

"I have to work tomorrow—" She wished she could swallow her words as quickly as she had said them because of the way his gentle, grey eyes had suddenly dropped.

"But I get off at eight— If you don't mind it being an evening thing?" She quipped trying to salvage the conversation.

His eyes lit up and a lopsided grin spread across his face.

"Eight is perfect. I'll meet you here?" He asked excitedly.

She nodded a yes and smiled as she watched him practically skip out of the diner. As he opened the door to leave he turned around and smiled at her.

"See you tomorrow, Tess."

Chapter Two

"Hadley, can you cover my last table? I really need to be out of here by eight." Tess asked as she took her apron off and started changing in the break room.

"Yeah sure, what's up? Got a hot date?" Hadley joked.

"Actually—" Tess broke off as a rosy, pink color invaded her cheeks.

"No way!" Hadley exclaimed. "With who?" She demanded excitedly.

"Well I don't know if it's truly a date—but with Nathan."

"Oh sweetie, that man has been drooling over you since the day you arrived. He definitely thinks it's a date, even if you didn't." She giggled. "I'm happy for you, you deserve some fun, and Nathan—he's a good guy."

"Really? You think so?" Tess asked modestly.

Hadley reached for Tess's hands and looked her in the eyes. "I know so." She said with a friendly smile.

"Thanks."

She turned to look in the mirror, fluffed her wild curls a bit, coated her lashes in mascara, and applied a little gloss to her lips. It had been awhile since she had been on a date, and she was feeling her nerves rising. She silently told herself to take a deep breath, took one more glance in the mirror, and exhaled deeply before she turned to leave.

"Wish me luck."

Tess walked out of the service door and saw Nathan leaning against the building. He stood there, unaware of her presence, so she took a moment to study him. His body was well built, with broad shoulders and a narrow waist, athletic, but from his clothes you'd never imagine him being much of a jock. He had a strong jaw line and his warm, grey eyes glinted under his tousled light brown hair. He was definitely a fine specimen to look at that's for sure.

Something more than his looks intrigued her. She hadn't noticed it before, but when he was still, she could see something in the way he held himself. Something that most men didn't carry, a burden of some sort—a tortured soul who worked every day to be a bit better. She was startled when he looked up at her and smiled.

"Hey there, how was work?"

She shook her head, forcing herself out of her reverie. "Hi, well you were right, it was a mad house there today." She spoke nervously as she stepped closer and he motioned for her to follow him.

"Yeah, that's the thing with living here, everyone appreciates our little town during the warmer months. It's the perfect place to sightsee, or to spend a few days with your family."

"Is that necessarily a bad thing?" She spoke shrewdly.

He turned somewhat startled. Her tone was as if he had offended her.

"No, that's not what I meant at all. I just mean, this place gets crawling with tourists, and it's great for business during summer—but I wish people could see how great this place is all year long. I've spent my entire life here, so I suppose I'm a bit biased, but Sitka—it's a great place."

She nodded that she understood. "So where exactly are we going Mr. Suppan?" She eyed him suspiciously.

"How do you know my last name?"

She laughed halfheartedly before answering. "You sit in my section at least three times a week. I think I ought to know your last name by now after all the receipts you've signed."

"Ah—yeah." He chuckled.

"You never answered my question." She remarked.

"I wasn't planning on it either." He winked with a crooked smile.

She narrowed her eyes at him but on the inside, she couldn't help but feel giddy. He was challenging in the best possible way.

She hadn't realized how far into town they had gotten when she heard the buzz of noise and laughter. She broke her eyes off Nathan and looked ahead at the street. It had been transformed. This morning where there were small bins of produce and flowers lining the street, now was a carnival. Lights, cotton candy, children running and laughing, and some screaming from the top of the looming Ferris wheel. People filled the street, all laughing and enjoying the cool summer night. She giggled in unbridled delight. She knew she should not act this way at her age, but it had been years since she had been to a carnival, and she loved them.

Nathan looked over at Tess, he watched as her eyes widened with glee and darted to their surroundings. He watched as a smile spread across her face; she was absolutely breathtaking and he was finding it difficult to concentrate with her so close to him.

"It may not be much, but it's sort of an annual thing around here, and people really get into it." Nathan spoke as he put his hands in the pockets of his jeans.

"Hmmm— you said you wanted me to have fun, right?"

"Yes…?" Confusion crossed his face as he saw the fixed smile and determination in her eyes as she reached for his arm and pulled him into the sea of people.

He laughed as she led him directly to the games; she stopped at the shooting range.

She leaned against the booth and turned to look him dead on. He couldn't help his eyes from wandering. She was completely enrapturing in the way she perched herself against the booth with her long legs shimmering under her tattered jean shorts in the carnival lights and the way tendrils of her hair fell across her subtly bronzed face. He gulped discreetly as his eyes passed over her breasts, he tried desperately hard to look away immediately. He attempted not to notice the way they looked under her low-cut white blouse or the way her brown leather jacket with rolled up sleeves clung to her in a 'I'm-too-sexy-for-my-own-good' kind of way.

"If I win, you have to ride the carousel with me. If you win—"

"If I win—I get a second date with you." He finished as he winked at her and gave the booth manager four dollars to play.

"Alright, deal." She said as reached her hand out towards him.

He shook her hand and grinned impishly. "I should warn you—I'm a pretty good shot."

She nodded lightly in acknowledgment and picked up the gun. They looked at each other once before they heard the bell to begin firing. Tess lined up her shot, pulled the trigger and made the bullseye in each of the target zones with every single shot. She put the gun back down on the table and looked over at Nathan's zone. He was right, he was a good shot—but she was better.

"Wow—I have to say, I'm honestly impressed." He said as he exhaled and scratched his head in disbelief. He knew he hadn't held back, he had every intention of trying to impress her.

She tilted her head back and laughed softly. "Us southern belles gotta learn how to take care of ourselves." She said in a thick southern drawl with a nod and a wink.

Nathan shrugged his shoulders and laughed. She was funny, a genuine kind of funny. It surprised him and if she wasn't already attractive, it made her that much more interesting. She was a serious girl who didn't take herself so seriously, and he liked that about her.

The booth manager handed her a small teddy bear with a pink ribbon tied around its neck. She took it and was quickly at the side of a little girl at the end of the booth who had been playing against them as well.

"Hi there, my name is Tess, what's your name?" She crooned in a tender voice as she crouched down to the child's level.

"I'm Susie. I like your bear." She whispered shyly.

"Do you? Well you know, I was thinking, this bear is really special, and could use a good friend."

"Really?" Susie asked hanging onto every word Tess said.

Nathan couldn't help but feel the same as Susie; he too was hanging onto every word Tess was saying. Something about her just demanded attention and he was more than willing to indulge.

"Would you mind being this bear's friend? I think you'd take exceptional care of him." Tess asked, holding out the bear towards the little girl.

Susie scooped the bear into her arms, holding it close to her chest.

"What do you say Susie?" Her mother asked.

"Thank you." She said through a grin that spread so widely you could see that not all of her teeth were there.

"You're very welcome Miss Susie, it was a pleasure to meet you."

Tess smiled as she walked back towards Nathan who was standing there staring with his mouth slightly open.

"Are you always like that?" He finally asked.

"Like what?"

"I don't know, just so—"

She smiled shyly and lightly knocked his shoulder.

"It's your turn to hold up your end of the deal!" She shouted as she took off racing towards the carousel.

"Come on." She said with a slight wave of her hand, beckoning him to come towards her.

He didn't hesitate this time. He jumped onto the carousel and pulled himself up on the horse next to hers.

"I love carousels, always have ever since I can remember." She explained as they waited for the ride to start.

She jumped a little as the ride lurched into motion and the walking lights dimmed. She smiled as the song played cheerfully and the horses began to glide through the air as the carousel spun. She exhaled as she spread her arms wide and leaned backwards, letting the motion fill her body. She giggled like she was young child again as she embraced the liberating feeling it gave her.

Nathan stared in amazement at the charming creature next to him. He had only ever known Tess as the waitress. Always polite and kind, and she always had this maturity about her, but tonight he saw a different side of her. Here she was this young child at heart, just dying to be free. He couldn't help but smile as he watched her enjoying herself.

"That wasn't so terrible, was it?" She cajoled as they walked down the crowded street.

"Nah—it wasn't *so* bad." He said with a playful nudge.

As they stopped and waited in line for the Ferris wheel, he noticed how the ride operator stared at Tess. The way his eyes traveled up and down her body and how he smiled salaciously, probably imagining inappropriate thoughts about her. Seeing someone eye her like that made a strange pit in his stomach. Was it jealousy? Possession? He had no right to those feelings— Tess wasn't his, and yet, he couldn't help how tense the situation made him. Did she even notice the kind of stares she elicited? Did it bother her?

He hadn't realized how lost in his thoughts he had become until she nudged his arm bringing him back into reality. He jolted momentarily before he helped her into the cart and took a seat next to her.

"You okay?" She asked carefully, as the ride slowly pitched forward.

He shook his head lightly. "Yeah, just spaced a bit." He put his arm behind her, anything he could do to draw her in closer. "How about you? Have you had, dare I say, fun?"

He surprised her. There was something about him that was captivating probably because it didn't quite make sense. Here was this guy who seemed to carry the world on his shoulders, a guy who seemed to beat himself up for things that were probably well beyond his control. And yet, he sat beside her and prodded *her* about having fun. She laughed quietly.

"What's so funny?" He coaxed softly.

"Nothing. I just haven't had this much fun in—well, I don't know how long."

"So Tommy was right. You don't do much but work, do you?" He questioned softly trying not to insult her.

She shifted her weight to lean forward and look out. Their cart was nearing the top and she had a good view of the carnival below. She saw the lights, could hear the music playing, and faint sounds of children screaming and laughing. She watched as they chased each other along the street holding sparklers, simply enjoying life— the way she wished she would.

She turned her head back towards Nathan. "We're grownups. When did that happen, and how do we make it stop?" She sighed in vexation as she lightly collapsed back into his chest.

He knew enough not to say anything, especially not to point out that from tonight he could gather she was still a kid at heart. Instead he waited patiently for her to continue to speak.

"Sometimes responsibilities take over and you can forget to slow down and enjoy what it means to live your own life." She looked over at him not knowing what to expect for a reaction. But he just sat there intently listening, and running his fingers lightly along her arm in a comforting way.

Something about him made her feel contented, and well, safe. She suddenly became aware that she basically said she doesn't know how to have fun. She felt her cheeks inflame as she wanted to bury her head in embarrassment.

"Kind of pathetic, huh? A girl forgetting what it's like to have fun?"

Nathan snorted. "Tess, you're the last thing from pathetic. If I didn't know any better I'd say you looked like you were enjoying yourself tonight."

"You're right I was, and still am—"

He cut her off mid-sentence. "Then don't worry about getting caught up in the tediousness of adulthood. Enjoy life when you can, and make the best of a situation. I know I don't know you that well yet, but from what I gather, you're not hopeless just yet." He gave her a friendly wink. "You still have time to enjoy life, and there are perks to being a grown up you know."

"Oh yeah? What's that?" She raised a satirical brow as she spoke.

He took his hand and intertwined his fingers with hers. "Well for starters, there's this."

She looked up at him and studied his eyes. It was as if she was trying to read his mind, maybe even his soul. It sent chills down his spine, and he tried to regain his focus, instead of concentrating on the tingle he could feel emanating in his hand.

He felt his mouth dry as he fumbled for words. "I just mean, of course there will always be responsibilities and what not, but when you're a kid you don't get to experience other things. Like your first beer," she giggled lightly, "or finding a career that you're passionate about, where you come home every day knowing you honestly enjoyed work, or even just the simple fact of coming home to your loved ones. Building a relationship with someone, getting to know them fully and they you." He paused as he continued to trace her hand gently with his thumb. "I don't know about you but I think the intimacy of a relationship can be something similar to a child's imaginary friend. They know all your secrets and still choose to stay with you. And if you find the right person, maybe they can help remind you what it's like to be a kid again."

He pulled her in closer and lightly pressed his lips to her hair as she leaned into him. She wasn't sure what it was about him, but she could already feel herself succumbing to him. Maybe it was because all of what he said was a reflection of what she would stay awake dreaming of at night.

"Thanks for tonight Nathan. I really did enjoy myself." She said from the stoop.

He stood close to her and her breath altered as her heart started to race a little. She forgot what it felt like, the beginning of something new and exciting.

"I'm glad you had fun. Do you think I could ask a favor of you?"

She cocked her head to the side wondering what it could be.

"Go on a real date with me this weekend. One where we get dressed up, I drive, and I pick up the bill."

"So tonight wasn't a real date?" She said sardonically. He hadn't expected that answer. His eyes widened and he tried to back pedal fast.

"No—I mean of course it was. I just meant a different kind of date."

She smiled knowing he was losing this battle. It was cute the way he tried to fumble around with the right words to say.

"Fine, I'll go as long as we agree it's a second date." She said with a determined nod of her head.

He sighed in relief. "Agreed." He let his finger trace the back of her hand as he spoke. "I had a lot of fun too, Tess."

She knew he was just delaying their night. It made her smile but the fact-of-the-matter was she was getting tired of waiting for him to make a move, and she blurted out, "Aren't you going to kiss me?"

He looked taken aback. He was planning on just leaving even though all he wanted to do was kiss her, but he didn't want to push her. He thought holding back was what women wanted. When she asked he was shocked, but not to the point that he wouldn't take advantage of a beautiful girl asking him to kiss her.

He took a step closer to her and put his hand along her neck under her ear, and with his other hand he placed it on the small of her back and gently pulled her in close to him. He lowered his face closer to hers letting the warmth of her breath caress his skin and send flames through his body.

She let her hands rest gently on his arms, and could feel his muscles contracting. Kind of like the way her stomach was tightening in reaction to his lips moving slowly and gently with her own. She closed her eyes and let herself get lost in the kiss, and when he finally pulled away she felt her breath shorten and she gasped for air.

"Goodnight Tess." He whispered placing a chaste kiss on her cheek before turning to walk away.

"Night Nathan." She said as he slowly let go of her hand and walked down the steps and off into the dark.

She put her fingers to her lips, memorizing the warmth of his lips, as if they had burned right into hers. A smile crept across her face.

He had to contain his excitement as he walked out of sight, but he couldn't hide the smile that was spread across his face. He was glad his back was to her; he would be embarrassed if she could see the boyish grin on his face. He had dated girls before, but none of them ever made him feel this way—none had ever kissed him like *that*.

Chapter Three

He knocked a few times before he heard her voice through the door.

"Door's open, come on in. I just need a minute. Sorry, I'm running late!" She called from her bedroom down the hall.

"It's no problem at all, besides I'm kinda early." He said as he stepped in and looked around her living room.

It was very simple; no TV, just a small, old radio in the corner, a couch in the middle, and a coffee table with a small vase containing a few lilies. Under the window was a small bookshelf containing only two novels: *Wuthering Heights* and *Romeo And Juliet*. He laughed silently to himself; he remembered sleeping through that part of English class.

He turned his attention to the fireplace. It seemed like it hadn't been touched yet, and above it were candles that lined the mantle. He liked the simplicity of her place, but couldn't help wondering if she was running from something. Running would explain a lack of personal items, or maybe instead of running, maybe she was searching for something that she hadn't quite found yet.

His attention snapped back when he heard the soft clacking of her heels walking towards him. She was breathtakingly-heartbreakingly-gorgeous. Her hair was pulled to the side, and she wore an olive-green, cocktail dress that clung tightly against her body. Her long legs shimmered in the light, accentuated by the tall, beige pumps, and he couldn't help but stare at her figure. She had subtle curves that sashayed when she walked and her smile was something he knew he would never recover from. He forced his mouth closed realizing he had suddenly become the Ferris wheel operator.

"Wow. You look sensational." He said as he reached an arm out towards her pulling her closer.

"Thank you, you don't look so bad yourself." She said with a wink and kissed his cheek softly. "Is that for me?"

"Oh, yes." He shook his head at himself as he handed her the single, long stem, red rose.

She took it and gave him a small grin before taking in the scent of the rose. She smiled inwardly to herself noticing that he had removed all of the thorns from the stem.

"Well, are you ready?" He asked handing her a coat that was hanging by the door as he started to lead her outside.

"I'd like to say yes, but it's hard to be ready for something you know nothing about." She chided playfully.

He chuckled. "Fair enough."

Her mouth opened in shock. "That's it? 'Fair enough'? You're still not going to tell me what we're doing?" She asked as she let him lead her down to his car.

He opened the passenger side door for her. "No. I'm not going to tell you, what would be the fun in that?" He goaded lightheartedly.

She rolled her eyes and huffed as she got in the car. She kept her face in a scowl at him until he couldn't see her as he walked around the car. When he was out of sight she let herself smile. She couldn't help it; she was excited and nervous all at once.

"I do need to make a quick stop at the marina, if that's okay?"

"Sure, that's no problem. Want me to wait here?" She asked as they pulled up to the dock.

"No, why don't you come with me, I don't know how long this will take."

"What exactly are you doing here?" She inquired as she followed him down the dock.

He surprised her when he quickly spun around to face her once they reached the bottom of the ramp.

"Do you trust me?" The smile on his face reached up to his eyes.

Cautiously she spoke, "Yes, but I guess the better question is, should I?"

He shrugged lightly as if it were a fair point well made. He walked around behind her and covered her eyes.

"Take a few more steps forward and then turn left." He whispered in her ear.

His hot breath curled around her ear, and a shiver rippled through her. She did as he asked, carefully walking towards the unknown. She mentally chided herself for wearing the tallest heels she owned.

He took his hands off her eyes and waited for her to open them and see what was in front of her.

She slowly opened her eyes not knowing what to expect, but what she saw was jaw dropping.

Tied to the dock was a wooden sailboat that glimmered in the reflection of the moon. Along its mass were hundreds of little white lights that traveled around the edge of the boat. In the cockpit was a small table set for two, silver covered plates, and three skinny, white candles. She gasped at the sight; no one had ever done something like this for her before.

She turned towards him. "It's beautiful! Did you do all this yourself?" She asked in disbelief as he led her closer.

He hopped aboard and reached down to help her up. She let her eyes wander around them taking it all in. He smiled intrinsically knowing he had done a good job.

"It was my idea, but Tommy helped me put up the lights. This is the MARTHA II. I had helped get her back into tip-top shape, but the owner unexpectedly decided to move to Florida to be closer to his kids and grandchildren and so he sold her to me."

"Wow." She wrapped her arms around his neck. "You're kind of amazing."

He pulled her in closer and wrapped his arms tightly around her, a feeling he had only dreamed about a week ago.

"So, you like it?" He asked.

"Nathan, I love it. It's wonderful." She breathed out.

He lowered his head down towards her and chastely brushed his lips against hers.

"Well I know the marina is nice, but what do you say we get out on the water?" He said as he smoothed a strand of hair away from her face.

"I think that sounds nice." She took a seat on the starboard side of the boat, leaning against the railing watching the water as Nathan prepared for their leave. It was a calming sensation, sitting there letting the sea breeze flow through you, and to hear the sound of the water rushing past the boat. She understood why Nathan spent so much time here.

"I still can't believe you did all of this for me." Tess said ardently as she took another sip of her champagne and looked out on the water.

"Well to be honest Tess, I've never known anyone quite like you."

"What? Someone who is witty, completely charming, and—"

"Compassionate." He said pragmatically.

"I was going to say intelligent." She said bashfully as she glanced down at her hand that was playing with the neck of her champagne flute.

He reached across the table and took her hand prompting her to look at him. "You are definitely all of those things and more."

She gazed up into his grey eyes; they looked smoky and smoldering in the twinkling lights. Nathan was a stranger, not in the 'I just met you' sense, but still, he didn't know her and yet he so blindly complimented her without question. She wondered if he always trusted people at face value or if he was just desperate to believe in someone. She remembered being like that once; putting her faith in everyone but herself. She hoped one day she would find that trust in others again.

She thought of Bobby, her ex, he might have been the closest thing she felt to love. But that ended the night she caught him cheating on her with a waitress at the local diner. Actually, it may have ended long before then, she wasn't sure anymore. Since that day she never really thought of love. She knew it could happen for some people, but she didn't think it would for herself. It hadn't for her mother and father, they always fought, but maybe that was their love. The idea of that being all that love is—it's heartbreaking. She needed to know there was more to it, and maybe Nathan was the one to show her.

"I've always wondered, what brought you to Sitka? I mean, don't get me wrong, I love the place, but it's not exactly a star attraction, nor that easy to come by."

His voice pulled her back to the present. She shook her head ridding her of her thoughts and regained her focus as he stood up and walked over to take a seat next to her.

"I think maybe that's why I like it. I loved my home, well I loved the idea of it."

"What do you mean?" He gently stroked the nape of her neck with the back of his fingers.

She smiled to herself knowing that he had his hands on her every chance he could tonight. "Ever feel like you just don't belong? Like you're a bird among squirrels."

"A bird among squirrels?" He quipped back testing the phrase. "I don't think I follow."

"Just so different from everyone. I grew up in Beaufort, North Carolina. I was an only child, my parents are still together, probably at each other's throats mind you."

Nathan chuckled softly.

"But I don't know, I just always dreamed of being somewhere else. I was always so different from everyone down there. Southern people I swear." She rolled her eyes and chuckled softly. "Even though I was raised there in that 'southern' way, it's not the life I wanted. I don't want the same life as my parents. The social obligations and forced conversations, always having to say no when all you really want to do is scream 'hell yes'." She shook her head and giggled. He felt his breath falter slightly at the sound of her giggle; he would give anything to hear it again and again.

"I never connected with anyone, probably because I was always off day-dreaming of the day I would leave that place. But of course, I was beginning to follow the path of every Dawson. I went to college and got my bachelor's degree, but by then I had met a boy. By twenty-three, I was engaged and wedding plans were well on their way. It took me until the moment I was trying on wedding dresses to realize I was exactly like my mother. She grew up in Beaufort, and got married straight out of high school. She never did anything for herself; she just stayed stuck in this position. And I mean, I suppose if you find the right person, and you can live with that, then more power to you. But I don't know, I just felt like I needed to experience life." She said with a lavish sigh.

"So, you left him and came here?" Nathan asked trying to fill in the pieces. Despite his best efforts he felt himself enunciate the word 'him' out of jealousy. The thought of her being with someone else pained him in way he had never felt before.

"No." She shook her head and laughed lightly. "I had this epiphany, but I was too chicken to do anything about it. I had never lived anywhere but Beaufort, and with Bobby, well, everything would be easy. My life would be planned out—so I got into a routine. I tried to accept that I would never leave and I tried my best to like it there. I started painting or doing odd hobbies to pass the time and concentrate on wedding plans. I guess I got so focused on trying to like it there that I didn't even noticed that something changed."

"You loved him though, so what happened?"

"What always happens? Life."

He waited patiently for her to continue, he could tell she didn't like to think about it, and he didn't want to press her.

"Well one night I went to visit my friend Vanessa at the restaurant she worked at, we were going to go get drinks, and I was going to ask her to be my maid of honor." Tess smiled at the distant memory of what could have been.

"But when I walked in the back to get her, I saw Bobby and her together. Right there in the break room. I was so ashamed and angry, I packed what I had and left.

At first I didn't know where I was driving to, I just started driving west. I couldn't think straight."

"That's awful. I couldn't imagine someone putting you through that." He said quietly as he stroked her exposed back lightly with his knuckles. How could anyone stray from the goddess sitting next to him?

She glanced over at him. His words were so sincere like he truly found it unbelievable and abhorrent for someone to hurt her. She found the idea comforting and charming in a way.

"Actually, what's awful is how long I let that charade of a relationship go on for. Bobby was bad news long before I found him cheating; but I guess when I saw him cheating it sounded like the best excuse I could find to leave him. I'm fairly certain what I felt with Bobby was never love. I know that as much as I tried to fight it, I never wanted to be stuck there. Seeing him with Vanessa was just the nudge I needed."

She thought back to that night, she remembered smiling as she pushed the door of the break room open, excited to ask Vanessa to be her maid of honor. The door was quiet as it slowly swung open, she suddenly felt the air sucked out of her as her eyes widened. Vanessa's legs were wrapped tightly around Bobby, with his pants hanging low on his waist, and his face buried in her neck. She stood there for a moment, stunned into a paralyzed state. It was long enough that when Vanessa opened her eyes their eyes met for a millisecond. As soon as their eyes met, Tess turned and ran out the door.

She didn't wait around to see what happened next or if Vanessa even told Bobby she saw them there.

She rushed home in a fury and started throwing things into her bags knowing this was her chance. Her mother walked in on her and tried asking what had happened. Tess told her and assumed she would understand, but her mother shocked her by saying he made a mistake and that you learn to forgive men of their needs.

"What? Are you insane? Forgive them of their needs? If you're about to marry someone you'd think they could keep it in their pants!" She barked.

"Men have stronger needs than us women, darlin' it's not as if they don't love us, they just sometimes need what we can't provide." Her mother acquiesced.

Tess stared at her mother with her mouth open and a dumbfounded expression on her face. The calmness in the way she truly believed what she was saying was beyond Tess.

After being momentarily stunned into silence, Tess found her voice again. "I'm sorry that Daddy went looking elsewhere and that you were okay with it, but I'm not you Mama. I don't want that for a life. To be wondering if he ran to another woman's arms each night, I just can't."

She stepped forward and placed a hand on her mother's shoulder in comfort.

"You can and you will. Now young lady, unpack your things. I'll call Bobby and have him come pick you up." She shrugged off Tess's hand.

Tess's eyes widened at her mother. She couldn't believe her.

"You have no right to interfere Mama. I am an adult and an independent woman. Let me find my own way for once." She grumbled in an impassioned plea.

"Sweetheart, there is a difference between being independent and being unspeakably sad."

Tess took a step back and shook her head, wounded by the words like a swift kick to the gut.

"No Mama, I won't follow in your footsteps and live in a loveless marriage. I won't live in this godforsaken place any longer! I will *never* be *you*." She grabbed her bags and strode towards the doorway.

"You're making a mistake."

Tess stopped in her tracks and tightened her jaw. Her mother would never understand and she could spend the rest of her life trying to explain, or she could walk out that door. Her shoulders sagged with a resigned sigh as she spoke, "No, I'm correcting one."

She started off west, trying to forget about the details of the night. She knew she should be absolutely heartbroken, and it scared her when she realized she wasn't. What she felt when she saw Bobby and Vanessa together wasn't a heart breaking, it was anger that she had stayed for so long, anger that she hadn't left a long time ago.

As the highway stretched out in front of her she began to cry. It wasn't until she was about three hours away that she dawned on the severity of what she had just done. She probably broke her mother's heart, she left the only place she ever knew, she didn't have more than a few hundred dollars in her bank account, and she didn't have a plan. She just started driving.

Everything in her body told her to turn around, go home, but something small was building in the back of her mind; the idea that she had the ability to start over. To have the life she had only ever dreamed of. A smile spread across her face as she pressed her foot down on the gas pedal.

West was the direction she was heading. She didn't really have a destination in mind, but when she had road-tripped through Alaska and along the Canadian border with her friends, she recalled liking it there. She remembered the adventures they had together, and she remembered Sitka. It was a small town in Alaska, one that most people would pass by without a second thought, but she remembered the quiet town. Sitka was the port they stayed in for a seaplane tour of Baranof Island to see some of Alaska's backcountry. They enjoyed their visit so much that they extended their stay to spend a few extra days in the sleepy town. Something about it felt like home. She finally had the room to breathe.

Sitka it would be then. She would find a way to get to Sitka and begin a new life.

She arrived in the small-town weeks later and instantly began to work on this new life of hers. She traded in her car for cash. It wasn't much, but it was enough to put a down payment on a small cabin as well as a few months' worth of rent, just enough to buy her time to look for a job. She knew she needed income quickly when she came across the Spar, a little diner right on the water next to the marina. She spoke with the owner and to her luck, he said yes. She assumed it was probably because he felt sorry for her. When she thought about it, she must have seemed pretty pitiful back then. To this day she still didn't have much, but she did have something invaluable—a new life.

She shook her thoughts away and snapped back into the conversation. Nathan didn't say anything about her long respite, nor press about what had been said to her mother. She was grateful for both.

"I got on the highway and somehow made it here." She said with a sigh.

"For whatever it's worth, I'm sure your mom forgives you, even if she hasn't made that clear. And what you did was courageous if you ask me."

"Courageous?"

"Not many people have the—excuse me for the lack of a better term, but most people don't have the balls to leave home. I know I didn't."

She giggled lightly.

"I'm glad you made it here though." He said looking into her eyes with a warm expression.

As she tipped her face up to meet his gaze she realized when she left, there would have been no other place for her to go. Sitka had called to her and she was beginning to understand why.

"Me too."

Chapter Four

Nathan pulled in the sail a few hundred yards from shore and threw down the anchor. Tess looked out over the water and realized they were no longer alone. Twenty or more boats littered the water next to them.

"What is everyone doing here?" She asked as she looked around.

"They're all waiting." He said glancing down at her.

"Waiting for…?"

He took a seat beside her before pulling her coat up over her shoulders and tucking the blanket tighter around her legs. With her exposed skin protected from the cool night air, he wrapped his arm around her.

"That." He nodded and pointed off towards the mainland and that's when she saw it.

Suddenly the night sky started to fill with small glowing dots, like hundreds of fireflies, and the water was becoming incandescent. She cocked her head to the side trying to figure out what it was. She gasped subtly when the boats next to her began to send lights up into the night. The lights were sky lanterns; all of the boats were sending them up into the night sky, illuminating the water below. She could see small children hanging off boats pushing tiny rafts with candles out into the water.

She was suddenly in a world of light; it was the most beautiful thing she had ever seen. It was as if they had crossed a threshold and entered into a world of make believe and enchantment, a world where they took up arms and arrows to defeat the darkness. In this moment they partook in a shared fiction of magic and wonder. She made an audible gasp in delight.

"It's staggering." She pronounced as she craned her neck to see everything.

"Want to let one go?" He asked proffering a small lantern in his free hand.

"For me?" She asked.

"Here hold it like this." He said as he placed it into her hands.

He took a lighter from his pants pocket and lit the coal underneath the lantern.

"What do I do now?" She asked, her eyes bright with excitement.

He gently placed his hands under hers, and with a gentle nudge he helped her lift it into the sky, sending it on its voyage into the night air.

She smiled candidly before leaning in to kiss him passionately.

"Damn." Was all he could say as he tried to catch his breath after she pulled away.

She blushed slightly as she sank back into the seat. She continued to stare up into the sky watching the lights dance along the air, and the lights that flickered in reflection on the still water.

"Why do they do this?" She asked looking back at Nathan.

"They've done it for as long as I can remember. It's our annual sky lantern festival, it marks the end of the carnival, but it's more for the soul."

"What do you mean?"

"It's a way of letting go. Everyone has things they regret, things to be remorseful of—this ceremony is about letting go of it all, and getting a second chance. Everyone sends his or her wishes of a new start into the sky. Lets the heavens figure it out."

"That's kind of perfect." She smiled.

"I thought you might like it."

Nathan continued stroking her arm as they sat in silence watching the last of the lanterns float off in the distance. He glanced around and noticed how they had long out-lasted the other boats on the water. He knew that's because he didn't want this night to end. She was there, in his arms, he could breathe in her intoxicating scent. He found it difficult to hold a conversation when all he could think about was running his hands all over her.

As if she could read his mind she turned in his arms to look up at him. He smiled down at her as she reached her hand up and gently pulled his face in towards her. She kissed him softly at first, savoring the way their lips molded against each other. Her lips parted subtly giving Nathan access, allowing his tongue to play with hers.

Nathan let out a guttural groan low in his chest as he pulled away from her and leaned his forehead against hers. His hand cupped under her ear holding her in place as he spoke, "You're really going to have to stop kissing me like that. I am trying to be a gentleman and you are making it impossible."

With a shy nervous tone, she whispered out, "So don't be."

He looked into her green eyes, their color had shifted slightly to a deep green that reminded him of the forest on a cool, foggy morning. After staring momentarily, he crashed his lips back into hers. He kissed her feverishly with a desperation he had been keeping at bay.

Nathan tore away from her, jumping to his feet and reaching his hand out for her to take. He smiled down at her with a devilish smirk as he pulled her from her seat and led her down into the cabin.

Tess stood at the base of the stairs watching as Nathan flicked on a small row of canned lighting that illuminated the small interior. Her face flushed slightly as she looked over at the perfectly well made bed with dark, green, satin sheets under the cream-colored comforter.

Nathan turned around and stared at Tess as she observed her surroundings. Desire pumped through his veins at an uncontrollable rate as he admired the subtle way she shifted on her feet. The way her hip popped out and the way her dress clung so closely to her body. He found himself envious of her dress, wishing he could be that close to her.

The thought spurred him forward. In three large steps he was standing in front of her, desperately trying to control his ragged breath. He gently grasped her coat in his hands and helped her out of it.

She looked up into his steely, grey eyes and watched him intently as he reached behind her and tantalizingly slowly unzipped her dress. Still watching him closely, she noticed how his eyes darkened in admiration as she gently shimmied, forcing her dress to fall and pool at her feet.

Her face heated slightly when she heard Nathan suck in his breath at the sight of her in her black, lace bralette, matching lace panties, and heels.

After eyeing her salaciously, he reached forward cupping his hand under her ear on her neck. He tilted her head to the side, running his nose along her jaw and down her throat. He placed a warm kiss on her neck as he breathed her in.

"You are a temptress." He spoke in a low deep voice that sent shivers down her spine.

Her hands shook slightly as she slowly undid the buttons of his ivory dress shirt. He leaned back to smile down at her as she tugged on his sleeves pulling his shirt off of him. Tess rocked back on her feet gently before leaning forward to place a kiss at the base of Nathan's neck.

He closed his eyes and tilted his head back giving her access. He groaned in appreciation as she trailed kisses along the width of his chest. Her hands slid down his sides making him shiver under her touch. Her fingertips teased along the waistband of his jeans causing his dick to twitch and strain against the material.

"Fuck." He huffed out under his breath.

He could feel a smile on her lips as she continued to run her tongue in small circles around his peck. He grabbed her roughly by the throat and kissed her passionately as he pushed her back against the wall of the cabin.

Nathan grabbed under her thighs and lifted her up, hooking her around his waist. She wrapped her arms around his neck and tightened her legs around his torso. Her stomach clenched at his carnal desire, sending a pulse right down to her core. She could feel her core thumping and her arousal causing a small pool of wetness to form in her panties.

He groaned as his lips left hers and he began kissing and sucking her neck. He smirked intrinsically knowing he would surely be leaving a mark or two on her neck, staking his claim on her as his. He pushed back from the wall and carried her the few steps over to the bed and gently laid her down.

He reached behind her back and unclasped her bra. He kneeled up between her legs as he slowly pulled off her bra. Nathan sucked in his breath as he watched her breasts spring free. They were the perfect size to hold in the palm of his hands and her small buds stood erect, teasing him. He growled appreciatively as he leaned forward and circled her nipple with his tongue while his hand massaged her other breast.

Her back arched slightly off the bed under his touch, she moaned as she rolled her hips against him. She could feel his hard cock in his pants and she welcomed the friction it caused against her skin.

Nathan let out a breathy moan against her skin as he spoke in hushed tones, "I want to taste you. Can I?"

Her face flushed desperately warm at his question. She brazenly rolled her hips against him in response.

Nathan groaned as he pushed himself further down the bed, slowly planting kisses down her stomach down to the waistline of her black lace panties. His hands skimmed down her sides and hooked onto her panties.

He looked up at her under hooded eyes. "Say yes."

She reached down and gently pushed her hand through his tousled hair, squirming slightly at the way his breath curled against her skin. She nodded her head as she breathed out, "Yes."

Nathan smiled triumphantly as he pulled her panties down. He stood up at the edge of the bed as he pulled her panties off and tossed them to the floor. He stared down at her for a moment savoring the mental pictures he was collecting. There she lay on his bed in nothing but the tall, beige heels that accentuated her calves. She was nothing short of a goddess and utterly gorgeous.

Reaching forward he gently spread her legs as he got down on his knees between them. He placed hungry kisses along the inside of her thighs, trailing up to her core.

She shivered under his touch and jostled slightly as he placed a kiss at the top of her entrance. He slid a finger parting her folds and murmured against her thigh, "You are so wet for me."

Tess moaned as Nathan's tongue penetrated her. His tongue swirled around her clit and sank in and out flicking at her insides. She bucked at his onslaught and she could feel his hot breath chuckle against her as he wrapped his arms under her by the hips forcing her to stay still.

He continued to lick and suck between her folds as he unwrapped one of his arms from her and inserted a finger and began pushing it in and out. She moaned loudly as she rolled her hips against his face. He eyed her as he watched her hands shoot out to her sides and ball up the sheets in her fists.

Her insides began to clench around his finger and she gasped when he inserted a second. Her face heated impossibly warm as she felt her arousal spilling out onto his tongue.

He continued to suck on her clit as he pumped his fingers in and out with strained force. He flicked his fingers up hitting her g-spot repeatedly as he watched her come completely undone around him.

Tess cried out as her orgasm ripped through her, arching her back off the bed and her core quivering as she came down from her high. Nathan sucked at her juices until she was completely spent.

He placed a kiss on her inner thigh and smiled against her skin as he whispered, "Good girl."

Tess flushed as she reached for his hand and he pulled her to her feet. He grabbed her by the nape of the neck and crashed his lips into hers. She could taste herself on him and squirmed as a new round of arousal clawed at her insides.

"You are delectable." He whispered to her.

She smirked as she deftly undid the button of his jeans. She gently slid the zipper down and pulled on his jeans to come half way down his butt. With a bravado she never knew she had, she reached into his pants and rubbed his hard dick against his briefs.

Nathan groaned low in his chest as Tess pulled her hand back out and grabbed the waistline of his briefs. She yanked down grabbing his briefs and jeans as she went and dropped them at his feet. He dutifully stepped out of them and kicked them to the side.

Tess reached down to pull her heels off and tossed them to the side before she looked up at him under thick lashes and slowly traced her hand down his chest. She watched as his chest began to heave in ragged breaths as she continued to trail down his torso. She sucked in her breath giving herself silent courage as she grabbed his hips and sank down to her knees in front of him.

His eyes widened in palpable shock. He knew being with Tess in this way would be incredible, but she was beyond anything he could have ever imagined. She wasn't breaking under his touch, and she challenged him back as his equal.

With her hands steadying her on his hips she glanced up at him as she took his cock in her mouth. Nathan's head fell back as he grunted at the feel of her warm mouth around his dick. She began to pump her mouth along his cock, taking him deeper and deeper.

He looked down to see her staring up at him as she continued to pull him deep into her mouth.

"Fuck that's hot." He breathed out as he wrapped his hand up in her hair.

Holding her by the back of the head he began to thrust his hips, pushing his cock to the back of her throat. He pumped his hips repeatedly, appreciating how her tongue flicked along his shaft with each thrust.

He pulled out of her and reached down grabbing under her arm and pulling her to her feet. She was breathing fast, her lips were swollen and red, and her hair was disheveled. She looked absolutely fuckable. He crashed his lips against hers in a hurried kiss before tearing away and kissing down her neck.

She moaned into him feeling his animalistic desire for her. He stepped them backwards and laid her back down onto the bed. He crawled on top of her, pushing his way between her legs. He kissed her hard, invading her mouth with his tongue.

He hovered over her and broke away from her lips. "Be mine." He breathed out the words as a command or a question, he wasn't sure which. All he knew was that she was made for him and he'd be damned if he ever let another man near her.

Tess ran her hand through his hair and placed her hand on his check prompting him to look at her. "I'm yours."

He turned his face into her palm and kissed the center of her hand as he positioned his cock at her entrance. He looked at her face to look for any sign of hesitation and when he saw none he gently thrust into her.

She gasped as she stretched around him, accommodating his size. He stilled inside of her, allowing her a moment to take him in. He swore under his breath, she was incredibly tight and warm around his cock.

He pulled out and gently thrust into her again, letting her juices coat his cock as he began to find his rhythm. She closed her eyes and tilted her head back into the sheets as Nathan began to pick up speed. He leaned forward and placed a small kiss on the corner of her mouth as he continued pumping in and out of her.

Her breathy moans filled the cabin as he flattened his chest against hers and placed his forearm by her head. He leaned forward, his thrusting slowing as he kissed her softly and passionately. His hips continued to move against her as they kissed. He moved from her lips and trailed kisses along her jawline. He buried his face in her neck lightly trailing his tongue around the dark hickey that had started to form.

Her body tingled under his tongue and her core clenched around his member as she felt herself tumbling down her climax. "Nathan." She breathed out.

Nathan groaned feeling her orgasm shudder around his dick, milking him. He thrust into her twice before stilling, reaching his own peak.

He lifted their entangled hands up trying to memorize this moment. She sighed softly as she nestled further back against his chest. The satin sheets pulled up against her skin mixed with the warmth from his body sent shivers down her spine. Nathan dropped their hands down, squeezing them around her shoulders as he craned his neck down to kiss the top of her head.

"You are incredible." He spoke softly.

She draped her free hand on top of his arm and lightly traced circles with her fingertips. "You aren't so bad yourself."

She knew Nathan was smirking smugly to himself even though she couldn't see his face. It made her smile widely. Never had a man made her feel this way. To feel so incredibly safe and cherished to the point that she felt free. Free to let herself get completely lost in the moment and just let go. Nathan worshipped her body, he lusted for her and still she knew at any moment she could say no and he would respect that. This man would surely make her come completely undone at the seams.

Chapter Five

"This is our what, sixth date? And you never talk about yourself. I think it's time to put you in the hot seat." Tess murmured dryly as she tried to tame her hair in the wind.

"I do too talk about myself." Nathan thought out loud as he wrapped up a rope.

"You do not. The only things I really know about you are things I already knew." She gaffed back at him.

"Well that's just because I like hearing you talk more." He winked down at her as he finished tying up the sails.

She stood up to face him; she grabbed his hand as he was getting ready to drop the anchor. "Come on, please?" She asked through thick lashes and her big, doe eyes looking up at him.

He sighed petulantly knowing that look would end up being the death of him.

"Alright fine, but if I talk, then you have to promise to jump in with me."

She drew her hand back and put both hands on her hips. "Look I may act tough and well—I am tough, but I don't do water that basically has ice cubes floating in it." She said adamantly.

Nathan laughed as he shrugged his shoulders. "That's the deal. Take it or leave it." He wasn't sure what he was hoping for as a result. On one hand talking about his past wasn't his favorite subject, but on the other hand, the look on her face about the deal would almost be worth it.

Tess crossed her arms and pulled her lips down in a pout. "Fine."

Nathan couldn't help but grin. The girl just couldn't resist a challenge.

"Well to tell you the truth, I don't have much of a story. I grew up in Sitka and every summer since I was eleven I've been working out here in the marina." He noticed the way she tilted her head and listened intently to what he was saying. He knew she wanted him to be open and honest with her and he really did endeavor to be. "I, uh, started working out here cause I needed to breathe."

She gazed up at him patiently waiting for him to tell her his story.

After dropping the anchor, he took a seat next to her. "When I was ten my mom was diagnosed with early onset Alzheimer's. At first, she would forget things like taking her pills or where she parked her car, but as months went by she started forgetting why she went to the store, or where the store was in relation to our house. I'd be on my way home from school and I'd find her wandering around the park."

Tess's gaze softened and she lightly touched his arm to show her support. Nathan glanced down at her hand and patted it before he fixed his gaze out on the water.

"It'd take me hours to convince her to come home. She didn't like to listen to me. She would argue with me saying she needed to wait for her son to get out of school."

She squeezed his arm. "Where was your dad with all of this?" She flinched when she said it; she knew how accusatory it must have sounded.

"He uh, he'd be in the bar. Getting himself wasted." There was a fleeting bemused expression that fluttered across his face as he spoke. "He'd come home around two or three every night. He started drinking when she got real sick, and he just couldn't shake the habit. He wasn't around much to help out. I guess I can't really blame him now."

"What do you mean?"

"Well when I was younger I'd be pissed at him—I mean *really* pissed for making me take care of her. I was furious that he would put that kind of responsibility on me, that he made *me* be the adult in the family. I couldn't understand how he would just go sit at the bar all day and leave me alone with her, but now that I'm older, I can see why."

Tess looked up at him with smoldering eyes, he could tell what he said bothered her.

"That's not what I meant, at least not like that." He held up a defensive hand.

"Then what *did* you mean?" She arched a brow inquisitively.

"That it must have been hard watching the love of your life forget you."

Her face immediately slackened and she dropped her head, *oh.*

"Don't get me wrong, I'd never condone that behavior, but I couldn't imagine watching my love forget who I was or forget the life we shared together. I think drinking himself silly was his way of trying to forget how broken his own heart had become."

Tess kept quiet as she thought about how awful it must have been. To know love and then to watch the one you shared it with forget— there aren't much worse fates.

"But back then I didn't see it that way. I saw it as he left me to take care of my mom while he went to the bar. He left me to take care of a woman who on most days had no clue who I was. There were days I'd sit there for hours letting her tell me all about her son Nathaniel. She'd tell me how much she wished we could play together because she knew I would get along so well with him." He tried to hide the hurt with the faint hint of a smile.

"I'm so sorry Nathan, I had no idea." Tess said as she put her arm through his and hugged him tight wishing she could somehow ease his pain or provide him with a source of solace.

He kissed her hair. "I know you didn't, not many do. I don't talk about it much. Not because it hurts, but because I've come to terms with it and I'd like to leave the past in the past."

He directed his eyes back out onto the water. Tess understood it then, at least part of it anyway. The reason why he looked like he carried the weight of the world on his shoulders—was because for most of his childhood, he had. He said he liked to leave the past in the past, but she knew better. She knew the past always has a way of catching up to you. She shuddered slightly as a fleeting thought blazed through her mind.

She shook her head regaining an inward focus on Nathan. She knew for as tough as he may seem, he stared out at the water like that for fear of her seeing the one thing he didn't want someone to know—that he was sad. Just a poor lost boy who was dealt a terrible hand.

Nathan's sudden admission startled her out of her reverie. "God, I was such an angry kid. I'd get in fights at school or take out my aggression on a trashcan in a back alley on my way home from school. I was just pissed at everything and everyone. I couldn't understand why my mom had this disease, or how she could actually forget me. But I'd fight and get pissed, and when I'd get home, I would care for her as I always had. I would talk with her for hours, help her take her meds, make her dinner, and help her get ready for bed. We fell into a routine for about a year doing that, but the last few months things got really bad. She'd start fighting me when I'd ask her to take her meds. She would yell and scream for my dad or for me, and every time I wasn't enough to calm her down." He shut his eyes at the memory and sighed heavily as he reopened them. "I guess my neighbors finally had it, so they called a home. They came out there and took her away. She was there for about a week before she passed away."

Tess sucked in a sharp breath and bit her lip trying to hold back tears.

"That was the first summer I spent out here. The water called to me I think. Something about it calmed me down. Once my mom passed, my dad quit drinking. He tried to be around more, but I was still so angry that I spent all of my time out on the water. It was just easier, you know?"

"I don't know how you did it out here, all this water, the immensity of it terrifies me." Tess spoke incredulously as she gazed out onto the water.

Nathan chuckled. "I think that's what I loved most about it. The water is so immense that I didn't matter. And I needed to not matter."

Tess looked up at him cagily hoping it would prompt Nathan to further explain.

"I mattered to my mom. It was my job to take care of her, and I felt like I let her down. Out here, on the water—I don't matter, so there's no one to let down."

"Nathaniel Suppan you take that back right now." Tess said with fervor shaking her voice.

Nathan's eyes widened in disbelief.

"What? What did I do?" His tone was earnest and desperate.

She took his face in her hands. "You matter Nathan. Don't ever say that you don't. And how could you possibly think you let your mom down? Do you know how incredibly strong you are for being able to take care of her and show your support through something like that, especially at that age?"

She softened her voice as she stroked his cheek with her left hand. "You are one of the bravest, strongest persons I know."

He leaned in to kiss her quickly before pulling her onto his lap. He gently wrapped his arms around her waist and pressed his forehead to hers. Her proximity soothed him in a way he didn't understand. Her scent, her touch, it sent shivers down his spine and warmed his chest.

"Thanks Tess, that means a lot. And I didn't mean it as harshly as it sounded. I never had suicidal tendencies; it was more about liking the anonymity of it." She pressed her head forward and nodded in acceptance. "Ever since I could get out here on the water, it felt like I could be at peace—at least for a little while."

She sighed contented with his revelation and wrapped her arms around his neck. "Alright, enough with the heavy. Tell me more about you."

Nathan frowned slightly at her mercurialness but decided to disregard it and try to lighten the mood. "I spent the rest of my summers out here on the water. I went to college, got my associates degree, went through the academy, and now I'm waiting for them to put me on active duty."

"Being an officer, is it something you actually want to do?"

"It can be rewarding. Like I have a sense of purpose, but do I love it?" He hesitated briefly. "I don't know."

"Don't you want something to love?"

He stared back at her. The statement hit harder than he ever would have expected. He couldn't find the right words so he just looked down at his hand lightly tracing the top of her thigh.

When he didn't answer she tried to change the subject realizing she may have gone a step too far.

"So where does Tommy fit into all of this?"

Nathan smiled to himself. "Tommy's been around since I was I think six. We grew up together. He's like a brother to me. You know, he's the one who finally convinced me to ask you out."

"Oh really?"

"Well that's putting it nicely. It's more like he said something to the effect of 'if I didn't get my butt in gear I'd lose you', and well it worked." He grinned.

Tess pursed her lips and smiled. "Well remind me to thank him someday."

"Oh no, you cannot tell him he had any part of this. He'll never let me live it down."

She cocked her head to the side and in a playfully taunting voice said, "Oh, now I most certainly *will* thank him."

"Now you've done it." He teased back as he picked her up bridal style in his arms and stood on the edge of the boat.

"Nathan! What are you doing?" Her voice started to rise with panic and laughter.

"A deal is a deal."

"Nathan! No!" She screamed as he jumped with her in his arms into the water.

He popped up out of the water first laughing hysterically. Tess popped up next sputtering, "Oh, you think that's funny, huh?" She asked as she gasped for air and her teeth began to chatter.

"Yeah, I do." He said mockingly coy.

She scowled at him before swimming over and climbing on his back while pushing his head down into the water. They played like that for what felt like minutes or hours he wasn't sure. It reminded Nathan of childhood. Playing in the water just because you could. Grownups didn't do that anymore, and after today, for the life of him, he couldn't understand why they didn't.

"Here's another towel. I know you must be chilly." He said as he handed her a thick towel from below deck.

"Thanks. So how come you went into the academy?" She asked as she tried blotting the water out of her hair.

She could see Nathan visibly stiffen at the question.

"You don't give up do you?"

"I don't have it in me." She narrowed her eyes and her expression turned somber as if her admittance was just a matter-of-fact.

Her bravado made him halt suddenly. "I don't think I've ever met someone quite like you." He chuckled softly before continuing, "I imagine I probably never will."

"No, you probably won't." She crinkled her nose and smiled up at him.

More than anything he wanted to be honest with her, but he wasn't sure if he was ready to let her in on all of his dark secrets. He knew that there was a real possibility that if she knew of all the darkness in him, that he may not be able to ask her stay. And he wanted so badly for her to stay and to maybe even love him one day. But at what cost? Her love would have to brave some pretty extraordinary circumstances; after all it's difficult to love someone like him. Someone who has yet to really figure out what it is they are meant to do or accomplish. Letting her know the deep dark secrets before he could show her any of the good stuff—well that wasn't a chance he could take. Not yet anyway.

"I got involved at the academy because I want to help people." He suggested.

She could see in his eyes that he wasn't telling the whole truth, but she didn't feel like it was her place to press the matter.

"Well I think it's really valiant of you. Sitka would be lucky to have a man like you watching their streets."

⸻ ••◆◆•• ⸻

"Again? Alright, thanks Tommy. I'll be there in bit." Tess sighed into the phone as she grabbed her purse and his keys.

She knew her way to the hospital all too well now. It had become habit to make the trip. She backed Nathan's Impala out of her driveway and began down the road with the sound of studs grumbling in protest against the pavement. She didn't make it more than five minutes before she had to pull the car over. She put it in park and climbed out, slamming the door behind her. With her hands over her head, she took a deep, steadying breath. She didn't know how many more calls like this she could get.

In the past six months since Nathan had been promoted to active duty, she had been in and out of the hospital eight times with him. Nathan was always putting himself in dangerous positions, more dangerous than necessary. He would never admit to being reckless, but she could see it in Tommy's eyes. She knew that even Tommy was scared for Nathan.

She couldn't understand his behavior, how he would willingly put himself in those situations. His disregard for his own safety was unsettling and cruel. She couldn't comprehend how he didn't see how draining it was to her, how much of a toll it took on her own sanity to keep receiving these phone calls. She wasn't sure if she could bear another day like this. Then again, she thought that every time, and every time she would be sitting in the waiting room right beside Tommy.

She let out a prolific sigh before lowering her arms and climbing back in the Impala. She shook her head as she turned the keys and the car roared to life. It took her seven minutes to get to the hospital and when she pulled up, Tommy was sitting outside on a bench waiting for her.

"How bad is it this time Tommy?" She asked as she walked up to him.

He dropped his eyes to the ground not wanting to look her in the eyes. He wouldn't dare tell Tess, but she scared the daylights out of him, and he knew she was going to be pissed. But more than that, he knew it was his job to watch Nathan's six, and it was his job to make sure Nathan made it back to Tess each night. Somehow, he kept failing both of them.

"S'not so bad." He mumbled as he moved a piece of salt around on the ground with the tip of his boot.

"Don't lie to me Tommy." Tess said in a heady voice with narrowed eyes knowing she could get Tommy to spill.

He threw his hands up. "Alright, alright. I'll tell you, but that's only because I'm sick of driving his sorry ass to the hospital. I'm worried about him too, Tess."

She sighed once before sitting down next to him on the bench. She rubbed his hand gently in reassurance. "I know Tommy."

Tommy shrugged. "He got in the middle of a bar fight. I told him to let it go, but of course he didn't listen. All I know is he took a few blows to the gut. Probably bruised a rib or two, and someone stabbed his leg with a piece of broken glass."

Tess flinched at the abhorrent idea of Nathan in a fight.

"What am I gonna do Tommy?" She relented, her green eyes glistened with tears and her face looked ashen.

He patted her on the knee as he spoke, "You're gonna tell him to knock it off because you're the brave one out of the two of us." He chuckled trying to lighten the mood. "And because just maybe he'll listen to you. Cause he sure as hell won't listen to me."

She shrugged her shoulders. She knew Tommy was right, but she still didn't want to have this conversation. She knew it could turn into a fight. As much as he needed to hear the truth about his actions having consequences, she still loved him, and she knew there was something going on that he wasn't telling her about.

She rocked forward standing up with as much assertion and courage as she could muster.

"Alright. Wish me luck." She said while facing the hospital doors.

"Break a leg."

Her face whipped around so fast that Tommy nearly spit the gum out from his mouth.

"Poor choice of words Tommy?" She chided playfully.

"Oh no, that was definitely pun intended." He chuckled softly.

Tess shrugged her shoulders and laughed. She could always count on Tommy to put a smile on her face.

Tess held her hand on the doorknob hesitating to go in. She knew bruised ribs would be bad, but she had to put her mean face on right now.

She closed her eyes tightly as she took a deep studying breath before bursting through the door. "Nathan, how could you?"

Nathan looked up at her horrified. Of course, Tommy sent her in. The big baby couldn't keep his damn mouth shut.

"Tess, I can explain. Look I thought I could handle it on my own—"

Her hand went up mid-sentence. "Save it. Nathan, you promised you wouldn't do anything so reckless anymore. You promised you were done. I swear Nathan, I can't do this anymore. I can't keep getting these phone calls." Her voice was starting to lose its potency.

"I am done. I promise Tess, that was the last stupid thing I'll ever do." He pleaded with her.

She inched closer to his bed while looking him straight in the eye. "It better have been because so help me God, if I ever get a phone call like this again—I *will* leave you." That was it. That was the one last shred of leverage she had left.

His stomach turned. He hadn't realized how serious she was before. She had told him time and time again, but he hadn't listened. He didn't understand how his actions were selfish, that what he was doing was really hurting her.

With her uncanny ability to read his thoughts she continued, "And it's not just me Nathan, Tommy is worried too. You're scaring the both of us. To be honest, we don't know what to do anymore." Her voice was shaking fiercely now, all of her vigor completely vanished. "*I* don't know what to do anymore," she whispered.

He took advantage of the respite in her thoughts and pulled her onto the bed with him. He wrapped his arm around her pulling her close. She sighed heavily as she sank back into his chest.

He flinched slightly in pain. "I'm so sorry baby. I promise I won't scare you again. I swear it." He whispered in her ear.

She wanted to fight it so bad, but all she could think about was how happy she was that he was alive. Happy that she was there in his arms and for a moment, everything was okay.

"Damn it." Nathan muttered under his breath as he tried to reach for his pills but was drawn back because the pain in his ribs was too severe.

Tess walked in to grab his pills for him. "You know you wouldn't be in so much pain if you hadn't been so rash."

"Yeah Tess, I know. You tell me every damn day." He sneered acidly.

The look on her face was as if he had slapped her. He wanted to eat his words immediately regretting them.

"Tess, I didn't mean—"

"Here." She grabbed the bottle of pills and shoved them towards his chest before storming out of the bathroom.

He threw the bottle of pills into the sink in a fit of anger. She was only trying to help. He knew she was equally, and understandably, both worried and angry with him. He didn't actually blame her— it was just the pain talking. He knew it was time to tell her the truth. He would lose her for good if he didn't.

He opened his front door. She was standing next to the railing of the porch with her back to him. Her arms were wrapped tightly around herself, locking her thick sweater around her trying to protect her from the chill in the air. He knew she was *really* pissed. She only ever gave him the silent treatment when it was really bad. Anything lesser and she would have been in there holding her own, but for her to just walk away—he knew she was reaching her limit.

He stepped closer to her and hesitantly placed a hand on her back. "Tess?" He cooed softly.

She turned further away from him trying to hide the tear she was wiping away. Nathan sighed resignedly.

"Tess, I'm sorry about what happened in there. I didn't mean to snap at you the way that I did. You were only trying to help." He spoke in a low solemn voice.

"You're right, I was." She spun around to face him, her eyes were bright with an ember smoldering behind them. If it weren't such a serious moment, he would almost laugh at the intensity of her look. There was that fire he had admired so much in her.

He brushed her arm softly. "I know, I'm sorry. I'm an idiot."

She gaffed slightly as she rolled her eyes. "That's putting it nicely."

"Yeah, I guess I deserved that."

She looked down and kept her eyes glued to the floor. She didn't want him to keep looking her in the eyes. If he did, she knew he would see straight through the tough act she was trying to put on.

"I think it's time I told you something." He breathed heavily with his admission as he beckoned her to the porch swing behind them.

Chapter Six

It was close to midnight when he was walking home from the marina. His dad told him he had to be home at ten, but he got distracted again. It was the third time this week he missed curfew and he knew his dad was going to be pissed. He went to take a shortcut through the back allies, and that's when he heard him.

At first it was difficult to make out what he was hearing. He heard a young boy crying and screaming, but it wasn't until he got closer that he could finally discern what the boy was pleading. *"Please don't kill me."*

Nathan crept closer, peeking behind the alley wall so he could see what was happening. His heart began thumping heavily in his chest. Two men who must have been in their early twenties were laughing as they took turns kicking something on the ground.

Nathan's eyes strained to see through the shadows to look upon the ground. It took a few seconds for his eyes to adjust to the darkness before he could finally see. On the ground was a young boy, probably only a few years younger than himself, maybe eleven or twelve years old. He was lying on the cold, wet ground in nothing but his white briefs that were stained black from the sludge on the ground. His pale body was visibly covered in bruises, cuts, mud, and blood—lots of blood. Nathan could see a gash on his head with blood streaming down the side of his face. For a brief moment he swore the boy looked straight at him.

The moment only lasted a millisecond before the young boy's eyes were drawn back to his attackers. In one of the man's hands was a knife; in the other man's hand was a pistol. The young boy whimpered in fear. The man with the knife laughed as he crouched down closer to the boy. He took his knife and slid it across the boy's arm. He screamed out in pain, and Nathan watched as blood gushed out of the open wound. The other man laughed harder and then kicked the boy swiftly in the gut once more.

"Please! Pl-please stop!" The young boy pleaded and cried.

The men looked at each other and nodded, the one with the knife bent back down. It was so fast Nathan could barely see him do it, but in a matter of seconds, the man with the knife had carved a symbol into the boy's chest. Nathan couldn't see what it was from where he was, especially since blood from the shallow cuts started dripping down covering the symbol. The boy hollered in crippling agony.

Nathan flinched at the sound. It was the most blood curdling noise he had ever heard.

"Please don't kill me!" The young boy pleaded with vigor for his life, but it was useless.

The man with the gun handed it over to his shorter but well-built friend. Nathan watched as he then held it up and shot off two rounds into the young boy's head. Nathan visibly shook with each pop as he blanched with terror before doubling over to hurl. Everything he had in his stomach was now laying on the wet ground in front of him. His heart beat erratically as he wiped his mouth and then wiped his forehead removing the bead of sweat rolling down. Nathan raised his head to look up, both hands on his thighs as he tried to steady himself on his feet. His mouth hung open in horror as he watched the men howl with laughter. They playfully swatted at each other before taking off and jogging down the alley.

How could those men be so cruel? What was their purpose? Was this just a game to them?

Nathan was slowly creeping towards the young boy when he heard the sirens. He could hear policemen over their PA systems yelling at the men to stop running and he got scared that maybe they would think he was a part of it. Nathan got so scared that he turned on his heel and ran all the way home without looking back. He snuck in through his window and crawled into bed still in his wet clothes, pulling the covers up to his chin, and silently cried himself to sleep.

"That's what you've been keeping from me?" Tess cocked her head to the side and regarded him intently.

Nathan's head hung low as he breathed out, "I didn't know how to tell you."

"Don't you trust me?" Tess sounded hurt and betrayed.

Nathan's head shot up. "That's not why I didn't tell you Tess. I was just so ashamed that I never did anything. I stood by and watched, and then when I could have told the police everything, I ran! I was a coward!"

He shook his head to himself in disbelief. Of course, she would believe this was her fault. She gave him so much more credit than he ever deserved.

She held his gaze looking back and forth between his eyes trying to understand her own thoughts and feelings as she processed what he had just told her.

She shrugged slightly; the sight of anguish on his face was sobering. "You were just a kid, Nathan. A kid who saw something horrific. No one could blame you for not doing anything and running, you were *just* a boy."

"Don't defend me Tess." He said vehemently.

"What do you want me to say Nathan?" She jumped up to her feet and held up her arms in question. "Do you want me to say 'Nathan you are such a coward, how do you live with yourself'?"

He hung his head low. "Yes. It's the truth." His voice was so soft she could barely hear him.

With one hand she gently lifted his face towards her and he eyed her warily. "Well you're not going to hear it from me. Just because you didn't do anything doesn't make you less than a man, it makes you smart.

Nathan, if you had tried to intervene, those men would have had no problem killing you."

"You can't know for sure that that would have been the outcome."

"No, but it was a possible outcome. I'm glad you didn't try anything. Yes, you ran, but you were a scared, traumatized, little boy."

She could picture it clearly, visions of a young boy staring wide-eyed and pale at a gruesome scene in front of him. The thought of it was heartbreaking.

Tess took a seat on his lap as they sat in silence for a few moments before Tess spoke up as a new thought crossed her mind.

"Is that why you've been so careless? Retribution?"

Nathan couldn't look at her. He couldn't give her an answer because he knew it was the truth, but he didn't want to say it out loud.

Tess took his silence as his omission of guilt, so she pressed on. "Did you think that by taking risks or getting yourself beat to a pulp, would somehow make amends for what happened? That's not how it works Nathan. You don't need to be punished, you didn't *do* anything wrong." Her voice was incredulous as she began to finally understand the depths of his wantonness.

"But I did, Tess. I did do something wrong. Don't you see that?" He said poignantly as he moved her off of him and stood up to walk over to the railing.

She hesitated a moment before making a move. She wasn't sure how but she knew then and there it would be her life's ambition for Nathan to see that he wasn't the villain in this story.

"Have you visited his grave?" She questioned as she walked towards him.

"What? No, no I haven't." He eyed her, surprised by her question.

"Then that's the only thing you've done wrong. That's the only thing you *can* control. Tomorrow, you and I are going to the cemetery to pay our respects."

"Tess, how is visiting a grave going to help?" He stared down at her with a perplexed and slightly reserved expression.

"Do you like T.S. Eliot?"

He shook his head with a subtle roll of his eyes. She was possibly one of the most mercurial women he had ever met. What the hell was going on in her head?

"The poet, right?"

"Yeah," she laughed, "the poet."

"What about him?"

"T.S. Eliot once wrote, 'I will show you fear in a handful of dust— We don't actually fear death, we fear that no one will notice our absence that we will disappear without a trace.'"

Nathan stared blankly at her trying to understand where she was headed.

"Nathan, the only amends you need to make is showing that boy that his absence has been noticed. That *you* noticed. Go to his grave and show him that someone out there cares for him, even when in his life he was shown such an absence of love that night."

He looked down at her. How could she take this so well, how could she be so understanding? He should have given her more credit; she could handle anything.

He put his arm around her pulling her close and kissed the top of her head.

"Thank you." He murmured.

"Come on Nathan. You can do this." She coaxed in a tender soothing voice as she sat by his side in the Impala.

He took the key out of the ignition slowly and turned to face her. "I don't think I can Tess."

"That's why you have to do it. You've been living with this for so long, it's time you let go. For him."

She smiled sweetly at him and patted his hand before she stepped out of the car.

He sighed loudly; he knew she was right.

She waited in front of the car for him holding a bouquet of flowers in one hand with the other hand outstretched for him to take. He let her lead him to the tombstone of Andrew Martin.

In Loving Memory of our little boy
You will forever be in our hearts

His heart stopped for a moment and he felt his throat constricting. Suddenly he wanted to be anywhere but there. Every inch of him was screaming to turn and run in the opposite direction. He was jolted back from his reverie at the sound of her voice.

"Hi Andrew, my name is Tess. You don't know me, but that's okay. Andrew, I am so sorry for the evils in the world, for what evil did to you. You were just a boy, something like this should have never happened, but it did, and I am so sorry for that."

Without looking she squeezed Nathan's hand before continuing, "Andrew, I'm here with Nathan. He was there that night, and he saw what happened. He was just a little boy then. He was so scared—like you. So he ran. He was just a scared, little boy who's been paying for his mistakes ever since." She hesitated for a moment before she carried on, "He's a police officer now, you know? He's out there protecting little boys and girls just like you. He's making sure nothing like what happened to you, happens again. But, Nathan is struggling Andrew. He feels like he is responsible for what happened that night."

Nathan stiffened at her words; he did feel responsible.

"Nathan is making this town a better place, but Andrew, I need you to let Nathan know you're not angry. That you don't blame him. Give him some sign that it's okay. Please."

Tears started to form in Nathan's eyes. He wasn't sure he believed in signs, he wasn't sure Andrew could forgive him, but he was sure that he loved Tess. That in that moment she had more faith in him than he had ever had in himself.

Tess looked up at him and smiled with a nod of encouragement. He took a deep breath and cleared his throat.

"Andrew, I just wanted to say I'm sorry. I'm so sorry I didn't do anything that night. I'm sorry that I didn't do anything when it mattered most. I don't think I can ever make up for that night, for what happened to you, but I promise I will try and help as many people as I can."

Tess rubbed his arm in support. She gently brushed the light layer of snow off the top of the tombstone and laid the white lilies they brought in front of it. She brought her fingers up to her lips and blew a kiss and said goodbye. She tugged lightly at Nathan's arm signaling it was time to go.

"Bye, Andrew." Nathan said as he turned to follow Tess.

They walked quietly back through the cemetery with her arm in his. As they walked through a patch of lilies, pelargoniums, amaryllis, and cyclamen popping out from the fresh layer of snow, all vibrant with color, all of different shapes, and sizes—Nathan heard a noise.

He stopped in his tracks. Tess turned around to ask why they stopped, but he held up a hand to signal to be quiet.

"Do you hear that?" Nathan asked after a moment.

"Hear what?" She whispered back, looking around.

"That noise? I swear I heard someone whistling." He shook his head.

"Nathan, there's no one around."

Nathan swiveled his head around craning his eyes trying to find who was whistling.

"There. I heard it again, didn't you?"

As soon as he asked, a gust of wind blew in fiercely. In its wake, petals from the vibrant flowers lifted into the air and swirled up high around them.

Tess giggled in pure delight, and Nathan felt a calm wash through him as they watched the petals dance around them.

Nathan looked over at Tess. She was there next to him with arms stretched out wide and her face lifted towards the sky. The petals swirled around her, caressing her skin as they continued their dance. She had the most beautiful smile that Nathan had ever seen. She commanded his attention in a way he didn't know was possible. Seeing her look so happy, he couldn't help but smile too. He threw his head back and let the wind blow around him.

"Thank you, Andrew." Tess spoke in such a quiet voice that Nathan barely heard her.

His head snapped back down at Tess who was still smiling up at the sky.

A sign?

He wondered to himself. Is this what Tess was talking about, sending a sign to let him know that Andrew was okay? He started to laugh. He never believed in this kind of thing, but with Tess, she made it possible. She made miracles happen.

A weight had suddenly been lifted from his chest and for the first time he felt like he could breathe again. She made it possible for him—she saved him.

He laughed and laughed and lifted Tess into his arms swirling her around. She giggled with him. When he set her down he kissed her with tenderness and love.

Her lips quirked up in a smile. "What was that for?"

He held her hands in his. "For being you. I love you, Tess Dawson."

"Let's do something crazy today."

Nathan gently moved the hair away from her face as the side of his lips started to curl up. "Like what?"

"I don't know, anything. Bungee jumping?"

That surprised him. For someone who was worried about his safety twenty-four seven, why she would willingly suggest something so extreme was a complete conundrum.

He laughed. "Yeah, no. I have a strict policy against doing something that people won't feel sorry for you if you die. No one has ever said, 'That's too bad about that guy who wanted to tie a rope around his ankles and jump off a bridge.'"

Her lips turned down into a pout, which made him laugh even harder. "Fine, I tell you what, grab a coat and I'll take you somewhere."

She grinned obviously pleased with herself. "Where to?"

"Does it matter?" He challenged.

She eyed him suspiciously for a moment before answering, "No, I suppose it doesn't."

He put the Impala in park and looked over at her. "What do you say to a hike?"

"Thimbleberry Lake?"

"It's nice, peaceful, and there's a much smaller chance that you'll die while hiking." He smirked.

She threw her head back slightly and laughed mockingly.

He chuckled. "Thank you for that courtesy laugh, I appreciate it."

She just gave him a lopsided smile and patted his hand in mirth.

As they hiked out towards the lake she beamed with a smile stretching across her face and breathed deeply inhaling the fresh, early, spring air. She could see why he liked this place. She glanced over at him often, he seemed content out here but she could see something was bothering him. Maybe he needed the fresh air more than she did. Maybe what he really needed was a chance to get away. She knew taking him to visit Andrew's grave wouldn't be the end-all cure, but she had hoped the joy she saw in his face as they were leaving—she hoped that would have lasted longer.

He stared off in the distance but from the corner of his eye he could see Tess watching him. She stared so intently at him. He knew that more than anything she wanted him to be okay, like she was willing it into existence. She wanted him to be the good guy, and he wanted to be that for her. But there was still something heavy and dark in the pit of his stomach. He promised her he would stop acting like a jackass and would be more careful, but the truth was, more often than not he would find himself dreaming of revenge. Even if Andrew had forgiven him, he couldn't forgive those men in the alley. It was almost as if it were a thirst he couldn't quite satiate. He wanted revenge so badly and the depravity of the thoughts of what he would do to get it, terrified even himself.

He cleared his throat as they gently padded along the trail. "Tess, is revenge or vengeance or whatever, well is it really so bad?"

He turned to look at her. He knew that by watching her he would learn. He would look to her, examine her reactions to things and then he would understand right from wrong. Knowing Tess helped him know whether or not he was on the right path. He was grateful for that and he needed to look to her once more to know if he needed to fight these feelings with every fiber of his being.

She took a moment to consider his question and sighed. "Well, I guess it depends."

"On what? What makes revenge justifiable or good?"

"I think it depends on what lengths you go to get it, and if you're willing to give up everything for it."

He eyed her carefully trying to understand.

She looked at him. "The way I see it, there are two types of revenge. I believe there is revenge or justice in being able to move on." She shrugged her shoulders knowing he wouldn't understand that one. "Moving on from whatever injustices you suffered is revenge in itself because it proves or shows whoever wronged you, that they no longer can affect you. That you are stronger than they will ever be. Taking that power from them is devastating to them."

She frowned slightly to herself at her own words. She hadn't realized until they were already out of her mouth that maybe she was talking from experience. That maybe being with Nathan, being happy with him was her own source of revenge against her past. The thought had never occurred to her before then.

He cleared his throat once more breaking her from her reprieve. "And the other kind?"

She sighed slightly and her voice was soft and hesitant as she focused back on Nathan. "The other kind of revenge is what you want. It's the kind that I pray you never go after." She let her eyes wander off into the distance as she spoke, "Nathan, you want the kind of revenge that would make you do things that go against everything that you are. The kind of revenge that there's no stopping because once you go down that road, you'll find that it was wrong. You'll go down that road just to see that it wasn't enough, that it only made things worse. And that's something you won't come back from."

They came to a stop by the lake's edge. He took a deep breath and nodded once and then stared off into the distance. After a few minutes he wrapped his arm around her and drew her into him. He inhaled the scent of her hair and kissed the top of her head and whispered, "Will I ever measure up to the kind of man you deserve?"

She grinned to herself as she nuzzled in close to his chest. How did he not understand that he had already done so much for her? "The fact that you continuously ask yourself that is more than anything I deserve."

She stayed back on the trail to take a last-minute picture of the lake and when she came out to the clearing she saw him. She saw him more unmistakably than she had ever before. He was perched up against the Impala. He wore dark jeans and his faded work boots. His dark grey thermal clung tightly to his torso and the olive-green button up hung loosely at his sides. He leaned with one leg bent against the car with both hands in his pockets and he stared off into the distance. She could see it there in his face that he was doing everything in his power to be the good guy. To be the kind of guy that she would be proud of. She smiled to herself thinking how lucky she was to find someone who wanted so badly to measure up to something. She only wished he could see for himself that he was the right guy for her. That he was the savior in her story. The only person he needed to prove anything to was himself. She just prayed that one day he would learn that. She quickly snapped a picture of him before she caught his attention and he smiled over at her.

Chapter Seven

"Can I ask you something?" Nathan asked as he took a seat next to his captain at the bar.

"You're off duty Nate. Go home. Spend time with that girl of yours." Captain Marx spoke as he took a swig of his whiskey.

Nathan looked at his knotted hands on the bar in front of him. "Actually sir, it was her idea that I come talk to you."

Marx looked over at Nathan and eyed him apprehensively. "Oh? And why is that?"

Nathan gently cleared his throat. "Sir, do you know why I joined the force?"

Marx shook his head no. Nathan took a deep breath and proceeded to tell Marx about Andrew Martin and what had happened to him. Marx sat patiently and quietly listening to Nathan's story and when he finished,

he took another swig of his whiskey and looked at
Nathan. "And now you're wondering if you ever faced
those demons, could you get your revenge and live with
it?"

Nathan played with the rim of the bottle of beer
that was set in front of him. "Yeah, yeah I guess I am."

Nathan was silently grateful that Marx had said
it for him. Perhaps revenge was one of the greatest and
most influential traits of someone in law enforcement.

Marx's lips turned down in a slight frown as he
considered what to say. "When I was a rookie, must
have been twenty-two or twenty-three years ago now,
my partner and I responded to a call about a possible
meth lab. The place was an old abandoned shipping
warehouse down by the dockyards. Sure enough, it was
a whole operation. Real scumbags there too." He paused,
his lips snarling up at the memory. After a brief moment
he seemed to shake it off and cleared his throat.
"Anyway, we went in, arrested a couple of the guys who
were too high to even question us being there. It was
routine, easy even, but then something went wrong."

It was Nathan's turn to sit quietly as he waited
for Marx to continue.

"My partner and I didn't think things through,
this was too easy. That's because we were only dealing
with the bottom of the food chain so to speak. We hadn't
realized that the head honcho running the operation was
actually there in the warehouse hiding. He let us arrest
his grunts so he could hide out, but my partner was being
nosy and started to go through the computer files
looking at where the deliveries were going. He thought,
well we both thought, that this could be our big break. If
we took down this warehouse and managed to get a list

of all the distributors, we would have cracked possibly the biggest drug ring this town—this state, has ever seen."

He sighed lavishly before continuing, "Once the guy realized we weren't just arresting his guys and leaving, he stepped out and shot my partner. Two rounds: center mass and head shot."

Nathan paled instantly thinking of Tommy.

"I didn't have enough time to react. The shots were still ringing in my ears and I remember looking down at my partner who was lying there in his own blood. When I looked up I saw the guy heading towards me with his gun raised at me. I don't know if adrenaline kicked in or what. Honestly, I don't even remember going for my gun; but I somehow pulled the trigger first. I shot him three times center mass and he went down."

"I'm sorry about your partner."

"Me too. He was a good guy. And he was right, that case was one of the biggest cases of my career. But it didn't come without consequences."

Nathan looked over at Marx who was studying his empty glass. "What do you mean?"

"That night, back at the station, I remember walking by my captain's office and there was a woman in there crying hysterically. I realized then it was the mother of the man I had just killed. I had never met her before and yet that's who I'll always be. In her story, I'll always be the person who handed her the worst day of her life."

Nathan swallowed hard. "How did you— How did—"

Marx tapped his glass to signal for another. "Go ahead and ask."

"How did you get past it? I know it was self-defense and you did what you had to do, but how did you get past it?"

"The answer is simple. I didn't."

Nathan's eyes widened momentarily and then he dropped them back down to watching his fingers play with his now empty bottle.

Marx grimaced slightly as he spoke, "I didn't get past it. I merely learned to live with it. There's a difference, and not in a good way. For a long time, it consumed me. I understood that what I did was justifiable. I also understood that he was a bad dude, but I couldn't help myself. I couldn't reconcile my guilt from my self-preservation and duty as an officer. I found myself searching and wanting to know everything about him. I could tell you every street he ever lived on, what grades in school he got, the name of his first girlfriend. I wanted to know it all. I *needed* to know it all. And then a week or two after it all happened, I got a package."

He sighed once more as he rubbed his eyes. "It was from his mother. She sent me everything she could find of his, including a ledger with the name of every distributor he ever worked with. What his mother did, it was more than anyone should have to do. I was grateful for it but I couldn't help but imagine how it must have felt to write the name of the person who took her son's life. I studied her print, imagining all the places her hand shook as she wrote it." His expression looked pained. "So, you tell me, how do you get over something like that?"

He scoffed into his drink as he took another sip. "Believe me, if I had the answer to that I probably wouldn't need a drink every night after a shift."

Nathan pulled up to his home and smiled softly as he noticed the headlights of the Impala wash across his front porch. She sat there on the edge of the steps waiting for him. He climbed out of the car and ambled towards her. "How did you know I'd need you?"

She reached for his hand and gently placed it on her heart. "I just didn't think you should be alone tonight."

He studied his hand on her chest. He could feel the steady rhythms of her heart beating against her chest. The gentle way it rose and fell with her breath soothed him. He smiled amorously as he let his hand travel up her torso until he wrapped his hand up in her hair and pulled her face in close to his. He leaned down and pressed his lips to hers.

They walked slowly into the house together, their legs and hands becoming a tangled mess of passionate and hurried touch. His lips continued their lust-filled assault against hers as he tore at her clothing, pulling her coat off her shoulders and letting it fall to the ground. He continued walking them further into the house while her hands shook slightly as she worked on undoing the buttons of his shirt.

In a grunted breath he pulled his mouth from her lips and began kissing down her neck as his hands laced the bottom of her cable-knit sweater. He grabbed the hem of it and pulled back quickly as he lifted the sweater over her head.

She smiled softly as she watched his eyes swallow her whole. She shuddered ever so slightly, the way he looked at her warmed her core and made her panties dampen. He licked his lips subtly as his eyes wandered over her. Her wild, red curls were chaotic around her face, her lips were bruised and plump from his frantic kisses, a slight rose color dusted her cheeks as he watched her chest rise and fall as she struggled to regain her breath. His eyes wandered south and a small smirk formed in the corner of his mouth as he salaciously watched her breasts rising and falling beneath her teal, lace bra.

She took his small reprieve to finish the last button on his shirt and she pushed it down off his shoulders. She softly trailed her fingertips across his bare chest, watching the way his chest pumped in rhythm to his strangled breath. She watched as small bumps rose underneath the trail her fingertips left as she continued tracing down his chest.

She loved the warmth of his skin under her touch, the ripples in the subtle definitions of his muscles. She grinned inwardly as she continued to trace down along the left side of his V and trailed her finger down along waistband of his jeans that hung low on his hips.

Her fingers teasing so close to his dick elicited a low growl from his chest and he reached out and pulled her into him crashing his lips into hers once again. He pushed against her, making her take small steps backwards as he made quick work to undo her bra and pull it from her body. He pushed her back one final step until she felt her back connect with the cool hardness of the wall behind her.

Nathan moaned desperately as his left hand tightly cupped her breast in the palm of his hand. His right hand continued to paw down her side making his way to her butt and he gripped her tightly. His rough passionate movements did something to her and her breath quickened as a long slow moan escaped her lips.

His lips curled up into a smile against her lips, he loved that she shared his same reaction. The way he could be animalistic with her and she wouldn't break. She challenged him back and their mutual need for each other was something he would never get used to or tire of.

He brought both hands down and cupped her tightly around her butt and lifted her up, hitching her to his waist. She clasped her arms around his neck and continued kissing him as he carried her into his bedroom.

When he felt his legs hit his bed he stopped and gently placed her down on the ground next to it. He trailed warm kisses down her neck and chest and let his hands cup her breasts. Nathan briefly let his eyes meet hers and smiled when he saw her head tilt subtly back and her eyes closed in ecstasy. The sight of her made him groan as he lowered his mouth to her breast. He gently sucked and teased her nipple as his hands continued massaging them.

Leaving her breathless he tore his lips away from her breasts and placed two gentle kisses on the flat of her stomach before he undid the button and zipper of her jeans. He gently pushed at the waistband and slid her jeans down past her butt. His breath hitched as he watched her slowly shimmy her jeans down and off, kicking them to the side.

"Damn, baby." He breathed out as he stared at her standing there in front of him in nothing but her teal, lace panties. He felt himself harden at the sight of her.

She giggled seductively as she undid his jeans and pushed down roughly on both his jeans and briefs. She smiled victoriously when his hard member sprang out as his clothes fell to the floor.

Nathan growled once more as he lifted her up roughly allowing her legs to wrap tightly around his torso. He could feel the heat from her core teasing him desperately. He pushed them onto the bed as he kissed her passionately, letting his tongue invade her mouth.

He pulled back slightly letting his forehead rest against hers and huffed out in jagged breaths, "I need you now."

She grabbed his face and pulled him in for kiss. "Take me."

He moaned against her mouth and trailed his hand down in between them. He smiled inwardly as he pulled her panties down and her legs parted under his touch. He began gently massaging inside her folds, her softs moans becoming more ragged. The sound of her pleasure made his dick convulse as he shoved a finger inside of her.

"Fuck baby, you are so wet."

She purred against him as she closed her eyes and softly bit down on her bottom lip as she let her hips rock in motion to his finger thrusting in and out of her.

He buried his face into her neck, planting wet hard kisses as he pushed a second finger inside of her. He loved the way she moaned audibly, the way she felt, how her body quickened at his assault, stretching her and pleasuring her.

He continued sucking on her neck as his fingers continued fucking her. Using his thumb, he began massaging her clit forcing her to cry out.

"Nathan!" She screamed as she neared her breaking point.

Hearing his name on her lips excited him even more as he pounded his fingers inside of her getting her closer to her release. Her back arched and she cried out as she orgasmed and tumbled down her high.

Nathan grunted in satisfaction as he watched her ride it out, once he knew she was finished he gently removed his fingers drawing them up to his mouth. He smiled wickedly waiting for her to open her eyes and watch as he sucked on his fingers tasting her.

"You taste so good." He murmured.

Tess blushed at his admission and wrapped her arms around his biceps as he lifted himself and slowly entered her. She winced briefly as she felt her core stretch around him, and let out a low breath as he pushed himself in to the hilt.

Gone was the frantic need to fuck as he placed a gentle loving kiss on her lips and pulled up to watch her as he slowly and gently thrust in and out of her. His eyes fluttered slightly at the feel of his cock buried in her walls. He could feel her juices coating his shaft as he continued to pump in and out. He smiled as he smoothed her hair away from her face and gazed into her eyes looking up at him under thick lashes.

"I love you, baby." He whispered through uneven breaths.

"I love you too—harder please, I need you baby." She whispered. She knew they both needed this. They needed each other desperately and roughly.

Nathan smiled, he didn't need to be told twice. He began quickening his pace, forcing his dick all the way in with each thrust. Her moans allowing him to go harder and harder.

He quickly drew out of her and turned her on her side. Up on his knees, he grabbed her leg and hitched it over his shoulder. Holding onto her thigh he entered her deeply causing her to cry out.

"That's it, baby." She huffed.

He smiled as he pumped in and out and let his free hand tug gently at her nipple. He loved playing with the small bud and began palming her breast as he felt himself nearing.

"Come with me baby girl." He commanded softly as he pulled his hand away from her breast and to the front of her slit. He massaged her clit again as he thrust in, he could feel her insides clenching around him, and he groaned in pleasure.

Tess screamed out as she orgasmed once more with him still inside her. He smiled as he pumped into her twice more before finding his release and letting his seed spill into her.

They stayed still for a moment in those positions, catching their breaths. He squeezed her thigh gently as he kissed her calf that was still hooked on his shoulder as he gently pulled out of her.

Her breath hitched slightly at the feeling of being empty. She smiled up at him seeing the grin that spread across his handsome face.

He rolled over gently laying his body on hers, and leaned down to kiss her once more. It was a soft impassioned kiss filled with post-coital bliss. She smiled as he pulled back and she gently combed her fingers through his unruly hair.

"Thank you for being here tonight." He murmured quietly.

She let her hands travel up and down his arms and she lifted her head so their eyes could meet. She let him stare at her; she knew he needed this moment. She knew he needed to know he could count on her to be there. He needed her and she needed him. The butterflies in her belly danced and her core throbbed gently and she knew she would never get enough of him.

With her right hand she gently pulled his face towards her and she kissed him. She let her lips move softly against his, letting her warmth sear right through him.

After their long kiss he finally pulled away from her and looked her in the eye once more and whispered a plea, "Never leave, okay?"

Her lips curled up and she nodded as she answered, "Okay."

⸻ ••◆◆•• ⸻

The deafening clap of thunder made her yelp as she spun around in the darkness. A flash of light illuminated the dark hallway as lightning struck outside. She stared down the long passage and saw at the end of the hallway, one of the tall windows was open and the curtains blew fiercely in as the wind and rain howled outside.

Her chest heaved in and out as adrenaline coursed through her veins. She wasn't sure where she was or why she had this sickening feeling in the bottom of her belly telling her she wasn't safe.

"Tessie." A disembodied voice whispered through the darkness.

Thunder clapped and rumbled again and again. She spun around in circles looking for where the voice came from, but it was too dark to see. The only glimpses she got of the hallway was when brief flashes of light seeped through the windows.

"Tessie." He called to her again. She recognized his voice this time and she strained her eyes, but no one was there.

She stayed in place, spinning around in circles looking for any clue, when suddenly the window next to her imploded in. She quickly raised her hands to her face and turned as she crouched down to protect herself from the shattering glass.

Once all of the glass clattered to the floor she lifted her hands and stood up. She gasped and tried to stifle a cry when she saw him standing outside of the window. He stood there, with his face covered by shadows in the pouring rain, watching her. A flash of light danced across his face and she watched his lips turn up into a sinister snarl.

It only took a brief moment for her to react and when she gained function over her body she willed herself to run. She bolted down the hallway and through the house.

The lightning was becoming more frequent and helped illuminate her way. She ran through the house, she still wasn't sure where she was but she knew she had to keep running. The hallway stretched on and she entered what she could only assume was a living room. There was a large fireplace on the far wall and couches and chairs were all covered in dust cloths. The scene in front of her was surreal, like a set out of a horror film cast in a haunted inn.

Her eyes scanned the room quickly looking for an escape route or a weapon, she wasn't sure which. As her eyes darted around the room she cried out again when she saw him standing outside the nearby window watching her. She didn't know how he could have found her here in this place.

She turned on her heel and took off down the dark corridor once more. Only glancing back briefly over her shoulder, she knew he was following her. She couldn't see him but she could feel him getting closer.

"Tessie."

She pushed harder against the wooden floors, forcing herself to sprint down the hallway. Halfway down the corridor she unexpectedly tripped over something on the ground. Before she could catch her balance, she felt herself fly forward and skid across the floor.

She sat up and grasped her ankle, wincing in pain. The pain subsided almost immediately when she saw the thing she had tripped over begin to move. All color drained from her face as she peered through the darkness to what lie in front of her.

She leaned forward and tilted her head. Once lightning illuminated the passageway she recognized what she saw and her eyes grew wide and she fell back on her arms. She shook her head violently whispering, "No, no, no."

She stared unblinking as the girl on the floor rose to her feet and stepped forward leaning over Tess who was still on the ground. The girl was barefoot in ripped jeans and her arms were strapped around herself in a dirtied straightjacket. Her reddish-brown hair lay limply around her face in matted clumps of dried blood and dirt smeared her pale, fair skin. As she stepped closer to Tess and stood in the light from the window, the girl cocked her head to the side and eyed Tess intently.

Tess felt the air evaporate from her lungs as she tried desperately to suck in new breath. The girl stood hovering over her now and her bright, green eyes glared at her with feral intensity. She knew this girl.

"I'm nobody!" The girl said with a freakish ability to read Tess's mind.

"Who are you?" She tilted her head side to side waiting for Tess to answer but Tess stared on, eyes wide in terror, unable to speak.

"Are you nobody, too?"

When Tess still didn't respond, the girl slowly paced in front of Tess with her large eyes and her head bowed slightly. "Then there's a pair of us—don't tell!" She exclaimed wildly looking down at Tess. She then crouched down in sharp jagged movements and leaned her face in directly in front of Tess—a face that mirrored her own.

"They'd banish us, you know." She whispered as the corners of her mouth lifted into a deranged smile.

Her pulse quickened as her heart beat frenetically against her chest. She sat up quickly in bed as she wiped the hair away from her face and felt the cool sweat against her skin. She squinted her eyes trying to adjust to the darkness. Her momentary confusion slowly receded when she realized she was still in Nathan's bed. She looked down and saw that he was still lying there next to her with his arm draped across her waist.

She felt an icy chill course through her and she could no longer bear it. She pulled her legs in towards her chest and began to sob into her hands.

"Baby?" Nathan stirred next to her. It only took him a second to realize she was crying.

He scrambled into a sitting position and pulled her onto his lap. He kept one arm wrapped tightly around her while the other stroked her hair.

"Baby, what's wrong? Please don't cry. Talk to me."

Nathan's soft cooing voice only made her sob harder. She turned her face into his chest and continued to weep.

Nathan felt his breathing hitch; he had never seen her like this. It was so unlike her. He was out of his depth and had no idea how to help her.

"Tess, you have to help me out here. Tell me what's wrong or tell me how I can help. Come on baby." He implored.

She stopped crying momentarily and sniffled. "This helps."

He sighed conservatively as he clutched her to him and continued to stroke her hair soothingly.

After what felt like an already achingly long time he felt her shudder beneath him as she relented to a fresh wave of sobs. He had never seen someone cry so desperately hard. He could feel the front of her thin t-shirt dampen with her fallen tears. He crooned to her softly, "It's okay baby, you're safe. You're okay."

He held her in his arms for another half an hour until her sobs finally exhausted themselves. He gently tilted her head back so he could look her in the eyes. Her nose was red and tear streaks marred her flawless, fair skin. He hated how absolutely beautiful her eyes looked right now when tears still lined them.

With his thumb he gently brushed a lone tear away. "What happened?"

She sighed apologetically. "I had a nightmare."

"A nightmare?" He tested the word. It seemed unbelievable that a mere nightmare would cause this kind of reaction.

He waited for her to tell him about it, but she kept her lips in a tight line and her eyes swept across the room looking anywhere but at him.

He sighed heavily and buried his face in her hair at the crook of her neck. "If you don't want to tell me about it that's okay, but baby it was just a dream. You're okay."

"Oh Nathan, I wish that were true." She whispered so quietly he couldn't make out what she said.

"What?"

She shook her head slightly and just hugged him close. He shifted their bodies and scooted down in the bed so he was lying by her side facing her. He lifted his hand and brushed her cheek softly.

"You can tell me anything. You know that, right?"

She smiled faintly and nodded yes as she leaned her face into his hand and sighed.

"You're not going to tell me though, are you?"

She giggled almost inaudibly. "Let's just say I won't be reading Dickinson anytime soon."

He raised a brow. "You had a literature nightmare?"

She narrowed her eyes at him. "Don't tease me, I can't control my subconscious."

He laughed slightly. "I'm sorry, I don't mean to poke fun, I just find it unbelievable that's all."

She sighed inwardly, grateful that he seemed to accept what she said. She wasn't lying, but if she was, it was a lie of omission. She knew that made her a hypocrite, but she made a promise to herself that she wouldn't taint her new life with anything from her past. She shook her thoughts away and refocused on their conversation and pursed her lips at his remark.

"Forgive me, please?"

She rolled her eyes and sighed dramatically. "Alright, you're forgiven." She appreciated that he was letting this go and helping her move past it with his lightheartedness.

He smiled but then his face turned serious as he regarded her intently. "I've just never seen you so upset. You're always so strong, I just didn't know what to do."

She clasped his hand in hers and gently kissed his knuckles. "Just having you here was enough."

He smiled reluctantly. "Good. For a moment I thought you might renege on our deal."

She arched an inquisitive brow. "Our deal?"

"The one about you never leaving?"

"Oh." She giggled.

She rolled over and pressed her back to his front prompting him to wrap an arm around her and pull her in close. "I'm not going anywhere."

She could feel his smile against her neck as he breathed her in.

Chapter Eight

"Is that the last box?" Nathan hollered from Tommy's truck.

"Yeah it is! I'll be there in a sec!" She yelled back as she looked around her empty living room.

There wasn't much there in the first place, but it was her home—the first place that felt like home to her anyway. A small part of her would miss the tiny cabin. She took a moment before locking the door for the last time. When she turned around she saw Nathan leaning up against the truck, both hands were tucked into his pockets, and he had a grin that spread across his face as he watched her. She smiled to herself as she tucked a loose strand of hair behind her ear—boy did she love that man.

She took off full speed towards him. He stepped towards her holding out his arms to catch her. She jumped into his arms and gave him a light peck on the lips.

"Are you ready to go home?" He asked her.

She took a final look around. "Yes, I think I am."

Tommy climbed out of the driver's seat and clapped a hand down on the bed of the truck. "Come on you love-sick teenagers, I'm sure you'll have plenty of time for that later."

Tess looked over Nathan's shoulder and playfully stuck her tongue out at Tommy. He let out a loud, billowing laugh and climbed back into the cab of the truck. Nathan shook his head at his friend as he gently placed Tess back down and offered her his hand helping her into the truck.

She slid over into the center and Nathan put his arm around her and smiled. He couldn't imagine anything better than this, having his girl and his best friend with him, he considered himself one lucky son of a bitch.

————— •••••• —————

"Hey, I know we just moved your things in yesterday, and I know this might be too much, but I thought I'd ask anyway. I want you to meet my dad Tess."

She stood up from the floor where she had been organizing their now collaborative record collection. She was happy for the distraction; knowing she only added three records to his collection made her a little sad. She walked over to him and put her arms around his neck.

She tilted her head playfully. "Technically, that's not a question."

He briefly narrowed his eyes at her.

She smiled coquettishly up at him ignoring his expression. "Bout time. I was beginning to think you were ashamed of me or something."

"No!" He gasped in amusement. "It was just the opposite. I was trying to keep you safe. My dad—he can be a bit…gregarious?" He offered.

"I like gregarious people. But anyway, I would love to meet your dad."

"Really?" He gave her that radiant-all-teeth-showing grin that Tess couldn't help but laugh.

"Invite him over for dinner. We can cook something up in a few hours."

"I'll go call him right now." He kissed her forehead before leaving the room.

"Now that the steaks are grilling can you come help me in here really quick?" She hollered outside.

"Yeah sure, but first—" His voice trailed off as he clicked a few buttons on the radio.

She snapped her head up when she heard "Do You Love Me" start to play.

She laughed as she watched him dance around the kitchen to the beat of the song. It was the oddest thing. She felt like she knew Nathan—she knew his habits, knew his styles, knew he could be rough yet gentle, but this—this was something else entirely. He was grinning from ear to ear as he mouthed the lyrics and reached a hand towards her.

She shook her head laughing. "Oh no. No way."

"Come on Tess, enjoy the music." He said with a wink as he pulled her closer.

She shrugged her shoulders down in defeat and started to move to the music. They laughed and danced around the kitchen doing the twist. As she spun around Nathan couldn't help but stare, she was a wild, gorgeous, adventurous woman full of surprises. She was always amazing him and he loved it.

As the song ended, she chuckled softly as she went back around the counter to continue her work.

"Do you always do that?" She asked slightly out of breath.

"Just with the girls I'm trying to impress." He shot her a wink as he chomped down on a carrot.

She glared back at him venomously and he laughed.

"Alright, you caught me. Yes, I always do that. The music just *speaks* to me." He said in a real cool cat voice.

She laughed at the absurdity; it was so uncharacteristic of him. On any other given day of the week she'd find him listening to all the classics like Led Zeppelin, Bad Company, or Foreigner. To find him dancing and singing along with the Contours—well it was just downright strange.

"Alright, well my dancing fool, do you think you can hold down the fort while I go change?"

"I think I can manage," he stifled a smile as he spoke, "but are you sure you don't need help getting undressed?"

She whipped her head back to look at him. "I don't think we have time for *your* kind of help." She cajoled with a wink.

Nathan chortled and shrugged his shoulders apologetically. "Better this way anyway. Wouldn't want my dad hearing you scream my name from the driveway."

Tess's mouth opened wide in shock, she took a step closer and reached to smack his chest playfully. Nathan caught her arm in the air and grabbed her wrist tightly pulling her into him.

Before she could give him a quick retort, he leaned down and smashed his lips into hers. He could feel her fight against him, but when her mouth parted slightly he used this moment to let his tongue dart in and deepen the kiss. He felt her relax against him and he used his free hand to wrap gently around her throat holding her in place. She moaned softly under his touch, kissing him back while feeling her temperature rising.

Nathan pulled away unexpectedly and leaned his forehead against hers.

"The things you do to me woman." He breathed out.

Tess giggled quietly as she tried to catch her breath. Nathan kissed her temple and quietly whispered in her ear, "Your screams and moans are for my ears only."

She shivered at the way his comment curled up around her ear and settled down in the core of her body. The man did things to her that she did not appreciate when she was supposed to be meeting his only family for the first time.

She rolled her eyes playfully and pushed off of him. She sashayed her hips as she walked out of the kitchen, sneaking a quick glance back at Nathan. She smiled to herself watching him curse under his breath as he quickly readjusted the bulge in his pants and looked away from her, determined not to follow her into the bedroom.

"Hey Pops, thanks for coming." Nathan shook his father's hand as he welcomed him in the house.

Nathan's father was only a few inches shorter than his son. His pale, blue eyes glistened under his unruly, salt and pepper hair and his strong jaw line was similar to Nathan's. After shaking hands with his son, he thrust his fists into the pockets of his black denim jeans. Neither would admit it, but the two of them were more alike than either of them realized.

Nathan's father silently followed Nathan through the house to the back yard.

"I'm glad you called." He said as he took a seat at the table that was set up on the deck in the back. "Where's this Tess you're always going on about?"

Nathan took a seat next to him and offered up a beer. He waved it off and pointed to his water.

"I'm good."

"Tess should be out any moment, she was just getting ready when you showed up." Nathan gave an indiscernible smile to himself when his dad refused the beer.

"So, is she handling you okay?" He asked coolly.

Nathan practically spit out his beer. "What is that supposed to mean?"

"Just that you don't always make it easy on people. She's got to be a hell of a woman to get anywhere near your heart. Not that I blame you."

Nathan tugged at the label on his beer. "Shit, just jump right in, why don't you?"

His father chuckled and shrugged his shoulders. "Look Nate, after your mother passed, you were angry. It was understandable, but I saw all the hearts you broke along the way. You never wanted to let anyone back into your own heart. Probably just protecting yourself. So, all I'm saying is I'm already impressed with this Tess girl."

Nathan shrugged. "Well you're right. She is one hell of a woman and I absolutely don't deserve her." His lips curved up slightly at the thought.

"Hi boys, I hope I'm not interrupting—" Tess said as she immerged from the house. She was dressed in an oversized, long sleeve, plum, sweater dress and a pair of brown riding boots that came up to her knees. Her wild curls were pulled up loosely in a bun and she beamed with that smile.

Both men stood up instantly. "You're not interrupting at all. Tess, this is my father. Pops, this is Tess."

"Evenin' Tess. Thanks for having me over. I've been looking forward to meeting you for a while now." He said as he shook her hand and gently kissed her cheek.

"It's a pleasure to finally meet you Mr. Suppan."

"Please, call me Jack, Mr. Suppan was my father." He flirted innocently.

"Well Jack, I've heard so much about you. It's nice to put a face to the name." She smiled inwardly to herself thinking if it weren't for the eyes and the height, she might be looking at Nathan's future self.

"All good things I hope." He huffed as he patted Nathan on the back. Nathan grinned slightly, never lifting his eyes from the beer he was sipping on.

They sat at the table for an hour laughing and talking, Jack telling stories of Nathan's childhood, at least the parts you would tell a stranger.

"Well I think that's about all I can handle reliving my childhood. I'm gonna go clean up. You okay out here?" Nathan asked Tess quietly as he stood up.

She nodded a silent yes and smiled up at him. "There's pie in the fridge if you want to bring it out when you're done."

"I love pie! Especially pumpkin." Jack said rubbing his stomach.

"So I've heard." She winked back at him.

"I'll leave you two then. Behave." Nathan spoke directly to his father with narrowed eyes.

Jack lifted his shoulders as if to say 'Hey I wouldn't do anything of the sort.'

Nathan kissed the top of Tess's head, she leaned into him and quickly closed her eyes savoring the feeling before he headed back inside.

"Walk with me Tess?" Jack asked her as he stood up from the table.

"Of course." She said as she followed him off the porch into the back yard.

They wordlessly walked through the trees that lined the yard and into the forest. Tess silently cursed at herself for not wearing leggings under her dress. The forest was damp and the leaves were in the early stages of budding as they fought the frigid cool air that would blow through. She jumped slightly when Jack cleared his throat.

"I don't know what Nathan has told you about his mother, but uh—he didn't have an easy childhood growing up." Jack spoke tentatively as he put his hands in his pockets.

Tess smiled, Jack really was one to jump in headfirst, and she admired that.

"Nathan told me everything." She reassured in a gentle voice.

"Oh." Jack responded somewhat dazed.

"He doesn't blame you, you know." Tess said glancing over at Jack. "Not anymore anyway."

Jack looked at her questioningly.

"He told me about the drinking, and that he was angry. He felt betrayed like you left him to take care of his mother." Tess began. "But as he got older, he realized that wasn't your intent."

Jack raised his eyebrows.

"He knew you were trying to mend a broken heart. He understands now how hard it must have been for you, so he doesn't blame you."

Jack laughed lightly. "That kid has always been understanding. I have no idea where he gets it. Even so, Nathan had to take on more than any kid should. He was so lost after his mother died."

Tess put her arm through his as they continued walking.

"When his mother passed, I tried to clean myself up, stop drinking, and be there for him. I know I was late, but I wanted to do right. But that wasn't really what Nate needed."

"What do you mean?"

"I think he just needed time. He was an angry boy who needed his space. I think that's why he took to the sea so quickly."

"He told me he spent a lot of time out there."

"Ha! That's putting it lightly." Jack scoffed.

Tess looked up at him hoping he would elaborate.

"He'd disappear for weeks at a time, just out there on the water. When he felt like getting away, he would. A real son of Poseidon, that one." He chuckled to himself before continuing, "It was hard never knowing if he was coming home, but then again, couldn't blame him either."

"That must have been hard on you, I'm sorry." She squeezed his arm softly.

He looked down at her and stopped in his tracks while softly patting her hand on his arm. "No Tess, I'm sorry."

"For what?" She asked in a surprised tone.

"For what happened to Nathan. He grew up in a way that a kid shouldn't and it made him guarded. I'm sorry for how hard you've probably had to work to get him to let you in. But I have to say Tess, I've never seen him this way." He paused a moment before he carried on, "He's happy, he seems content—finally. Tess, you've had such an influence on him. The progress is astounding. You've had a profound effect on him. I hadn't realized it then, but I get it now. When he was growing up he needed time and space, but most of all he needed a force for good in his life. I think that force for good may have been you. You saved him Tess, and I will forever be grateful for that."

She smiled sweetly. "Can I tell you a secret?"

"Sure darlin'." He patted her hand gently once more.

"Your son was the one who did the saving, he saved me."

He looked down at her. "What do you mean?"

Tess tugged lightly at his arm to keep walking. "I don't know what you've heard about why I moved here, but I wasn't happy in North Carolina. I never felt like I was home. I caught my fiancé with my friend, and that night I knew I could finally leave town, but when I went to leave—my mom tried to stop me."

He waited patiently for her to continue.

"My mother said and did some things that I found unforgiveable, so in turn, I said some awful things to her Jack, truly awful. I packed my bags and left town. And somehow ended up here." She said looking and gesturing to her surroundings.

"When I got here, I was a wreck. I barely had enough money to get by, I didn't have friends, and for all intents and purposes, I didn't have a family."

She sighed fondly at the memory that was teetering on the edge of her mind.

"But there was a man, who would sit in my section at the Spar, three days a week. One of the sweetest men I had ever met. And this man, each day would make me feel a little more at home. He taught me how to live again Jack, he taught me how to enjoy life. That is something I will never be able to repay."

Jack smiled to himself; his son had grown into an honorable man.

"And you know something?"

"What's that?"

"Nathan is the one who convinced me to forgive my mother. We still aren't on speaking terms, but I no longer carry anger in my heart. And I owe that to him. So no, Jack, I didn't save him—he saved me."

Jack leaned in and gave Tess a kiss on the head. "Tess, I think I'm going to like having you around." He chuckled softly.

"There you two are." Nathan said as he stood on the porch watching them walk through the trees into the yard.

"Nathan, you better hold onto this one! She's a keeper."

"Don't worry, I plan on it." He smiled down at her as she approached him.

She kissed his cheek lightly before heading inside.

Chapter Nine

"Nathan, get your ass back in the unit until back up is here." Tommy seethed into his radio.

"Leave it alone, Tommy. I can handle it." Nathan hissed back as he peered around the dumpster into the shadowed alley.

He watched as three large men took turns pushing a smaller male around, passing him around like he was a rag doll. The men were toying with him.

"Like hell you can Nathan. If you don't want to use your gun that's three to one. You *will* lose."

"You and I both know that one there is Jackson."

"Nathan, I know. And I know exactly how badly you want this guy but stop. Think about Tess."

"Don't bring her into this." He said with anger rising in his voice.

"I'm going to if it'll make you stop and actually use your head." He snapped back.

Nathan felt every nerve ending in his body come alive. Heat invaded his face and traveled down his neck and his hands tensed into fists. Jackson was among the three men. He liked to leave his calling card on his victims—a symbol carved into their chests. This was the guy there that night in the alley, the night Andrew was murdered for sport.

A memory from a few weeks ago emerged from his peripheral as he watched the scene unfold in front of him.

"Hey Tommy, got your message, what's going on?" Nathan asked as he approached Tommy. His face was taut with bemusement at Tommy's body language.

Tommy was leaning up against the door of the morgue with his hands kneading his temples and his face in a contorted, penitent expression.

"I don't know anything for sure, except that I'm probably going to regret showing you this."

"Showing me what?" His eyes glowered hesitantly at Tommy.

Tommy sighed a ragged breath and motioned for Nathan to follow him into the morgue.

Nathan dutifully followed Tommy to the metal slab with a covered body on it. He furrowed his brows and looked at Tommy with a perplexed expression.

Tommy exhaled deeply before leaning over and pulling the sheet back. Nathan's eyes stared unblinking at the body on the table in front of him. He felt his heart begin to pump in overdrive and his breathing faltered.

On the table was a young man in his late teens to early twenties. The young man had a very thin and delicate physique with boyish features. His body was badly bruised and small lacerations covered his arms and his cheek. There were two gunshot wounds in his upper abdomen, but that wasn't the most striking significance.

Carved into his upper left pectoral, was the symbol of an arrow.

Nathan leaned back away from the table and looked at Tommy with stupefied horror. "Is this? Can it—" He struggled to articulate his words, but deep down he knew his suspicions were right and he knew why Tommy hesitated to show him.

Tommy nodded his head in concession. "Yeah Nate, we're pretty sure."

Nathan gawked at Tommy with his eyes flitting from him to the boy and back at Tommy. After a moment of silence, he shook his head and tightened his jaw. "What do we know?"

Tommy sighed as he reached for a manila folder on a rolling table next to the slab.

"John Doe, age nineteen. He was found in a back alley, beaten and shot, wearing only his briefs. DNA pulled two prints and a third partial."

"It's the same as Andrew?" Nathan was almost sure of it.

Tommy scratched his head. "Andrew had only one clean print and the other was a partial but at the time we didn't have anything in the database. I mean I wasn't sure this was connected, but I figured it was. The arrow, do you know what it means?"

"No, do you?" Nathan looked up surprised.

"Not definitively no, but there is a lot of lore behind an arrow symbol."

"Such as?"

"Such as the mark of hunters."

Nathan scowled in disgust. "Prey. That's all they are to him." Nathan wasn't sure why this affected him so much. He was a child when he witnessed Andrew's death, but even then he knew Andrew was considered nothing more than a game to those monsters.

Tommy nodded apoplectically. Nathan staggered backwards and clutched the edge of the counter to hold himself up right. He lifted his eyes and looked at Tommy and watched as Tommy's eyes bolted to the floor.

"What else Tommy?"

"We have a name."

"What?" Nathan hissed under his breath.

"Darren Jackson."

Tess stood quietly at the entrance of their bedroom doorway. She tilted her head to the left and sighed sadly as she stared at Nathan. He had his back to her as he sat on the edge of the bed with his elbows on his thighs and his head in his hands. She felt her throat constrict with unshed tears.

Quietly she climbed on the bed behind him and slowly wrapped her arms around him. With her front to his back she tightly clung to him and held him close to her. She felt his body sigh and slowly loosen under her grip. She pressed her cheek into his back and sat quietly holding him.

After a few minutes of silence, he stroked her arm and she took it as an opportunity to speak, "Tommy told me. Are you okay?"

He tightened at her words and with one hand he pulled one of her arms from him and clasped her hand in his. He opened her hand and turned her open palm towards him as he gently kissed her hand at the center of her palm.

"I don't know what to do Tess."

It wasn't long after the boy's body with the symbol carved into his chest popped up, that the lab was able to confirm Andrew's case was connected. After all this time, Nathan couldn't believe they had a lead. A lead that had quickly reached a dead-end. At least until he got a call about three men jumping a guy in the alley. Now that he was there watching, every bone in his body told him that Andrew's murderer was among them. Andrew was never the only victim—he was just a piece in a pattern. Nathan watched as one of the men took a swing at the guy and he heard something break.

Nathan felt himself wince involuntarily at the sound. His breathing became aggravated, he took a moment and un-holstered his gun, unloaded the magazine, and put it on the ground next to him. He knew it was a downright stupid idea to go in vulnerable, but Marx's voice was ringing in his head and he thought about what Tess said about revenge. He knew that if he got the chance, he would kill Jackson. He also knew if he did, there was no coming back from that.

"That's it, I'm going in."

"Nathan!" Tommy screamed through his radio. "Damn it! Get me that backup unit at the alley behind Seventh and Coy, now!" He ushered to dispatch.

Nathan pulled out his unloaded gun as he sauntered towards the men.

"Sitka Police, freeze!"

"Well lookie here." One of the men turned to face Nathan straight on, completely unphased by authority.

Jackson.

The other two stopped kicking the young man who was now sprawled on the ground whimpering.

It may have been over a decade, but seeing him now in the flesh, Nathan had no reservations. "Let him go, hands in the air."

"Or what?" Jackson retorted back with a gleam in his eye. He was egging Nathan on; he was looking for a fight.

"Let him go, *now*." Nathan spoke with an undercurrent in his tone.

Jackson howled with laughter. "Fine, let him go." He ordered nonchalantly to the two with him.

They both stopped laughing and looked at him flabbergasted.

"What?" One of them finally asked.

"Do I need to repeat myself? Let him go." He hissed back at them.

The two held up their arms and took a step back letting the man pick himself off the ground and run towards Nathan.

"Run through the alley, find my squad car, my partner is there. EMT will be here soon." He whispered to the man as he jogged past Nathan.

"Come on then, arrest us." Jackson taunted.

Nathan stepped closer; he could see in the guy's eyes that he was looking for a fight. But so was Nathan. Jackson looked weathered around the eyes, showing that he had aged since the last time he saw him, but so had Nathan. Nathan was older now, stronger now. Nathan's mouth turned into a subtle, grim smile as he put the gun back in its holster and waited for him to attack.

Nathan prepared for Jackson to make his move, and when Jackson lunged forward, Nathan caught him by the arm and swung him into the side of the building. He felt and heard as Jackson's body slammed against the bricks, but Jackson was a sturdy guy. He easily recovered and elbowed Nathan in the gut. When Nathan staggered backwards from the blow, Jackson took his moment. Jackson wailed on Nathan beating him down until Nathan could no longer bear his own weight and fell down on his knees.

Jackson spit out his own blood from a blow to the mouth that Nathan managed to get in. He looked down at Nathan and smiled.

Through an already bruised eye, Nathan looked up at Jackson and saw the smirk on his face. Even though he was weak, the years of guilt and rage over that night wouldn't allow him to lie down and take it. He leered quietly to himself and then looked straight up into Jackson's eyes. His lips turned up in a smile and blood stained his teeth.

"You hit like a bitch."

Jackson snarled at Nathan's defiance and bent down to punch him in the gut once more. Nathan wheezed as he doubled over in pain and spit out blood. But Jackson hadn't counted on Nathan's quick recovery.

With his head still down as he was bent over, Nathan grabbed Jackson's ankle and with all his strength he pulled on Jackson and flipped him onto the ground. Falling on the ground caused Jackson's head to slam down against the asphalt with a considerable thump. The hit was hard enough that it gave Nathan a chance to climb on top of him and pin him down. Looking down at him, Nathan slung his right arm back and rocked it forward, connecting hard with Jackson's face. The solitary blow was hard enough to knock him out, but he didn't care. He didn't stop as he repeatedly punched Jackson's jawline until his arm gave out.

When he was sure Jackson was utterly unconscious, he looked up at the other two men. Nathan smiled a bloody and wicked all-teeth-showing smile at them—daring them. Scared of Nathan or scared of the onslaught of sirens, the two took off down the alley and out of sight. Before Nathan could do anything more, he succumbed to the pain and adrenaline and slumped unconscious onto the ground next to Jackson.

"Two broken ribs, probable head contusion, lacerations to head and cheek, possible fractured wrist and hand." The paramedics said over their radio as they drove to the hospital.

Nathan opened his eyes and saw Tommy leaning against the wall in the room. Tommy rested his arms behind him on the wall and he stared down at his feet with a pensive look on his face.

"Hey Tommy." Nathan garbled out as he tried to sit up in the hospital bed.

"What the *fuck* were you thinking?" His voice so low it was almost a whisper. "I told you to wait for back up. They were on their way God damn it." Tommy's voice rose with earnest as he erected himself and walked over to take a seat in the chair next to Nathan's bed.

"I couldn't chance that he could get away again. You know that Tommy."

Tommy bowed his head. "Yeah, I know. I know what this meant to you, and for that, I'm glad his happy ass is rotting in a jail cell. But Nathan, man—when are you going to *think* about the consequences?"

Nathan thought hearing that Jackson was sitting in a cell would make him feel good—maybe even give him closure. But really all he could think about was the itching of his stitches, the dull ache of pain, and the fight he knew he was about to have with Tess.

"Tess mad?" Nathan asked ignoring Tommy's accusation.

Tommy rubbed his head with his hand. "Yeah, I suppose she is."

Nathan nodded figuring as much. "When is she coming?"

Tommy sighed despondently. "She's not Nate. She waited to make sure your scans came back okay, but she's not coming to see you."

"What?" Nathan's eyes burned with warm water and his voice cracked and withered.

"You knew this could happen. She told you she couldn't get another call like this. I'm sorry man, but I don't blame her for it." Tommy eyed the floor deliberately as he spoke.

Nathan stared at Tommy with wide, pained eyes.

"Nathan, you're reckless, and you just don't *think*. I get what you were trying to do. I get it. But at what cost? Your life?"

"I don't see it that way though." Nathan tried to explain.

"That's part of the problem. I'm sure Tess gets it too, but she loves you man. She doesn't want to get a call one day saying you're not okay, for real."

"I guess I don't blame her either." He sighed and looked down at the IV in his arm and then he lifted his eyes to Tommy and whispered, "She's really not coming?"

"No," Tommy spoke in quiet defeat, "she moved some of her things out Nate."

He laid his head back on his pillow, beaten.

"She's staying with Hadley for now, just give her some time." Tommy tried to offer his friend with a closed lip smile.

"Here's some tea." Hadley handed Tess a mug as she sat down next to her on the couch.

"Thanks."

"Tess, are you okay?" Hadley asked looking concerned.

"No, I don't think I am. I love Nathan so much that sometimes it hurts. I've never had someone that I cared for like this." Her lips turned up into a half smile as she spoke of him.

"You're smiling, doesn't that mean you should be there with him then?" Hadley questioned as Tess shifted on the couch.

Tess's smile receded quickly. "I can't Hadley. As much as I love Nathan, I can't do it anymore. Being a cop is scary enough, but to live in fear that he may not come home because of something *he* did—I just can't live with that."

Tess wiped a tear from her eye before continuing, "Nathan is a good man. I truly believe he thinks he is doing the right thing out there. And he is—I know he's protecting people and I know the risks that come with the territory. But with him, if I got that call one day that he's really not okay, I will always wonder if he got hurt because he was protecting someone or if he got hurt because he was looking for a fight and had found someone willing to oblige."

Hadley nodded in agreement. "I understand what you're saying, and I completely agree with you. I just want to make sure *you,* will be okay with this decision."

Tess's eyes began to fill with tears as she looked up at Hadley. "I don't know." She began to sob.

Hadley put her arm around Tess in comfort. "Oh sweetie."

Tess turned her face into Hadley and let her sobs take over.

They jumped when they heard a knock at the door. Hadley was the first to speak up, "You don't think that's him, do you?"

Tess tried to wipe her eyes. "I doubt it. I think he'll be in the hospital for a while—it was bad this time."

Hadley nodded and went to the door. A few seconds later she walked back into the room and gestured that someone was there for Tess.

Tess walked into the foyer to see Tommy standing there.

"Tommy, things didn't take a turn for the worse, did they?" Her voice quivered noticeably.

He shoved one of his hands in his pocket. "No, no of course not."

She crossed her arms. "Then why are you here, Tommy?"

"Ouch." He rubbed the back of his head with his free hand and chuckled softly.

Her eyes widened and dropped immediately. "I'm sorry, I didn't mean—"

"It's okay Tess, I know. I just, I just needed to see if you would please come to the hospital. He's a wreck. He knows he messed up."

That's what made her snap, the fact that Nathan *knew* what he was doing was wrong. He *knew* he was being careless with his life and he *knew* that she couldn't handle another phone call. She told him countless times what he meant to her and yet he disregarded his life with no remorse for how it would make her feel the day he didn't make it home.

"Do you know what the definition of insanity is? It's doing the same thing over and over again and expecting a different result. He keeps jumping into the same damn situations thinking that maybe this will be the day that he makes up for what happened to that poor boy all those years ago."

"I know Tess, trust me, I know. But this time *was* different. This time it *was* Jackson."

That made her pause for a moment. She knew that this would have been the one instance he would never and could never walk away from. But just because she understood, it didn't mean she could live with it.

"Tommy, I love him, you know that I do. But I needed him to choose me. To choose a life with me." She paused as she closed her eyes briefly in pain and shrugged. "And he didn't."

———— •• •• ——

It was late when she walked back down the corridor of the hospital wing. She knew she shouldn't have come, she knew she needed to leave him, but she needed to see with her own eyes that he was really okay first. She had to be sure he was alright. She wouldn't have the strength to stay away if she didn't just this one last time. The hospital lights were dim and it was quiet, but she could still hear the beeps and hisses coming from the machines.

She took a deep breath as she rested her hand on the handle of the door. She had to keep telling herself to stay strong, to look in on him and then leave.

She slowly inched the door open, his room was dark except for the lines on the heart monitor. She let out a sigh of relief as she watched the steady pace of his heart beat. Quietly she walked in towards him, she stood next to him and looked down at his face.

He was badly beaten. There were cuts sewn up on his forehead and cheek, his lip was busted, and his eye was completely encased in purple. She sighed heavily in forlorn longing as she started to cry. With her right hand she lightly traced the side of his face as she whispered, "Why couldn't you have just walked away?"

She watched him sleep for another minute and then she turned to leave, wiping her tears with the back of her hand.

"Tess?"

She stopped in her tracks at the sound of his low, groggy voice. She wanted to turn around and run to him, but she couldn't.

Nathan quickly tried to pull himself up. He stared at her, straining his one unharmed eye to focus. Her back was turned to him and he could barely make out her figure, but he knew it was her.

"Tess, I know—I know I messed up and I know you think you have to do this and that means I will have lost the only girl I have ever truly cared about—"

Tess swiveled around and cut him off, with one hand on the door she looked at him. "Nathan, you didn't lose me."

He tried to smile, but for the first time the light touched her and he caught a glimpse of her face and could see tears cascading down her cheeks.

"You threw me away." She whispered as she quickly stole out of the hospital room.

Nathan sat there in the darkness of the room stunned into bitter silence.

"Nathan, what are you doing?" Tommy asked as he walked into the hospital room.

Nathan was trying to pack his bag to leave but winced when he caught his wrist on his jacket. "I'm going to bring Tess home."

"Nathan, it hasn't even been two weeks. Your head has just barely healed, but your wrist and your ribs, those aren't healed."

"I don't care Tommy. I need her in my life. This has been the worst week and a half of my life. I can't live knowing I never even tried to make things better. Now are you going to help me or not?" He looked at his friend in aggravated earnestness for support.

Tommy shrugged in exaggeration. "Fine. What the hell, it's not like I could stop you if I tried." Tommy put his coat on the chair and began packing Nathan's bag for him.

Nathan smiled and slapped Tommy on the back with his good hand. "Thanks, you're a good friend Tommy."

"Don't thank me yet. You still don't know if you can get her home Nathan, you didn't see how upset she was."

Nathan's face dropped. "Actually, I did."

Tommy stopped what he was doing and looked up at Nathan. "What?"

Nathan tried to swallow the lump in his throat as he looked down at his shoes.

"She snuck in here the night I was brought in. I think she tried to sneak in and sneak right out, but I woke up."

"Why didn't you say anything?"

"She told me that I hadn't lost her—"

Tommy smiled and clapped Nathan on the shoulder. "That's great man!"

Nathan's head dropped for a moment and then he brought his eyes up to meet Tommy's.

"She said I hadn't lost her, she said I threw her away."

Tommy's head bowed.

"She's right, Tommy. She told me again and again to walk away and I didn't. I knew this could happen and yet, here I am."

Tommy's shoulders shrugged. "She wanted you to choose her."

"I know," he swallowed hard before continuing, "but that's why I'm going to do everything in my power to bring her home. I need to show her I can be the man she needs me to be, the man she deserves."

Tommy looked at him questioningly.

"I have to prove to her that she means more to me than any of this does. I can't keep going without her. I need her in my life and I'm going to prove to her that she needs me too. I know somewhere deep down she still loves me, and I'll do anything I possibly can to make things right."

Tommy shook his head. He had to give it to Tess, even if she didn't realize it, she knew exactly how to make Nathan see straight. Somehow, some way, even in her absence, she was making Nate man up to being the man she always knew he could be.

"I'll give you a ride to Hadley's." Tommy spoke as he slung Nathan's bag over his shoulder.

"Coming, just a sec." Hadley hollered at the door.

"Nathan." She gasped, "What are you doing here?"

"I need to see her."

Hadley put her head down and pulled the door in eliminating Nathan's view into the house. "I don't think so Nathan."

"Please Hadley, I love her." He begged.

She sighed and opened the door wider again. "Come in." She nodded into her house.

He took a seat on the couch, quickly letting his eyes dart around the room for any sign of Tess. "Thank you."

She held up a hand to quiet him. "Don't thank me. I have to tell you something."

Nathan squirmed in his seat. "Okay, what?"

"Nathan, you're an idiot."

He bowed his head. "I know, but that's why I'm here."

She held her hand up again. "Let me finish. Tess really loves you, I mean *really* loves you. And although she would be pissed at me for this, I believe you two belong together so I think I should tell you."

"Tell me what Hadley?"

"Nathan, Tess is in North Carolina."

His eyes widened, had he really driven her to that point, to the point she would return to that place?

"About a week ago she got a phone call. Her mom—well her mom had a brain aneurism."

He looked shocked; he hadn't seen that one coming. "Oh God. Why didn't she tell me? Why didn't she tell Tommy?"

Hadley stood up abruptly. "Because Nathan, you're an idiot."

Nathan stared blankly up at her. She had said that statement as if that was an explanation but he needed more.

She rolled her eyes at him. She wasn't sure if he was deliberately being obtuse or if he really didn't understand what she was getting at. "Do you know how many times I've been the one to console her when she's gotten a call that you were in the hospital?"

"No."

"Or how many times I've been the one to calm her down, because she hadn't heard from you and she thought maybe you were lying in a back-alley dead?"

"Well, no."

"You're right, you don't. So why on earth would she come to you with this, when you put her through that, yet again?"

"I...I..." He stumbled with his words finally understanding the implications of his actions.

"And as far as Tommy—Tess isn't cruel. She knew that by leaving you, you would need your best friend, and it wouldn't be fair to him or you for her to monopolize him."

Nathan bowed his head. Tess showed him unbelievable compassion and kindness and he couldn't even be man enough to show her, her own worth.

Hadley rubbed her temples. "Look Nathan, I know how upset she was, but I also know she loves you, and needs you right now. She's too stubborn to admit it, but I'm not going to sit around and watch it happen. You're going to go to North Carolina. You're going to be there for her, and then you're going to bring her home." She said jabbing a finger into his chest as she spoke.

Nathan jumped off the couch bounding for the door, halfway out he turned around to face Hadley. "Thank you. Thank you for being there for her when I wasn't."

Hadley nodded silently and gave him a small encouraging smile.

Chapter Ten

"I didn't always do right by your mother, Tess." Her father stared out impassively at the ocean as he spoke.

She walked towards him and placed her arms on the pier railing next to his and gazed out at the sunrise over the water.

"I'm so sorry for that, but I loved her Tess. I loved her. I swear to you, I did."

"I know Daddy." She said as she grabbed his hand in comfort. She looked back out at the water and tried to fight the unbidden tears.

"Tess?"

"Oh Daddy, I've made so many mistakes, before I left I said some truly horrible things to her."

"No one is perfect."

"But you didn't hear what I said to her—I broke her heart."

"We both know that your mother had forgiven you. We both know that you loved her, and that you will miss her. This guilt that you're feeling, this pain—it's not just because you lost your mother. There's something else tugging on your heartstrings Tess. Take it from a man who has more regrets in his life than he can count. You need to figure out what it is, and either fix it, or learn to let it go completely."

She stiffened and cleared her throat before speaking, "I just wanted to believe in it again."

"I'm sorry Tessie." He spoke in quiet understanding.

Her shoulders sagged down heavily. "How did I get here? How did I go from being the girl who chased a life I thought I wanted, to the girl who broke her family and now has to put it all back together? How did I fall so far?" She blinked back tears.

"Well somebody needed to be the adult in this family, and it sure as hell wasn't going to be me. And honey, you haven't lost that girl yet."

"That's the thing though Daddy. I found someone, and when he told me he loved me—when he showed me how much he cared, it was as if my entire world snapped back into focus. The funny thing was, up to that point, I hadn't even noticed it was out of focus to begin with."

He pulled her close to him and kissed her hair.

"Look Tessie, I know you felt like you needed to mend things with your family, the thing of it is, you can't fix everything—but you sure can come home broken. How are you really doing Tess? In Alaska, I mean." He asked her knowing she had been reticent before.

"I've made a mess of things." She sighed prolifically as she leaned into his chest.

He kissed her hair again and laughed. "I'm sure that just isn't true."

"It is though. I have no idea what I'm doing anymore."

"I know you and your mama didn't always get along or see eye to eye—"

Tess chuckled. *That's an understatement* she thought.

"But she did get something right."

She looked up at him quizzically.

"She used to tell you about the man in the moon."

"The man in the moon? That sounds familiar."

"She used to say that if you told the man in the moon your problems, that while you slept he would solve them for you. He could figure out any puzzle."

She smiled. "That's right, she did tell me that—right after Teddy Barrett broke up with me at the seventh-grade dance." She giggled fondly at the memory. "The next day Teddy fell in a pit of mud in front of everyone."

Her father joined in her laughter. "That's right, I forgot about that."

"I wish the man in the moon *could* solve my problems now." She sighed.

"Well how do you know he can't? Have you tried?" He asked.

"Well no, but you don't really believe in that do you?"

"I didn't, but your mama did. And that's enough of a reason for me to believe now." He smiled down at his daughter and squeezed her tight.

"Thanks Daddy."

"Mr. Henry Dawson?" Nathan asked as a burly man in jeans, rolled up denim button up, and a short beard opened the screen door.

"That's me, who are you?" He huffed with narrowed eyes.

"Hi sir, my name is Nathan Suppan. I just wanted to tell you how sorry I am for your loss."

Henry scratched his chin and grumbled, "But that's not what you're here for, is it?"

Nathan bowed his eyes quickly before stiffening up and looking Mr. Dawson in the eyes. "No sir. I'm here hoping I can speak with your daughter, sir."

Her father crossed his arms as he stared back at Nathan and eyed him conspicuously.

"So, you're Alaska." He said it as more of a statement rather than a question.

"I'm sorry?"

"You're the boy that has Tessie doing somersaults in her head for."

Nathan flinched reflexively. "I'm sorry sir, I know I'm probably not the person you want to see or deal with in a time like this, but that's why I'm here. I love your daughter, sir. And I want to be here for her.

I've made a mess of things and I know I have a lot to atone for."

He took a moment to mull over what Nathan was saying. He grunted once before he spoke as he ambled down the stairs.

"Maybe you're wrong. Maybe you're *just* the person I was hoping to see. Follow me."

Nathan's eyes widened in shock, but he didn't miss a step following her father around the house down to the beach.

"Sir?" He finally asked once they had gotten down to the beach and Henry had stopped walking.

"You see that pier right there? The one that connects to the day break?" He pointed off to his left.

"Yes."

"You'll find her out there. She walks to the end of the pier, and climbs down onto the daybreak. Follow it out to the end and you'll find her."

Nathan smiled gratefully. "Thank you, sir."

Henry eyed Nathan carefully once more and noticed a wrap around his wrist.

"Fair warning—Tess is somewhat of an avid climber. She found that spot when she was seven, she's gone back ever since, but no one else really goes out there. Rocks hard to get over and all." He fisted his hands in his pockets as he spoke.

"I'll manage." Nathan said determinedly as he headed out towards the pier.

He got to the end of the pier and saw the spot where she climbed down. There was a small opening between the pier and the rocks; she must have slid through it to get down. He shimmied his body through the gap, pausing only once to fight back the pain in his side.

Her father was right, Tess really was a spider monkey to get to where she was. He struggled here and there when he was forced to use his hand. The pain was nearly unbearable, but he managed, just like he said he would. He had almost reached the end when he spotted her.

She was sitting on the edge of one of the rocks that was jetting out of the side, with her feet dangling out in front of her. She sat quietly while she stared off into the distance. There wasn't a smile like there usually was. She looked sad. Her mouth was in a tight line; instead of that permanent grin he loved so much.

Her wild hair danced around her face, blowing in the wind. Even when she looked so sad, she was the most gorgeous human being he had ever seen. Her long legs glistened in the sun, he noticed how bronzed they had become in such a short time in comparison to her stark, white sneakers. His eyes traveled up past her tattered jean shorts to the oversized, soft, linen white, button up shirt rolled up at her sleeves. He noticed the way the wind tousled her shirt against her torso as she sat so incredibly still. He felt his chest constrict. He ached for her not just to be with her, but for the hurt she endured. For the fact that she felt obliged to endure it alone.

"Tess?" He called down to her.

She jumped at her name being called.

"Nathan, what are you doing here?" She asked as she stood up abruptly.

He held up his hands as if talking to a caged animal cowering in the corner. "Please don't go, I just want to talk to you."

She shrugged her arms. "Well you picked a place where you have me cornered. I suppose I don't really have a choice, do I?"

Hurt flashed across his face at her remark. "Tess, you always have a choice. I just would like to talk to you, I won't make you listen."

She took a moment to wrap her arms protectively around herself. She bowed her head and kicked a shell with her shoe before she looked up at him. "I'm listening."

"What you said to me that night in the hospital, you were right. And waking up each morning alone, and not having you there waiting for me—it was the worst feeling in the world. Worse than any ass-kicking I have ever taken."

"You know why I wasn't there though." A small pang of guilt flushed through her.

He scratched his head as he spoke, "I know Tess, and I understand. I took you for granted and I am so sorry for that. I continued to be reckless thinking you'd still be there at the end of the day." He hesitated slightly as if considering what to say next.

He took a deep breath and continued, "Everything leaves a mark, and I have received so many marks that I think my bare skin is no longer visible. But that is nothing compared to the marks I have left on others—nothing compared to the mark I left on you."

Her eyes gazed upon his, studying them, trying to decide how she felt.

His shoulders sagged down in defeat when she didn't say anything back. "Tess, I miss you more than you can imagine. Ever since you left, I feel completely incomplete. I know I don't deserve you, but I promise if you let me, I will spend the rest of my life making it up to you."

She cocked her head to the side and suddenly the steadfast look in her eyes was gone. Her shoulders fell down and she let out a distressing sigh. Nathan took the moment to close the gap between them and joined her on the rock she was standing on. He wrapped both hands under her ears and pulled her face in close to his and kissed her. As much as she wanted to fight it—she couldn't. Or rather—she wouldn't.

His hands held her face roughly to his as his lips moved with hers. He moaned inwardly, the feel of the warmth of her breath and the softness of her lips against his. She was made for him, and he for her. As his lips continued to move against hers, he felt a hot liquid melt between them. When he pulled away, he saw she was crying.

"Tess?" He said slightly out of breath.

"You were in the hospital again and then my mama—I just feel—I just—I can't *feel* Nathan, and it scares me." She sobbed into his shirt.

"Shhh…it's okay. It'll be okay baby, I promise. I am so sorry about your mom." He kissed her hair over and over again as he stood there holding her in his arms.

They sat on the rock together, with her legs draped over Nathan as he held her close letting her cry. An hour had passed before the silence was broken.

"I'm sorry." A tiny voice said.

Nathan looked down at Tess. "What are you sorry for?"

"For crying like this, and for leaving."

He squeezed her close. "Don't be sorry for either—as long as you come home with me."

"Nathan, I don't know—" Her small voice trailed off.

"Tell me you don't love me. Tell me that deep down you don't know that we are meant to be."

"Nathan, I do love you, but I just don't know where that leaves us."

"Thing is Tess, turns out you can't control your heart. The damn thing just does what it wants—and if you want this, come home with me." He purred against her ear as he placed a kiss on her head.

She gently placed her hand on his chest, pressing her palm against his shirt feeling for his heartbeat and then looked up at him. "And yours? What is yours doing now?"

He chuckled softly. "Aside from beating out of my chest?"

Tess smiled and looked back down at her hand on his chest. "Hey." He said as he lifted her chin so their eyes could meet.

"It's telling me that I will love you 'til kingdom come and that I need to do everything in my power to make you see that your home—your *real* home—it's with me."

She sat up quickly. "Nathan, I can't come home right now, my father, and—"

He brushed his finger across her lips gently to hush her. "I'm not asking you to leave this moment. My ticket wasn't round trip. I'm staying as long as you need to stay, and when you're ready, we'll go home—*together*. I just ask that you do go home, with me, whenever that may be." He smiled at her.

He could see that it was still hard for her to smile, but as small as it was, at least it was there. He wiped the hair from her face and stared into her eyes. There was a look she would give him, something only she could give. A look that said, 'you saved me'. He cherished that look. He never felt more alive, more loved than when she gave him that look. To imagine not ever seeing it again—was unimaginable.

———•••••———

Nathan sat on a park bench in the middle of the town square. He sat staring at the small ring he held in between his fingers. He smiled broadly as he watched the sunlight bounce and flicker off the thin, gold band.

"Ah love, one of the finer things in life." An older man said as he took a seat next to Nathan.

Nathan smiled in amused agreement.

"Love is the most important thing there is; finding the right person to spend the rest of your life with."

"I know I made the right choice." Nathan said as he placed the ring in his pocket.

"Love is funny that way, letting you think you had a choice. You never had a choice. Love finds you son—you don't find love. Love is tricky when there are so many variables in the equation. Destiny, fate, what's written in the stars, divine intervention, and well the simple fact that women are generally smarter than we are. And they're wily." He laughed and dipped his head as he continued, "Your sorry butt never had a choice. But, if you want to believe you had a choice in the matter, I'd say you made a good one."

Nathan laughed at the man's outward audacity. "Oh yeah? How do you figure?"

"Because she showed up. And she sure is pretty." He nodded in Tess's direction as she made her way towards Nathan.

Tess's hips swayed melodiously as she walked towards him. Her mint green, thin-strapped dress billowed softly in the wind and her hair tumbled down her back. When Nathan's eyes met hers, she tucked a strand of hair behind her ear and smiled coyly.

"She really is, isn't she?" He smiled back at the older gentleman before getting up to greet Tess.

"Hi, I'm glad you agreed to come."

"I almost didn't, but then I realized staying in that house wasn't what I needed." She said as she walked with Nathan.

"What do you need Tess?" Nathan asked stopping in his tracks.

"Fresh air, life—you." She smiled slightly as she put her arm through his and they continued walking.

Nathan sighed in contentment but was startled when Tess stopped abruptly after walking only a couple hundred feet. He looked down at her and saw that her eyes were transfixed on someone.

"Vanessa?" Tess cocked her head to the right as she watched a girl approach them.

Nathan turned his attention to the girl walking up to them. She was thin, a little too thin. Her hair was jet black and her skin was a pale, icy color, which felt a little out of place in North Carolina.

"Hi Tessie." The girl spoke almost inaudibly as she stepped closer.

Nathan noticed she was wearing a uniform with a nametag on and he realized why her name had sounded so familiar. This was Tess's friend, the waitress that Bobby cheated on her with.

Tess shifted her weight beside him and chewed on her bottom lip.

Vanessa glanced quickly down at the ground and then back up at Tess.

"Tess, I want you to know, I never meant to hurt you. I don't know how or why it happened, it just did."

Nathan had to fight back a million responses flying through his head, was that really the best she could do?

Tess removed her arm from Nathan's and crossed her arms in front of her chest. She took a defensive step back and looked down at her feet and then slowly back up at Vanessa.

"I believe you." She spoke with a steely resolve.

Vanessa smiled widely and tucked her hair behind her ear. "Thank you, Tessie. I've missed you so much."

Tess stuck her arm out in front of her to stop Vanessa from coming any closer. "Vanessa, I know now that I didn't love Bobby, and I also know that finding you two together gave me the freedom to leave, but don't mistake that for my forgiveness."

Vanessa shrank back. "But Tessie—"

Nathan could hear the conviction in Tess's voice; she was trying desperately hard not to tremble. "Vanessa, what you did was wrong, but I suspect you get that. And because of that, I, from the bottom of my heart, hope you find whatever it is you are looking for. If it is my forgiveness that you truly seek then I will give it to you. But I have to tell you, I think you're looking for something else."

Nathan felt his mouth open slightly in shock. Tess's honesty and her compassion were disarming.

"Tessie, not all of us can get out of here you know?"

Tess nodded. "Well then I hope you find a way to be happy here. We were friends once, and truthfully I guess in some really messed up way, I owe you."

"What for?"

Yeah, what for? Nathan thought to himself as he observed this bizarre confrontation. In what world would Tess owe this girl for getting into bed with her fiancé?

"Because of what you and Bobby did, I left and I found the thing I was searching for." She smiled hesitantly at Nathan before turning back to face Vanessa.

Nathan grinned obviously pleased with himself as he took the opportunity to step forward and wrap his arm around Tess in support. He was proud of the way she handled this, she was stronger than he could ever be. Probably more mature than he would ever be in a situation like this too.

Vanessa gave Tess a genial smile. "I have to admit Tessie, you do look happy."

Tess lifted her hand across her chest and squeezed Nathan's hand that was on her shoulder and she smiled. "I am."

Vanessa nodded and forced one last shy smile as she slowly backed away from them and walked off in the opposite direction.

Once Vanessa was out of sight Tess exhaled slowly all of her bravado evaporating.

"Quite the homecoming crowd." Nathan said flippantly trying to lighten the mood.

Tess couldn't help but laugh as she lightly smacked his chest. Nathan pretended to be hurt and fell back.

"Hey, I'm just saying, if I knew how well you reacted to tense situations, maybe I would have introduced you to a few of my exes." He eyed her as he watched her head turn to face him. The scowl on her face was priceless. He missed this, playing and joking around with her. He winked at her.

She pushed his shoulder and took off running towards the river walk. He chuckled to himself and took off after her. He caught up to her quickly and picked her up from behind and twirled her around. She giggled and screamed at his attack.

He couldn't help but laugh too. He felt like she had become lighter, like a weight had been lifted from her heart and she was beginning to be happy again.

He set her down and kissed her hair. "Come on, I have some place I want to take you."

She looked surprised. "Wait, this is my hometown. How have you already found a place you want to take me? Shouldn't it be the other way around if anything?"

He nodded. "Sure, if I wanted to be conventional, but I like to think outside of the box." He drew a box in the air with his finger as he spoke and then he looked over at her and winked playfully.

* * *

"Nathan, I don't think we're supposed to be here, we could get in trouble." Tess whispered as she followed Nathan up the spiral staircase of the lighthouse.

He chuckled to himself hearing her whisper before he turned to face her. "Are you kidding me? I'm already in trouble—I'm in love."

She shook her head at him and laughed at that face-splitting grin of his.

"Wow, I can't believe I've never been up here." She exclaimed as she peered out of the glass once they reached the top. Nathan led her out of the room to the exterior railing and stood quietly. She took a moment to soak it all in. To watch the gentle rays of the sun cast their last lights out on the water, and the small silhouettes of sailboats out at sea. It was peaceful here. She had forgotten the beauty of this place, and she was happy she had someone in her life that could remind her of it.

"Close your eyes."

"What?" She asked somewhat startled from her reverie.

"Humor me, please." Nathan crooned softly. "Please."

Tess eyed him cautiously before slowly closing her eyes.

"When you close your eyes, what do you picture?"

"What?" She asked again as she laughed nervously.

"When you close your eyes at any given moment, can you remember this? Us? How you feel about me? Can you remember how much I love you?"

Her eyes snapped open, something about his voice made her blood sing. "Nathan?"

He pressed his forehead against hers and his hand gently slid around her waist. "Will you always remember how you feel when I hold you?" He paused briefly rubbing circles around the small of her back. "When I kiss you?" His lips met hers as he tenderly kissed her. When he pulled back he asked, "Will you promise to always remember?"

"Nathan, what's going on?"

"Promise me?"

She took a deep breath and closed her eyes before answering, "Nathan, when I close my eyes I picture the carnival we went to and the way I felt that night, and every night after. And I remember our love. I remember the way you make me feel because you saved me, you saved me from myself."

He knelt down beside her proffering a gold band between his fingertips. "Then marry me, Tess."

Her eyes immediately shot open as she looked down at Nathan kneeling in front of her.

"Marry me, and I promise I will help you remember every day. You are this beacon of guiding light in my life, and for some reason I will never begin to understand, you chose to let me love you. And I feel like if I can convince you to continue letting me love you for the rest of my life, then maybe, just maybe—I will be okay."

She put her hands to her mouth to stifle her cry.

"Yes." She said through muffled tears, as she nodded excitedly.

He slid the ring onto her finger before standing up. He lifted her in his arms and held her tight as she giggled with joy.

She grabbed his face in her hands and kissed him passionately, letting her breath seep into his lungs as he walked them back inside the lighthouse. He pushed her back up to the wall and hitched her legs around his waist. The metallic wall was cold against her bare skin, but desire bloomed deep in her belly and pushed the chill away. Her kisses became more savage, like she needed them to breathe, and his hands caressed her body with a fierce ardor matching her urgency. His fingers tore at her dress as she shrugged his opened button up off his shoulders. She ran her hands up under his lightweight thermal as his right hand gently cupped her breast and his fingers stroked her softly. He moved his mouth to her neck and kissed her neckline down to her collarbone. She gasped for air as his tongue traced the contours of it. She continued to let her hands trail up his torso under his thermal and squeezed him in close to her. Grabbing under her thighs he pulled her from the wall and took a few steps back.

He gently laid her on the ground and stopped momentarily to gaze at her. Her red, wild hair sprawled out around her and her bright, green eyes were full of carnal promise. He quickly drew his thermal over his head and bent down to continue kissing her.

He paused briefly when he saw her eyes widen at the sight of his wrapped ribcage. She reached her hand up and gingerly touched the wrapping.

"It's okay. I'm okay." He whispered to her trying to ease her concern.

She furrowed her brows briefly as she trailed her finger along the top of the wrapping. When she saw Nathan shiver in appreciation, she seemed to accept his words and nodded to him.

He bent down and kissed her, letting his tongue entangle with hers. His skin hummed to the way her body felt beneath his as she gently rolled her hips against him in response to their heated kisses. Her exposed skin was warm under his and the material of her dress caused a welcome friction. He quickly undid his pants and pushed her panties to the side and then he entered her swiftly. Her eyes grew big with the fullness she felt and she stared at him. The moment of intensity was over, she softly raised her hand and with the back of her palm she gently caressed the side of his face.

"How do you always find me?"

He took his right hand and smoothed the hair away from her face and bent his neck down to kiss her tenderly. When he pulled back he spoke with ardent fervor, "Because I will never stop looking."

Tess closed her eyes tilting her head back and moaned quietly to the rhythms of Nathan's body against hers. She bit her bottom lip to keep it from quivering as she let her hands travel up and down his arms. His skin was soft and she felt the muscles contract and tighten in his movements. She trailed her hands around his chest to his shoulder blades, pressing herself further into him. He groaned low in his throat. His right hand landed on her knee and he slid it up her thigh. His fingers softly dug into her skin with his movements against her. He could feel her body quickening and tightening under him. He kissed her hard, pouring everything he had into her as he felt her come undone beneath him.

She whispered his name almost inarticulately. He groaned audibly and bore his face into her hair next to hers as they sank into ecstasy. After slowing his breathing, he eased out of her and rolled off of her, panting in the darkness of the lighthouse.

"God, I've missed you." He managed out as his heart slammed against his chest.

She quickly turned over next to him, and in a moment of pure intimacy and bliss, Tess snuggled so close to him that he was recompensed. He claimed her right then for payment for everything that he had ever lost.

"Here, I better let you take this," he handed her his button up as he spoke, "your father might not be too happy with me." He smiled smugly, clearly pleased with himself as pointed to her shoulder.

Tess laughed as she slipped his button up on. He was right; the strap of her dress was ripped. As much as she wasn't ashamed, she still couldn't imagine looking her father in the eye and having him know what they had just been doing.

Nathan stood there staring at Tess, marveling in the moment, knowing that *here* was the reward for remembering, he thought. This man had been awoken from the routine of the asylum. He hadn't gone crazy; he'd had a sudden bout of *clarity*. He'd cracked open his eyes and seen through the mist. Tess was his light. She was the purpose in his life. And now that he had found that, he would never let it go.

Chapter Eleven

"Mrs. Suppan—I kind of like the sound of that." Tess said aloud as she walked hand in hand with Nathan along the beach back towards her childhood home.

She felt the cool sand beneath her feet and the gentle salty breeze blow through her hair. This night would be a night she would tell her children and her children's children about.

"I think I like it too." He smiled that all-American-boy smile down at her.

She dipped her head and snuggled close to his chest trying to conceal her shy smile.

"Tessie?" A voice called to them from behind.

What is it with this town and people calling her Tessie? Nathan wondered to himself as he heard someone approaching them on the beach.

Tess stopped instantly and twirled around in her tracks breaking away from Nathan. "Bobby?" Tess felt her heart slam against her chest and a shudder rippled through her. This was the thing she feared most, here he was, standing right in front of her.

Nathan felt his hair rise at the sound of Tess's voice. He could swear he could hear the thumping in her chest as the color drained from her face. He watched how her entire demeanor changed instantly. Her eyes darted around them like an animal trying to escape its cage, and he noticed the not so subtle way her hands began to tremble at her sides.

Bobby took a step closer to her, letting his eyes adjust to her in the night. "Tessie I'm so glad you're home—" His voice trailed off as his eyes fixated on her chest. The button up had fallen off her shoulder and he could see the strap that had been ripped on her dress with the top of her breast slightly exposed.

"Who the hell is this?" Bobby boomed while eyeing Nathan and then looking back at Tess. He sneered at her and cast a leering look up and down her body before finally nodding towards her shoulder. "Looks like Vanessa isn't the only loose woman in town."

Tess sank back cut from his words. She fumbled quickly to try and pull the button up over herself and wrap her arms protectively around her torso.

Nathan instinctively stepped in front of her cutting off Bobby's line of sight. "Don't talk to her that way. She's none of your concern anymore. You lost that privilege a long time ago."

He eyed the man in front of him. He was the same height relatively, but he had light blond hair, brown eyes, and was clean shaven, whereas a light stubble decorated the bottom half of Nathan's face. He looked like he used to be a jock, or at least he had the build of a jock. Nathan imagined he was the type of person who never really let go of their 'glory days' in high school.

"Oh, and I guess now it's yours?" He quibbled back, breaking Nathan from his thoughts.

"As a matter of fact, it is. Tess has agreed to be my wife." Nathan forced his jaw into a hard line giving nothing away.

"Did she now?" He said as he peered around Nathan to look at Tess.

He looked back at Nathan with a sardonic sneer. "You have no idea what you got yourself into. She'll say yes to anyone. That stupid bitch is ungrateful." He spat out.

Nathan had been trying to keep himself in check since the moment Bobby arrived. Jealousy. Rage at what he done to her. The way Tess's voice shook as she said his name—you name it, whatever it was, Nathan loathed the guy. And now to hear him talk that way about her— he couldn't hold back. With his good hand he pulled back his arm and let it fly into Bobby's nose. He heard something crack once his hand connected with his face. As much as it hurt his hand, he couldn't help but smile appreciatively.

"Son of a bitch!" Bobby hollered in pain. He glared his eyes up at Tess. He looked up at Nathan as he spoke and then back at her, "You know you broke your mama's heart, that's what she died of."

Tess clamped down hard on her bottom lip fighting to hold back tears. A metallic taste invaded her mouth and she could feel herself getting weaker. Bobby always knew how to kick you when you're down. He knew exactly what to say to make it hurt, and to make it stick. He was truly talented in his weaponized torture of her emotional state.

Nathan grumbled low in his throat. He couldn't help it, he took one more shot, this time at Bobby's jaw. He saw him go down and start to cry out in pain. He wouldn't show Tess, but his insides were cheering.

Not saying a word to Bobby, he took a step back and grabbed Tess's hand as she stood there in shock.

"Come on Tess, let's get you home." He hauled her away from Bobby, practically dragging her behind him.

He waited until they were out of eyesight before he reached down and scooped her into his arms, wincing imperceptibly at his ribs. He knew what Bobby had said had wounded her. Perhaps that's why he hit him, or maybe it was just the smug look on his face. Old habits die hard apparently.

Nathan carried her all the way back to the house. Her father was waiting with the door open for them as he watched them approach from down the beach.

"What happened?" He asked as he followed them into the living room noticing that something was obviously very wrong.

Nathan gently sat down in a chair with her still in his arms. She had cried so hard, it had worn her out, and minutes later she had fallen asleep on their way back. He sat carefully so not to jostle or wake her.

"Bobby." Nathan's voice was harsh and clipped.

Her father moved to take a seat. "I never did like that guy."

When Nathan didn't respond, Henry took a moment to eye Nathan's bloodied hand. "Need a bag of frozen peas?"

Nathan chuckled softly. "Please."

He watched as Henry walked to the kitchen. He could hear her father rustling through the freezer as he spoke, "I suspect you got a decent shot in?"

"I broke his nose—and possibly his jaw." Nathan said a little embarrassed at his own brazenness.

"Well I'll be!" Her father howled in joy. "Not that it really matters, but what *did* Bobby say to get a beating?"

"He made a comment to the effect of Tess was—uh—getting around." Nathan stared down as he made the comment checking to make sure the button up was securely covering her shoulders. He hated that Bobby even indicated Tess got around. She wasn't like that. She was his, and his only. But being around her father, he knew she wouldn't want him to see her as anything less than his innocent, little girl.

"Bastard. You know what he did to Tess right?"

"That's why his nose is broken." Nathan snorted.

He laughed. "Very good. So, his jaw then?"

Nathan's lips formed a tight line. "He told her she was the reason her mother passed away, that Tess had broken her heart."

Her father immediately stopped laughing and sank into the couch as he scratched his head. "Bobby sure knows how to get 'em where it hurts, don't he?"

"Yeah. Suppose he's gifted that way." Nathan replied as he gently stroked Tess's hair.

Henry grunted as he shifted in his seat. "Did Tess tell you what happened between her and her mother?"

"She told me she said some hurtful things to her mom before she took off."

He folded his arms across his chest. "But she didn't tell you what got said or why she said them?"

"I never really pressed the point, I could tell Tess wasn't happy with herself. I wasn't going to make her tell me anything she didn't want to."

Henry shook his head and laughed quietly to himself. Of course, Tess never told him, because of course she found a way to make herself the bad guy. Sometimes he believed God gave her such a big heart that he forgot to leave room for plain sense.

"Well Nathan, you should know that what happened that night was my fault." He mumbled warily.

"What do you mean?"

"Tess had walked in on Bobby and a close friend of hers—"

"Vanessa. Had the pleasure of meeting her earlier this afternoon."

Henry raised his eyes. "Right." He grumbled as he leaned forward.

"Well she was real upset, starting packing all her things and her mother started in on her. She told Tess that men have stronger needs than women, and it was just something you got used to."

Nathan's head perked up, he hadn't heard about this before.

"See, her mama was referring to me. I loved my wife, I did, but I made some really bad choices, and I wasn't all that discrete about it. I thought I was keeping it a secret, but come to find out, both Tess and her mother knew all along what I was doing." He bowed his head in shame thinking about both his wife and daughter knowing the truth about where he was going to and coming from each night.

"Anyway, my wife told Tess she needed to accept it and go home with Bobby. She believed the only way Tess could be happy was with the life Bobby would provide."

He paused and shifted further back in the chair before he elaborated. "Bobby comes from old money. His family owns about half the town, and it's true, he could provide generously for Tess. What her mother didn't understand is that in return for that generosity, Tess would have to give up the notion of love with Bobby."

Nathan looked down at the woman in his arms. He couldn't imagine a world in which Tess was trapped in a loveless marriage. Completely bound to ridiculous notions of what a wife should be, and what a wife should accept as okay. Tess needed to be free, her spirit was never meant to be bottled up like that.

"What my wife said didn't sit too well with Tess. Tess got angry, told her mother she couldn't be like her in a marriage like ours. Tess said those things, but I think the anger she was feeling was really meant for me."

Nathan wanted to comfort her father, but he couldn't think of a single thing he could say.

"Her mama wasn't loved the way she should have been and I take full responsibility for that, but I'm glad Tess had enough sense to know she deserved better. And I'm glad that for whatever reason, it led her to you."

Nathan smiled warmly down at her in his arms. With his free hand he gently caressed the side of her face. "I'm glad too." He stared down at her for a moment with his hand still by her face. Something about her had changed. She suddenly looked so young, vulnerable, and defeated there in his arms. He didn't know much about love before he met Tess, but knowing how he felt about her, knowing how loving her made him feel—he knew that something more happened between her and Bobby. She wouldn't seem so small and fragile if she really hadn't loved him like she said.

"I have to ask, there's more to the story than just finding Bobby cheating, isn't there?" He flushed slightly, feeling like he was somehow betraying Tess by asking.

Nathan eyed her father as he watched him shift forward in his chair and rub his chin.

"I always suspected so, and truthfully I know I had to have blocked some of it out."

"I don't follow."

He huffed once before speaking, "There are certain behaviors that we have become accustomed to. Something I was raised with, something that I wish more than anything Tess had never been a part of. Southern standards in a household."

"Such as?" Nathan wasn't sure what her father was getting at, but he felt his temperature start to rise.

"Women around here were held to different standards for a long time. As my late wife said and as my own mama said, women were led to believe that it was okay for a man to wander to another woman's arms as long as he came home to you. Just as it is okay for a man to slap a woman around if it meant teaching her a lesson."

Nathan's face drained of blood instantly.

Henry shook his head and continued, "I never laid a hand on my wife nor my child. I grew up watching my daddy beat the livin' daylights outta my mama and I swore I would never do that to a woman."

Nathan tried to clear his throat but was unsuccessful as his words cracked under his tongue. "Are you saying Bobby used to abuse her?"

Her father's eyes began to water and Nathan could see his bottom lip start to tremble. "Tess never told me. We never discussed it, but I suspect he did. I didn't press her because either I didn't want to know, or I—or I just eventually blocked it all out. I'm honestly not sure. Tess, probably in large part from watching her mother stay silent about me for so many years, never told anyone. If I, or anyone else saw something, or mentioned one of her afflictions—she would tell a convoluted story of how she fell or was just plain clumsy."

"Afflictions?" The word stuck in his throat in disgust at the detached term. Nathan was pissed now. Her father stood by and watched his child get beaten and bruised and he never did anything. And he was angry with Tess, why hadn't she told him?

Henry gave Nathan a small contrite smile before he bowed his head slightly. "Nathan, my daughter, my little girl right there—she is the only good and decent thing I have ever done in this world. I cheated on my wife. I acted like a fool and an adolescent, but most of all I stood by and never questioned my daughter even when I knew the tells of an abused woman. Can you understand how that regret haunts every moment of every day of my life? The day my Tessie left here was the best day of my life and the proudest I have ever been. My daughter was the girl who fought oblivion and won."

Nathan carried Tess into her room and laid her down on the bed. He sat there patiently stroking her hair and watching over her as she slept. He figured she stayed asleep as a coping mechanism to shut out the world. All in just a week's time she had had to overcome her issues with him, her mother's passing and the guilt she feels, and she had to face a nightmare of epic proportions. It was more than any one person should have to deal with. He understood why she would want to stay barricaded in her mind.

He was lost in his thoughts when her eyes finally fluttered open. He could see her start to panic slightly as her eyes tried to adjust to her surroundings. "Are we at my dad's?"

He felt his throat dry hearing how small her voice sounded. "Yes, I thought it would be best to bring you here."

She sat up in the bed and pulled her knees to her chest. "Bobby?"

Nathan chuckled slightly. "He's probably nursing his wounds in a bar some place."

"You hit him?" She asked more as reassurance of her memory than as an accusatory statement.

Nathan looked down at the bed as he spoke, "Twice, actually." He paused momentarily. "Tess, why didn't you tell me?" His voice was hoarse and harsh in the dim light of the room.

His soft, grey eyes looked wounded, like she had betrayed him, but she had no idea what for. "I told you about Vanessa and how guilty I felt about my mama."

He eyed her warily as he spoke, "Not about them, I mean about Bobby."

"What about Bobby?"

"He *hurt* you." The words felt like a fire poker in his throat. In no world would he ever be okay with someone hurting Tess.

Her eyes glued themselves to her fingers that were playing with a loose string on her bed comforter. "I told you that you saved me in more ways than I could count." She whispered almost inaudibly.

"Tess—" He sighed in slight frustration.

"How did you find out?" She tried to change tack.

"Bobby's attitude started it and your reaction to him was a big red flag, but I wasn't sure until I talked with your father."

That caught her attention and she looked up at him with wide eyes. "My father knows?" She felt her breath falter completely as her chest heaved in and out.

"He suspected. He knows you lied and covered up your 'afflictions' as he put it. He says you never told him, but he's pretty confident."

"I never told anyone." She muttered as she pulled her legs even tighter to her chest.

Nathan put his hand on her knee hoping she would continue talking but she stayed silent.

"Tess, are you okay?" He was trying his damndest to give her the same look she gave him, the one that willed him to talk to her.

She shook her head lightly. "You know I asked myself that same question a thousand times. I thought to myself that I must either be insane or a masochist to be okay. To allow it to keep happening. Honestly that may have been my biggest fear: finally going mad from it all."

Flashes of the girl in a straightjacket appeared in her mind. She knew deep down if she had stayed with Bobby, that that would have been her fate eventually.

Nathan pushed a loose tendril of hair behind her ear waiting for her to continue.

"It started off as small things. First, he learned how to make everything my fault. Every argument or disagreement, he found a way to turn the tables and make me feel guilty. It was an art form actually. The way he knew exactly what to say to truly make me feel like an awful human being. It got to the point that every fight or argument I felt so sick with guilt, it would kill me. It would cause actual pain for me to think he was mad at me. I would spend hours groveling for him to forgive me, for us to just be okay again. I would find a way to get us back to 'normal' and in the days that followed, I craved him. I craved his attention—I craved for him to love me, to lust for me, and to want nothing more than to know that I was his—body and soul."

Nathan's face heated at the idea of her wanting to be anyone's other than his. His possessiveness over her knew no bounds, and he gulped slightly at the thought that he could share any characteristics with her abuser.

"It was insatiable the way that I wanted him to love me. But I think even that bored him. In his boredom he turned his attention to knocking me down a few good pegs. It started with my looks. I was already insecure and he found a way to show me every reason as to why I had insecurities in the first place."

Nathan stared over at her. How she could ever be insecure was beyond him, but maybe that's why she was so damn attractive. Because no matter how obvious her beauty was, she was so humble about herself, that she couldn't see herself the way everyone else did.

"Then he moved on to my dreams, my ideals— he made every attempt to show and *teach* me that I was living in a fairytale. That I was stupid and naïve to believe in anything other than what was standing directly in front of me."

"Tess, you know that's not true." He said aloud thinking how odd it was to hear, considering *she* had been the one to make him believe in things beyond what he could physically see.

She gripped Nathan's hand. "I know." She sighed softly before continuing as she stared back down at the piece of thread on her comforter.

"Bobby just knew exactly when, where, and how to twist the knife. He stripped me of everything that I ever was, everything that I ever believed in, until all that was left was my love for him. He alienated me from friends, my community, activities that I was involved in. He made it so all I wanted in the world was him, and all that I had in the world—was him."

She tried to swallow the thick lump in her throat. Remembering back to those times, feeling the isolation like she had—it was a horrible feeling she wished she could erase completely. More than that, she was ashamed of the thoughts that had accompanied those feelings. Thoughts she hadn't dared to say out loud, because once they were said, you could never take them back. She had wished he had hit her because bruises would heal, which would have been better than the mental abuse she endured. The body healed, but the mind and soul, they aren't always so lucky. If she really were to say that out loud, it would truly make her a masochist, right? Sane and ordinary people don't wish physical harm on themselves unless they are truly broken. Do they? And as time passed, she realized sometimes we get the things we hope for, and unfortunately, there's no way to return them.

She let her shoulders sag down as she continued, knowing that her past only got worse. "I don't know if he got bored again or if he just wanted to prove a point, but eventually he used sex as a tool. A way to exert his control over me."

"What did he make you do?" Nathan hissed out as he felt his hatred for Bobby exuding from his body in waves.

Tess's voice was barely louder than a whisper as she spoke, "He wasn't violent sexually, but I had to be available to him whenever he wanted and my sole responsibility was to please him. Sex was not a mutually enjoyed 'activity'. It was for him and him alone. I was there to perform, to do as he asked, and then I was discarded. Other times he would build me up just to reject me. To make me feel like less of a woman."

Tess hugged her knees again. Talking about her past with Bobby was something she prayed she would never have to do. He had hollowed her from the inside out. She was an asset, no more important or valuable than a car or a watch. She was constantly debased and degraded at his hands.

Nathan shut his eyes tightly and rubbed his temple with one hand wearingly. He knew in this moment if Bobby was standing in front of him, he would kill him. Tess watched Nathan intently and when he opened his eyes she diverted her own and looked back down at the comforter, ashamed of what she was going to say next.

"I stayed with him. I allowed him to make me feel the way I did because I thought without him, I would be nothing—which is exactly what he had always wanted. So, I stayed. And things got worse. It started small, if he was angry he would grab me by the wrist and his grip would leave bruises. If I wasn't walking fast enough he would yank on my arm and force me to catch up. If I wasn't listening he would grab me, pull me in close to his face and then shove me away."

"You know and understand that that's not okay, right?" He shook his head in disgust at another man's treatment of a woman—his woman.

"I think a small part of me did." She looked up at Nathan as she spoke in a hushed voice and then quickly dropped her eyes back down. "I knew enough that I should get away for a while. So, I went on a road trip with a couple friends. It was something we had all talked about, and, at that point, it seemed like something I needed to do. It was the same trip that I visited Sitka for the first time."

Thinking back to that trip, it was the first time in a long time that she realized she could be okay without Bobby. He left her dozens of voicemails, but being hundreds of miles away gave her courage that she normally didn't have; so, she ignored them. She started to remember what it was like to feel independent and have aspirations, but Bobby would never let that happen.

Nearing the end of the trip, Vanessa and Rachel wanted to go out and party on their last night in Canada before heading back into the United States. Tess wanted to enjoy a peaceful evening alone, so she stayed behind at the motel and took a long, hot, bubble bath. It was a cold night; it had been raining for two days straight, and she finally had the room to herself. She was relaxing in the tub, listening to the rain outside when she heard a loud thump as the bedroom door burst open. Bobby rushed directly into the open bathroom. He stood there, staring at her for a moment, furious, with his lips in a tight, straight line, and rainwater spilling off his shoulders.

"Bobby? What are you doing here?" She grasped the edge of the tub as she looked up at him in palpable horror.

His jaw was taut as he reached down with one hand grabbing her arm and the other grabbed her by her hair. He yanked her out of the tub and dragged her into the room. She cried and screamed as she tried to pull her hair from his grip. Her head was throbbing in response to the tugging, but he was so much stronger than she was. He pulled her into the room and threw her onto the bed. With his one hand still gripping her hair, he used his other hand to pin her down by her throat with considerable force.

She kicked and withered under him, trying to escape his ironclad grip, but he held her down, choking her.

"You stupid bitch. Did you really think I wouldn't find you?" He screamed inches from her face.

She shook her head violently as she cried, gasping for precious breath as she could feel her windpipe being crushed under the pressure of his hand. When he finally released her throat, she cried out, "I wasn't—I wasn't leaving you! I was coming back!"

She coughed as her throat slowly began to expand again, its walls sticking together.

He reached his left hand up and brought it down, smacking her back handed across the face. The blow was painfully hard and his class ring adorning his middle finger tore through the top layers of her skin. She turned her face into the bed, gripping her red, glowing, and now bleeding, cheek.

He reached down again and pulled her up by the forearm. She felt her legs quivering beneath her, betraying her. Her body convulsed under his touch and she was painfully aware that she was completely naked, only adding to the humiliation. He grasped her chin tightly with his free hand, forcing her to look him in the eye. She could see the feral intensity burning through his eyes. With his teeth clenched he leaned forward, breathing heavily into her face, "You. Are. Nothing. Without. Me." He paused briefly before smiling wickedly at her. "No matter where you go, I will find you. I have friends in really low places. You do *not* want to defy me again. I promise you—you won't like the consequences."

He shoved her away from him and crossed his arms as he looked on at her with ill-disguised disgust.

"Get dressed, and get your things. We're leaving."

Tess shook the memory from that night away. She recalled the story to Nathan and watched as every muscle in him tensed. She could see him starting to shake. She knew how much it was starting to affect him. She wanted to stop there but she knew she owed him her story. He deserved the whole truth, every ugly detail of it.

He wanted to look away from her. He didn't want her to see the venomous look in his eyes or the blood springing from the half-moon shapes his fingernails had dug into his closed fists. He didn't want her to see the violence lingering there just beneath the surface. He didn't want her to know the monster inside of him, a beast that could very closely resemble the monster she faced in that hotel room. It was these thoughts that kept him from asking the question for an answer he needed to know to in order to protect her.

"It got worse from there. I came home with him, and because I did, I gave him the green light to continuously abuse me. He mostly loved to toss me around and smack me. He only punched me once, but it was enough for me to never make the same mistake again."

"Only? You say it as if it was good that it *only* happened once." Nathan said disdainfully through clenched teeth. His hands gripped at his jeans in balled up fists as he tried desperately hard to gain control over himself.

"No, that is not at all how I meant it. I said only because it happened just one singular time, because," her voice quieted dangerously low as she continued, "it was more fun to toss me around and smack me. Too much damage and his toy was no longer fun to play with." She spoke absentmindedly.

Nathan stared at her with a horrified expression; her impassive tone was unsettling. How broken had she been and he had never even noticed.

"He sprained my wrist and broke the other arm." Nathan paled at the way she didn't even break her train of thought as she continued, "I learned to come up with stories. Most of the time my stories were ridiculous, and I think that's because a part of me was hoping by telling such absurd tales someone would finally ask. Someone would finally push for me to tell the truth. But no one ever did."

"I would have." He was so quiet she could hardly hear him. He played it over and over in his head, all the ways he would have saved her if he had only known her back then.

She gripped his forearm in comfort and forced a small-inhibited smile.

She sighed despairingly before speaking, "I stayed scared of him. Scared to speak up or speak out, and scared to leave. But when I saw him with Vanessa, I saw it as my way out. It was a public scandal now, and I could use it to leave. Granted, I snuck out of town when no one was looking, but it gave me the strength to do the thing I had been terrified to do for months."

He could feel his throat burning with a mixture of violence and extreme sadness. How could she not have told him? How did he not know how much she needed protecting? "Tess, I need to know how he found you on your trip—I need to know how you felt safe enough in Sitka and didn't tell anyone for your own protection?"

She tilted her head back slightly while closing her eyes and sighing through closed lips. She slowly opened her eyes to look Nathan in the eye. She could read the devastation and betrayal etched into his beautiful, steel, grey eyes.

"Nathan, I know it was risky not telling anyone about him, and I know I should have told you of all people—but I was desperate. I was desperate to put as much separation between me and that life as I could."

She watched his shoulders sag as he subtly shook his head. She knew he would always feel that answer was not good enough, but she continued sharing anyhow, "Bobby had some rough friends. Friends he met while at basic training at Fort Benning in Georgia."

Tess paused briefly, noticing the way Nathan's brow arched and his eyes widened slightly. She chuckled softly to herself as she answered his unspoken question, "Bobby never graduated. He failed out claiming a knee injury." Nathan's shoulders silently lifted in a 'that's what I thought' kind of way.

"Even though his time in the Army was short-lived, he made some lasting connections, with one guy in particular. His friend was really good with the tech stuff. I made sure never to post locations on social media and made sure my friends didn't either. I told them I needed the trip to be a break from social media, time to clear my head. But he was a hacker; he didn't need any help from us, and that's how he found me in Canada."

He waited patiently for her to continue. This friend explained how Bobby found her, but it didn't explain how she kept herself hidden for over a year.

"I learned from my mistakes, but I also know I've been lucky. When I left here, I emptied my bank accounts—not that I had much, but I took everything I could in cash. I sold my car along the way in some no-name town and took public transportation the rest of the way. Although I never tried to change my name or anything, I also don't use social media, and I only use cash."

It dawned on him suddenly, all of the signs he had missed. He knew in the beginning the thought crossed his mind, but maybe he just wanted to believe that she didn't have a haunted past like he did.

"I have a very small technological footprint. I know that isn't bulletproof, but I guess I relied on the public scandal. Bobby's family owns most of this town, I knew his family would do everything they could to hide his dirty secret. I knew, or at least hoped, that would prevent him for looking for me." She paused briefly as she looked over at Nathan and spoke with a small voice, "At least I was right?"

Nathan placed his hand on hers. "Tess I—"

They both turned their attention to her door; they could hear her father on the front porch. They heard his shotgun being loaded; it was enough for both of them to spring to their feet and head out towards him.

Henry stood on the edge of his front porch with his shotgun in hand, his breath curling up around him in the cool, dark air.

"Get off my property. I have more than a right to shoot you—I have a *desire* to shoot you. I'm giving you a fair warning, but that's it."

"Mr. Dawson, you're not going to shoot me. You know I'm the right man for your daughter."

Bobby stood out in the front yard, first staring down Mr. Dawson, and then he lifted his bruised face towards the sky as if he were playing God.

Henry laughed and pumped the gun once, "Ah, like hell."

"Daddy?" Tess called to him as she finally understood what was going on.

"Tessie, stay inside. I've got this."

Nathan instinctively pulled Tess around behind him as he took a step forward and stood directly behind the screen door.

"Come on Bobby. Take a step closer so I have an excuse to shoot you. Tessie, cover your eyes so you have *plausible deniability*." He enunciated as he gleamed wickedly.

Bobby started pacing out front, goading him. "Like I said, I don't think you're going to shoot me."

At that, Nathan pushed open the screen door and strode out to stand beside Tess's father.

"Ah, Bobby, I do believe you met my soon-to-be son-in-law, Nathan?"

"I don't know if you'd really consider it meeting someone when all they really got to see was a fist in their face." Nathan smirked.

Henry let out a billowing, raspy laugh before he shouted down to Bobby, "This one is funnier than you!" He motioned over at Nathan.

Bobby sneered, "Real winner your daughter has there. Coward won't even come off the porch."

"Nathan. Don't." Tess warned from behind the screen.

Nathan held his hand back towards her, urging her to stop speaking. "Stay out of this Tess."

She rocked on her heels. Her father stopped laughing and looked over at Nathan. Nathan quickly grabbed the shotgun from him. "I'm just going to set this down so you don't accidentally shoot me."

"You? What are you going to do?" He quirked back.

"I'm going to give this asshole the beating he deserves." He pushed up the sleeves of his thin thermal and started to make his way down the front steps into the yard.

Tess burst through the screen door. "Nathan. Stop. He's not worth it."

Nathan turned back momentarily. "Go back inside Tess."

From the tone of his voice Tess shrank back. She could see there was no possibility of getting Nathan to walk away.

Bobby stood there with his arms spread wide, egging Nathan forward.

Nathan walked right up to Bobby and popped him once in the face. As Bobby fell back clutching his nose, Nathan smirked. "This is going to be fun."

He went to lunge forward, but Bobby had beaten him to it and charged at Nathan, throwing him to the ground. Nathan was able to pick himself up and quickly got the upper hand, despite the dull pain in his ribs. Once Bobby got up, Nathan stepped forward and swung at his jawline again. Nathan heard a small pop after his hand had connected with Bobby's jaw. Bobby hobbled backwards and Nathan charged forward grabbing the back of Bobby's head and bringing it down hard and swift into Nathan's rising knee. The blow left Bobby doubled over, so Nathan took a chance to bring his knee up into his stomach a few times.

Bobby coughed up a spattering of blood and swayed back and forth trying to steady himself. Nathan sneered and wiped a bead of sweat off his forehead. He waited until Bobby was able to stand up straight and then rushed at him, catching his arm and swinging him around so that his back was to Nathan. With his back turned, Nathan pushed him face forward, slamming Bobby's head into a nearby tree. The blow was enough to collapse Bobby down at Nathan's feet.

Nathan huffed once in the night air trying to catch his breath. He steadied himself and walked back towards the front porch. As he walked up the steps, he looked at Henry who was laughing so hard there were tears in his eyes.

"You may want to call the cops. Let them know what happened and to send paramedics."

Henry tried to control his throaty laugh. "Sure will, but enjoying the hurt a few minutes more won't kill 'em."

Nathan shrugged and headed towards Tess. She stared at him standing in front of her. She eyed him wearingly with her arms crossed and then turned on her heel and stalked off back into the house.

Nathan rolled his eyes at himself; there he'd gone and done it again. Just when he got her to forgive him for doing something stupid, he went and beat the lights out of her ex.

He walked inside ready to start groveling. "Tess—" He was cut off by her pushing him towards a chair in the kitchen. She pulled out the first aid kit and a bag of something frozen.

"Sit down." She commanded as she quickly began tending to his hands. His knuckles were covered with small cuts speckled with sand, and she could see his wrist was red and swollen. She sighed exasperatingly as she worked on cleaning out and disinfecting the cuts.

Nathan sat quietly as she tended to him. He was waiting for her to yell or say something, but she continued to work silently. He mentally cursed at himself; the silent treatment was the worst. The things he imagined her to be thinking were running roughshod over his emotions.

She cleaned his wounds, wrapped them, and then she taped a bag of frozen vegetables to his wrist.

"When the paramedics come I want them to check your wrist; you may have re-sprained or broken it. It doesn't look good. May need to check your ribs too."

"Alright." He said guardedly as he held on to the bag taped to his wrist.

She sighed once more as her father walked into the kitchen and he cleared his throat slightly. "Cops and paramedics are on their way."

"Good." Tess said as she roughly shut the first aid kit. Her father shoved his hands in his pockets and kept his eyes glued to the floor while Nathan stared at Tess waiting for whatever was about to come.

She looked from her father and then back to Nathan. "So, are you two done now? You good?"

Henry raised his hands at her. "Tessie, it's not like he didn't deserve it."

She tapped her foot with her arms crossed in front of her chest and looked at Nathan waiting for him to say something but when he didn't she spoke up, "I didn't say he didn't deserve it. He had it coming, but I'm asking, are you two done now?"

Both of the men bowed their heads as if their mother had just scolded them. "Yes." They said in smarting unison.

"Alright then. Let's go out front and wait for them to arrive. I, for one, would like to be there when they haul the son of a bitch off."

Both Nathan and Henry gaped at Tess with their mouths hanging open as she stalked passed them to the front porch.

Nathan quietly sat down beside Tess on the front porch steps. He hesitated slightly as he exhaled. "Scale of one to ten—how mad are you right now?"

She turned to gaze at him with an expressionless look. "Nathan, I'm not mad."

"You're not?"

"Jealous, maybe. But not mad." She offered.

"What?"

She looked at him like he had a fifth limb. "What, you think I haven't thought about kicking the crap out of the man who abused me? Of course I thought about it. It was cathartic to see too."

Nathan shook his head and laughed.

"But just because it was fun to see, I still think it was reckless of you. You could have been hurt."

He stopped laughing instantly. His voice was rough as he responded, "You're wrong, Tess."

It was her turn to be surprised. "What?"

"You're wrong. That was probably the most in control thing I have ever done. I wasn't being reckless. Bobby was in serious need of getting his ass handed to him, and I was more than happy to oblige. He *hurt you,* Tess."

"What, and you think that gives you carte blanche?"

"No, but Tess, see this for what it is. He did more than hurt you—he *broke* you. He did horrible, unforgivable things, and you let him. You let him, and so did everyone else. And, instead of fighting and making him own up to it—you ran."

"Nathan, I—"

He touched her lips with his fingertips to signal her to stop talking.

"Running was the absolute best thing you could do at the time. I don't think you were a coward; I think you were smart. But the fact is, Bobby didn't learn. He's still the same jackass he was back then. He may not have followed through on his threats and searched for you like he could have, but Tess, what if I wasn't here when you bumped into him? Do you really think he would have simply allowed you to walk away?"

Tess dropped her eyes in silent agreement as Nathan continued.

"Me kicking his ass was far less than he deserved. What he deserves, what I really wanted to do—was put a bullet in his head."

Tess blanched indiscernibly at the gravity of his statement. From his tone, she knew Nathan absolutely meant it.

Nathan shifted next to her. "Instead, I chose to beat him to a pulp. Personally, I think that shows a great deal of control on my part."

Tess couldn't help it; she had to laugh a little at the irritatingly, smug smirk on his face. She looped her arm in his and rested her head on his shoulder, grateful to have him in her life.

Chapter Twelve

Tess stood at the bottom of the front porch steps with her arms crossed protectively in front of her as she watched Bobby glower at her from the back of the ambulance.

She watched as they stitched up a cut on his nose. She smirked to herself; Nathan really had done a number on him. She scolded herself silently for her brief moment of amusement and regained her focus. She continued to stare at Bobby and he glared right back at her. She knew if he had the chance, he would walk right over and strangle her. Perhaps that was the reason she continued to stare at him, because for the first time, she knew for certain there was absolutely nothing he could do to her.

She continued to watch from where she stood, her insides taking a victory lap as she watched an officer place a pair of silver cuffs on him. She knew how much of a hypocrite she was. It wasn't long ago that she told Nathan to give up on revenge, and yet, here she was dancing in triumph over the revenge she had finally gotten. Maybe it wasn't done at her own hands, but she knew in a small way she was responsible for what happened there tonight.

Nathan sat in the back of the second ambulance. He was surprised that they would dispatch two of them considering the injuries were relatively minor. Then again, Henry was the one who called it in and he did have a way of embellishing details. He looked over at Tess who stood stock-still with her arms folded and her eyes fixed on Bobby with a deadpan expression. She held her mouth in a straight line, and her eyes never wavered or blinked from what he could see. He had never seen her like this—then again, he had never really known the whole truth. Knowing what he knew now, he understood why she felt the need to watch him. In her mind she was probably thinking she was watching because it was fun or cathartic, but the truth is, she was observing to make sure he didn't come after her. A part of her was still scared of Bobby. Nathan wondered if he would ever truly get her to stop being scared. Being treated that way isn't something you get over. As much as he wished it, beating Bobby within an inch of his life wouldn't erase what had happened to her.

Tess silently watched as Bobby was driven off the property in the back of a squad car. She sighed heavily in relief to herself and then turned to see that Nathan had his eyes locked on her. She ducked her head slightly as she began walking towards him.

"How's your wrist?"

He took a moment to eye her before he responded, "It'll heal."

She took a deep breath and then took a seat next to him on the back of the rig. She held her hands between her knees and kept her eyes glued to them.

"I guess I was wrong about revenge. I guess sometimes no matter what we do, revenge finds us." She confessed feeling guilty about how happy seeing Bobby bloody made her.

Nathan looked over at her stunned. "Tess, you didn't do anything. This one was on me."

"Thank you, Nathan, but we both know you did this because of me."

"Damn straight, but not because I was fulfilling your revenge fantasy."

She turned her head to look at him quizzically.

"I did it because I love you—because I hate what he did to you, but most of all because I couldn't stand the idea of you being afraid of him. And the truth is, you would continue to always be afraid of him if something hadn't been done about it."

She dropped her eyes down to the ground in front of them. She never wanted to say it out loud or even to herself how afraid she was. Afraid that somehow, some way, he would find a way to drag her back here and keep her from ever leaving. The thought had crept into her mind and dreams on more than one occasion.

Nathan slid off the rig and stood in front of Tess. With his hand he gently lifted her chin so her eyes could meet his. "Tess, my job as your partner, your fiancé, your husband, whatever my title may be—my duty to you will always be making sure you feel safe, protected, and loved."

He watched as tears filled her eyes and her chest sagged slightly. "So, it's really over then?" As the words spilled out, she heard herself for the first time and realized that she had been holding her breath for the past two years. Because of Nathan, she was finally able to breathe again. Something she wasn't fully aware she hadn't been doing all along.

His lips turned into a half smile as he pulled her onto her feet and into his chest as he kissed her head. He stayed silent for a moment as he stroked her hair. "Yeah baby, it is."

⸺•◦●◦•⸺

"So, what would you say to letting me show you my favorite things about here?"

Nathan chuckled as he looked over at her. "And here I thought you didn't have any favorites about this place."

She rolled her eyes. "I wasn't entirely miserable growing up, you know. Now, are you coming or what?" She held out a hand for him to take.

He grinned up at her. She was standing in front of him in a navy-blue, rockabilly dress that flared out around her when she moved and white sneakers. Her hair was loosely pinned up which made him laugh to himself; it seemed no matter how hard she tried, she would never be able to tame that hair of hers.

"I admit it; it's nice here." Nathan spoke as he observed the waterfront that was lined with people and street performers all enjoying the sunshine.

Tess smiled widely. "It has its moments." She winked over at him. "Come on, there's someone I want you to meet."

She walked over to a crowd of people surrounding a group of dancers. Nathan watched as Tess weaved her way to the front of the crowd as she watched and clapped for the dancers. Once the song had ended, one of the dancers noticed Tess and took off running towards her. The man was in his mid-twenties, well built with short, brown hair, and he wore brown pants with a brown vest that covered his white, rolled up, dress shirt. He picked her up in his arms and twirled her around while laughing. The smile on Tess's face was priceless. Nathan wondered whom this man could have been to make her smile that way. And then the more unreasonable and irrational part of himself tensed at the sight of someone hugging her. He quickly tried to slap his subconscious down.

Once the man set her down he smiled at her and hugged her once more. "Tessie, I've missed you."

Nathan subtly rolled his eyes, he didn't think he would ever get used to that nickname.

"Ford, I've missed you too! Look, I want you to meet someone." She wrapped her arm in his as she led him over to face Nathan.

"Nathan, this is Ford, one of my very best friends growing up," Ford smiled down at her and patted her hand as she spoke, "and Ford, this is Nathan, my fiancé."

She giggled wildly as she held up her left hand to show Ford the ring. Nathan couldn't help the swell of pride and joy at her excitement.

Ford laughed and hugged Tess once more. "Well I'll be Tessie."

Ford looked back over at Nathan and stuck his hand out to shake. "So, this is Alaska?"

Nathan shook his hand and looked from Ford to Tess. "Does everyone call me that?"

"Pretty much." Ford answered through a big all-teeth-showing grin. Ford nodded for them to follow him out of the crowd.

"Mr. Dawson gave you the nickname when Tessie here told him she had found someone to love out there."

Tess grinned slightly as she stepped away from Ford, closer to Nathan and put an arm around him. He squeezed her close as he made eye contact with Ford, knowing full well he was having a one-sided pissing contest with her friend.

Ford chuckled so subtly that Nathan was fairly certain Tess didn't notice. He relaxed slightly, grateful that Ford didn't seem bothered by Nathan puffing up his chest for no reason.

Nathan looked down at Tess recovering from his sudden bout of jealousy. "Alaska, huh?"

Tess blushed as she looked back over at Ford. "My parents and Ford are the only ones who knew where I was. Ford and I grew up together; our dads were hunting buddies. Ford is the one who taught me how to shoot."

Nathan's mouth gaped open slightly as he looked up at Ford who just shrugged his shoulders in ill-disguised exuberance. "So, you're the reason I lost my very first shooting bet."

Ford let out a loud laugh. "That's my girl!"

Ford continued to laugh for a minute until it finally faded out and he looked at Nathan, then down at Tess. He stuck his hands in his pockets as he spoke, "You look happy though."

She looked down at the ground and smiled before lifting her eyes to meet Ford's. "Yes Ford, I think I am."

Nathan squeezed Tess in close to him knowing that he could claim responsibility for that.

Ford smiled and clapped his hands. "Well as much as I would love to stand here with you two heartthrobs, I have a show to get back to." He pointed over his shoulders as he asked, "Wanna watch?"

"Wouldn't miss it." Tess gave him her signature you-will-never-ever-recover-from-this smile.

"How's everyone doin' today?" Ford bellowed out as he stood in the center of the crowd.

The crowd cheered and hollered their responses.

"Well folks, I have to tell you, we have got quite the surprise today." He bellowed out as he slowly made his way around the circle. "See, one of our own has finally come home."

He smiled widely over at Tess and held out a hand in her direction as the music slowly clicked on. Nathan watched as she took a step back and sucked in her breath. "Oh no. Absolutely not."

"Come on Tessie, for old time's sake." Ford with an outstretched hand started tapping his feet and snapping his fingers while raising his eyebrows at Tess.

Nathan looked down at Tess who sighed once, looked up at him with a smile that said, 'oh well what are you gonna do about it?' and winked before she took off running into the center next to Ford.

Nathan's mouth dropped as he watched Tess and Ford perform a whole swing dance routine to the music. He watched as the two of them danced their way around the circle, Ford's feet moving to the music, Tess spinning circles around him. He watched as her dress flared out around her and a smile spread widely across her face. Tess took Ford's hand and together they danced around with gentle lifts and spins. Nathan couldn't close his mouth for the life of him. He stood there gawking at Tess, there was so much he never knew about her.

When the song ended the crowd cheered wildly. Ford took Tess's hand and raised it above their heads, together they bowed for the crowd. Ford turned and hugged Tess, giving her a peck on the cheek before she strolled back over to Nathan.

Tess bit her lip trying to keep her giggle from turning into full-blown hysterical laughter, but failed miserably as she took in Nathan's expression. His mouth hung open and he stared at her with bewildered eyes. She walked right up to him finally containing herself for a fleeting moment, patted his chest with her hand and whispered, "Guess you're not the only one with secret hobbies."

She fell back into a fit of laughter as she walked passed him. Nathan stood there for a minute more, completely dumbfounded. After a few seconds he gained control of himself again and closed his mouth brusquely, turned around, and ran up to Tess.

"You cannot compare my dancing in the kitchen to *that*." He held a hand back pointing at the crowd they had just come from.

Tess's head fell back in laughter. "Okay, maybe not, but the look on your face sure was priceless."

Nathan scratched his head. "Well I'll say, I mean I had no idea you could dance, and I mean—damn, you're good. Like *really* good."

Tess smiled and took her dress out at her sides in a courtesy. "Why thank you, kind sir."

"Cute." He teased playfully and stuck his tongue out briefly.

She giggled in response.

Nathan laughed as he wrapped his arm around her shoulder, and pulled her in close to him as he shook his head in shocked amusement. "You are full of surprises."

"So, what do you think of Beaufort?" Tess asked as they strolled hand in hand down the river walk.

Nathan looked out towards the water and then back at the downtown waterfront. Earlier today where there had been groups of performers and vending booths, the paths had now begun to clear. Small hanging lights weaved their way between buildings and he could hear a country band performing in the distance.

He smiled down at her. "Well, let's see, I saw you dance, which was," he paused momentarily, "well unexpected. Good, but unexpected. Sweet tea is sweet, the barbeque was great, and I have a new love for lighthouses." He winked gently as he continued, "Well, and, there's the whole bit of you agreeing to be my wife—yeah, I guess you could say I like it here."

Tess playfully nudged him as she led him closer to the band playing. She pulled up short of the crowd surrounding the band. They stopped close enough to hear the band, but far enough away to be alone.

Nathan placed his hand on the small of her back and pulled her in close to him. With his other hand he grabbed her left hand and drew it up between them and kept it there. He held her close to him and swayed her gently to the soft, country melody.

Tess sighed lightly and pressed herself close to Nathan's chest. She knew she had finally found peace of mind, because with him, she would be safe. She breathed in his scent as he continued to slowly spin them in circles. She wanted to remember this. She knew she would never want to rush this feeling with him; she wanted to take it slow, making it last forever.

She gently tipped her head up and chastely pressed her lips against his throat. She heard a low, soft moan escape his lips and she smiled to herself before tucking her head back under his chin.

"Nathan—I—"

"Yeah, Tess?"

"I just wanted to tell you I love you. Can we go home now?" She questioned in a soft murmur.

Chapter Thirteen

"How are you doing with all of this?" Nathan asked as he walked alongside Tess down the jet way.

"With what?"

"With being back here in Alaska? I know North Carolina wasn't necessarily what you wanted it to be, but it's still the place you grew up—your first home. It's okay to miss it."

Tess smiled. "With you there, for once it felt more like the home I always wanted it to be. But that was never meant to be my home. Right here, with you, in this little Alaskan town—this is my home."

Nathan smiled down at Tess and squeezed her hand tenderly.

"Nathan! Tess?" Tommy called from the waiting area while waving his arms over his head.

"Hey Tommy." Nathan patted Tommy on the shoulder as he stopped in front of him.

"Hi Tommy."

Tommy beamed at Tess with a face-splitting grin. "So, I suppose this means you changed your mind?"

Tess hesitated a moment for dramatic affect and rolled her eyes humorously. "Suppose I did."

Nathan hackled. "I think you did more than that."

Tommy looked back and forth between them. He waited for one of them to speak but he just watched Nathan eye Tess conspiratorially. "Oh, for the love of it, will you tell me what's goin' on?"

Nathan chuckled and looked from Tommy to Tess and shrugged his shoulders.

"I wasn't going to ruin you telling him." She responded to his look.

"Tell me what?" Tommy piped in.

"Why do I have to tell him?" Nathan rejected. He knew Tommy was getting ready to burst and he couldn't help but continue this charade. He was delighted that Tess was playing along.

"Tell me what?" He demanded again.

Tess smirked subtly ignoring Tommy and addressed Nathan. "Because he's your best friend."

"So, you could have told him too. You're his best friend just as much as I am."

"Will somebody tell me what the hell you two are yappin' about?" Tommy blurted out in vexation.

Tess sighed heavily in good-humored annoyance. She held her left hand out in front of her with a haughty grin.

Tommy grabbed her hand pulling it incredibly close to his face as he studied the ring on her finger with his mouth hanging open.

"I'll be damned." He muttered under his breath. Tess couldn't help but giggle.

"How the hell did you manage that?" Tommy peered up at Nathan.

Nathan looked taken aback. "Whoa, what's that supposed to mean?" He laughed.

"She was so pissed at you that she moved out. Then you come back a week later and somehow convinced her to marry your sorry ass? How the hell does that work?"

"I'm just that good." Nathan teased.

Tess joined in the laughter, but was quickly quieted by Tommy's finger pointing at her. She immediately stopped laughing and sunk back on her heels with a small pout on her face like a child who's been reprimanded. "And you, Tess—you were supposed to be the strong one here. You know, make sure Nathan stopped being a damn fool." He whispered.

"I think I've got that under control now Tommy." She whispered right back.

Nathan narrowed his eyes at Tommy.

Tommy ignored Nathan's glare and took a moment to think about it as he looked back and forth between them again. Then a grin spread broadly across his face and he grabbed them both in a group hug.

"Well congratulations! I knew she was the one for you when you first met." He beamed in pride.

Nathan shifted his weight. "You did not. You kept telling me if I didn't make a move someone else would!" Nathan huffed.

"I was only saying that to get your butt in gear, cause I knew, *she* was *the one*."

"Sure." Nathan rolled his eyes.

"I did!" Tommy exclaimed.

"Children, the both of you, I swear." Tess stood between them with her hands on her hips.

If Tess wasn't trying so hard to feign seriousness, Nathan would have laughed and told her that she was really getting the whole 'mom' thing down.

"Alright, alright. Let's get you two home." Tommy huffed as he motioned for them to follow him to where his truck was parked.

Tommy looked back as they neared his truck. "I call dibs on hanging out with Tess tonight."

Nathan chuckled and looked at Tommy with a perplexed expression. "You can't call dibs on her, she's *my* fiancé."

Tommy turned around quickly grabbing Tess by the arm yanking her towards him as he licked her exposed forearm.

Tess shrieked, "Gross!"

Tommy wiggled his eyebrows at Nathan, ignoring Tess. "See. Licked her. Now she's mine."

Nathan narrowed his eyes as he swatted at Tommy making him quickly dodge and run to his truck.

Tess chuckled loudly as Nathan's head snapped over to her. "Think that's funny, do you?"

She beamed at him and shrugged her shoulders. "Well it is a little."

Tommy bent over slapping his thigh with one hand and the other pointed at Nathan. "Ha!"

Nathan rolled his eyes and huffed loudly.

Tess closed the gap between them putting a hand on both Tommy and Nathan's shoulders. "Tommy, Nathan has something he wants to ask you. Nathan?" She playfully jabbed him in the chest. He winced back and mouthed to her 'ow'. She rolled her eyes before narrowing them, prodding him to ask his question.

He chuckled at her reaction. "Dunno if he deserves it now." He muttered quietly before shaking his head and clearing his throat. "So, Tommy, what would you say to being my best man?"

Tommy straightened up and looked surprised; happy, but surprised. That made Tess laugh. Why Tommy even had to question Nathan's loyalty to him was beyond her. Tommy wasn't just Nathan's childhood friend, Tommy was his family—Tommy was their family.

Now serious, Tommy straightened himself and shook Nathan's hand. "I'd be honored, Nate." Tommy patted Nathan on the back as he grinned boyishly at Tess.

------•◆◆•------

"Nathan, I was thinking; let's just elope." Tess said as she swiveled her legs over the couch and plopped down beside Nathan.

"Elope, huh?" He asked as he put his arm around her and traced her arm gently with his fingertips.

"Or at least something small. I don't want a huge wedding." Tess spoke as she cocked her head slightly to the left and stared out the window.

Nathan knew she wanted to do the exact opposite of everything she had ever dreamed up or planned with Bobby. Anything to shake the memory of him from her mind completely. As much he wanted to do that for her, he couldn't bear the idea of her waking up twenty years down the road, sad she never got the wedding she deserved.

"As much as I'd love to just run away with you and elope, just the two of us, I don't think we should deny your father the chance of walking you down the aisle. But if small is what you want, just family and a few friends?"

"I suppose you're right. If we get married this summer, we could have the wedding right here in the back yard, quaint and romantic."

"Tess, we can do whatever you'd like. Just let me know, and I'll make it happen."

"Is that so?" She challenged him.

He pulled her up onto his lap and let his eyes wander around the room a moment before answering, "Okay, anything within reason." He gave her a wolfish smile.

"Ah, you teased me." She leaned forward and gently kissed his lips.

After she kissed him, she got up and padded over to the bookshelf. He watched as she reached for one of her old books that she brought back from North Carolina, and she held it to her chest tightly.

"Baby?"

She stood there a moment more smiling down at *Gone With the Wind* as she slowly opened its pages. There, pressed between the pages, was a single

Casablanca lily. She gingerly held the flower with her fingers and walked over to Nathan.

"What's that?"

"It's a Casablanca lily. Growing up, my mama would take me to this garden on the outskirts of town and there were hundreds of these flowers. It was like walking into heaven; they were so beautiful."

"It's pretty."

"They celebrate life, you know." She smiled over at him. He leaned forward to stroke her back gently.

"Whatever we decide to do with our wedding, we should have Casablanca lilies in honor of our mothers, because I know more than anything, they would both be here if they could."

Nathan nodded in agreement and smiled back at her.

Chapter Fourteen

Tess peered through the window into the backyard. A simple wooden arbor entwined with ivy and Casablanca lilies stood at the entrance of the woods. In front of the archway were four small rows of white chairs and in the aisle, a bed of white petals lined the path. Off to the side were two long tables decorated with white linens and green centerpieces with lilies adorned on top. Nathan, Tommy, Jack, and Henry had worked tirelessly to string up fairy lights over the tables to make their reception absolutely magical. Tess smiled at their little back yard wedding; it was perfect for them.

She turned back to face the mirror. Her hair was pinned up with a few small, white, Egyptian star flowers placed in the bun that hung low to her neck. Her dress was an ivory, lustre, satin, v-neck gown with vine straps, a low back, and a sweep train. It clung to her chest and hips, framing her face delicately and accentuating her curves. Its long train pooled out behind her and she smiled widely; she felt like a queen in a magical kingdom.

She looked down at her hands that were visibly shaking with the knowledge that this was going to be the best day of her life. She smiled as she reached for her small bouquet of lilies. A piece of fabric surrounded the stems, binding them together, fabric from her mother's wedding dress. She smiled because in a small way, she felt her mother was there with her now, helping prepare her for this moment.

She heard a faint knock at the door. "Who is it?"

"It's me, darlin'."

She opened the door. "Hi Daddy."

"Hi gorgeous. Let me look at you." He said as he held her hand and looked at her dress.

"You are the most beautiful bride. You look so much like your mother." His eyes started to dampen.

"Aw, Daddy, don't. You're gonna make me smear my make up." She said as she dabbed gently at her eyes.

"Alaska sure is one lucky man."

"We're both lucky." She responded gleefully.

She smiled sweetly as she slowly made her way down the aisle, gently shuffling the white petals in her wake. Bouquet in one hand and the other looped in her father's arm. She tried to ignore the stares from friends and family in their seats, instead she gazed ahead at Nathan. He stood poised, straight and stern, with hands clasped in front; exactly as an officer should. But instead of his mouth in a firm hard line, he grinned that I'm-too-cute-for-my-own-good smile at her. He wore a tan vest over his ivory button up, rolled up at the sleeves, with a lavender tie to match her color scheme. She could feel his love for her, radiating off of him in waves. The way he stared at her with misty, grey eyes sent shivers down her spine. She knew she would never feel this way about anyone else. The butterflies in her stomach would now and forever, only dance for him.

To his left, Tommy stood in matching attire with his hands clasped in front of him. If Tess wasn't mistaken, she swore she could see his eyes getting misty too. She bent her head down with a small laugh; Tommy sure did love them both with everything he had. She regained focus looking up at Hadley, the closest thing she ever had to a best friend or a sister. Hadley in her lavender, tulle, ruffled dress smiled back at Tess in encouragement. She watched as Hadley discretely wiped a tear from her eye with the back of her hand while her other hand gripped a small bouquet.

Tess was startled when her father suddenly stopped. She was so lost in her thoughts, she hadn't realized they were standing under the archway now. Her father turned to Nathan while holding his hand out, with his other hand he clapped Nathan's shoulder and whispered in his ear, "You take care of my baby girl."

Nathan shook Henry's hand firmly and nodded a silent 'yes sir'. Then Henry turned back to hug Tess and gently kissed her cheek before walking away. "Your mama's watching you right now Tess, and she couldn't be prouder."

"Thank you." She mouthed silently.

"And now the vows. Nathaniel?" The justice of the peace looked to Nathan.

Nathan held Tess's hand in his, facing her as he spoke, "Tess, I promise to love and cherish you, every moment, of every day. I promise to make you laugh when you are sad. I promise not to ever scare you again with a phone call from the hospital. I promise to make you waffles every Sunday." At that, she turned towards their guests and gave a thumbs up. They all laughed in unison. "I promise to keep my singing to a minimum in the shower, and I promise to always find you and save you. And—I promise that for the rest of my life I will help you remember our love and what we shared here today."

Tess smiled back at him with water welling in her eyes. Before she could start, she dabbed away a loose tear and cleared her throat. "Nathan, I promise to love you with no regrets. I promise to always tell you the truth, even when it hurts." The crowd laughed once more. "I promise to make you feel young every day. I promise to dance along with you every time you play *Do You Love Me?*. And, I promise not to be mad at you for everything, when I'm really only mad at you for one thing. And, most of all, I promise to love you without question, each and every day, for the rest of my life— and then some."

"Do you have the rings?" The justice of the peace asked Tommy who was completely enthralled while listening to Nathan and Tess exchange vows.

"What?" He asked in a dazed voice. The guests howled in laughter.

"Oh right, the rings." Tommy said flushing brightly, somewhat embarrassed as he patted his chest looking for the rings. "Here," he said as he handed them their rings.

Nathan and Tess both shook their heads at Tommy; he wouldn't be Tommy if he didn't act this way.

"Do you, Nathaniel, take Tess, to be your lawfully wedded wife?"

"I do." He vowed as he gently pushed the ring on her finger.

"And do you, Tess, take Nathaniel, to be your lawfully wedded husband?"

"I do." She promised as she placed the ring on his finger.

"I now pronounce you, husband and wife. You may now kiss the bride."

Nathan took Tess's face in his hands and kissed her deeply. The crowd roared in applause for the newlyweds.

••◆◆••

Tess stood up from their table with a glass of champagne in hand. "To my husband Nathan, may you never steal, lie, or cheat—but if you must steal, then steal away my sorrows. If you must lie, then lie with me all of my nights. And if you must cheat, then cheat death so that we may be together always. Cheers." She raised her glass and everyone ushered cheers in unison.

Once she sat back down next to him, Nathan leaned over and gently pressed his lips to her forehead before whispering, "Brontë? Shakespeare? Dickinson?"

She turned in her seat to face him. "An old Irish proverb, actually."

Nathan shook his head and laughed. "I'm never going to catch up to you, am I?"

She smiled at him and lightly traced her fingertips along his cheek, "No, you probably won't."

He chuckled at her sincerity and brevity. He let his hand trail down her bare back, sending tingles straight through his body and down to his toes. He momentarily let his mind drift to the warmth of her skin and how it elicited arousing thoughts. He could tell by the way her breasts hung in her gown and how the satin clung to her hips that she was bare underneath. The thought excited him, but also drew on his deep-rooted desire to keep her hidden and saved for only himself. He groaned inwardly knowing he really needed to get her alone. He shook the dangerous thoughts from his mind as he reached over to grab her hand tightly. He leaned in closely and whispered in her ear, "'til kingdom come?"

She shuddered subtly under the warmth of his breath and promised, "'til kingdom come."

"Thank you for coming." They said to everyone as they slowly made their way out of the back yard.

"Tess!" Hadley practically screamed as she ran towards her.

"Hadley, thank you so much for being my maid of honor, and thank you for everything else." Tess said as she hugged Hadley.

"Of course Tess, and I expect you to return the favor one day." She leaned back and pointed in gleeful assertiveness.

"I would be honored to." Tess smiled and nodded.

Hadley turned her attention to Nathan as she raised herself up on her toes to whisper in his ear, "I knew you wouldn't let me down."

He smiled back at her as she walked away.

Tess looked at him quizzically. "What was that about?"

"Oh, nothing."

Tess turned her lips down in a pout. "I thought married couples didn't keep secrets?"

Nathan hesitated. "Uh—hey Mr. Dawson!" He was relieved for the interruption. He had to stifle his laughter because of the look on Tess's face.

"Hi Daddy." She hugged her father once more brushing off her pout.

He held her hands as he spoke, "You know, I think the man in the moon did a fine job of solving your problems."

"You're right, I think he did." She smiled up at Nathan who looked down at her amusingly.

Her father turned towards Nathan. "You're a good man, Nathaniel. I expect you to keep it up, and take care of her."

"I will, sir." Nathan held out his hand to shake his father-in-law's hand.

"Tess, will you promise to keep in touch?"

"I will Daddy."

"Thank you, sweetheart." He kissed her cheek once before he left.

"So, what was that about?" Nathan waited for him to be out of earshot before he asked.

"Wouldn't you like to know?" She said in a playfully sultry voice.

"Actually, I would—" He grumbled as his eyes darkened and he took a seductive step forward.

Her breath faltered; the way that man looked at her would be her undoing. She took a step back and craned her neck to see Jack walking towards them, trying to break from Nathan's intense gaze. She knew if he continued to look at her that way, it wouldn't matter that guests were around them, they would do unspeakable things right there for the world to see.

"Jack. Hi!" She called to him.

Nathan huffed at her for getting away with not answering. She just laughed and a grin spread across her face as she arched a brow thinking that two could play at that game.

"Hi darlin'. Son." He greeted them before continuing, "It was a beautiful ceremony."

"Thank you, Jack."

"When you two are back from your honeymoon, I'd like you to have dinner at my place sometime." He offered.

"You're going to cook?" Nathan asked dubiously.

"Yes, I will cook." He retorted.

"That's a wonderful offer. We will call you as soon as we're back."

Nathan shook his head still trying to understand. "You never cooked for me before. We lived off frozen dinners."

"Well, you didn't have a wife before. Plus, maybe I just like her more than you." Jack laughed and joked with Nathan.

Tess couldn't contain her laughter either. Nathan just rolled his eyes and sighed lavishly.

"Well, if you two are quite finished." Nathan scolded them, "Thanks for coming Pops."

"Wouldn't have missed it for the world." He hugged Nathan as he spoke, and then hugged and kissed Tess's cheek before leaving.

As Jack walked off they noticed Tommy sneaking out with the rest of the guests.

"Hey Tommy! Aren't you gonna say bye?" Nathan hollered to his back.

"I'll see you two off tomorrow. I wouldn't let you leave without saying goodbye first!" He yelled back.

Tess and Nathan both just shook their heads; Tommy did have his own way of doing things.

"Wanna go inside, Mrs. Suppan?" Nathan winked.

She smiled devilishly. "Race you there." She scooped her dress up in her arms and took off towards the house.

Nathan smiled to himself and laughed as he rocked back on his heels before taking off after her. She had only gotten to the top of the deck stairs by the time he reached her. He scooped her up in his arms, making her scream and giggle.

"I couldn't let you in there without fulfilling the husband's duty of carrying his wife over the threshold."

She laughed. "I thought we were unconventional?"

"We are—but some things are sacred." He kissed her before she could interject.

He carried her into their room, and her eyes widened ardently. Their room had been completely transformed. Hundreds of candles filled the wooden floor, flickering and bringing the room to life. Lining the shelves and nightstands were tall white candles, and their bed was covered in deep, red, rose petals.

"It's beautiful." She gasped.

"I thought you might like it."

He gently set her on the bed, quickly undid his tie, and shimmied out of his vest. She stood from the bed and turned her back to him. He gently clasped her zipper in between his fingers and with tantalizingly, slow movements, he dragged it down her back. She let the smooth satin ripple down her body and pool at her feet. She turned around to help him with his shirt. He felt his cock twitch at the sight of her bare body. She was sexy in a completely unprompted way and he knew he would never not want to look. One by one she undid his buttons with deft, nimble fingers and pulled his shirt from his shoulders.

He tilted her chin up to his face and leaned forward pressing his lips softly to hers. As they kissed he lifted her up, letting her wrap her arms around his neck and her legs around his waist. He gently leaned her back laying her on the bed of petals.

Nathan gently grabbed her wrist, pulling it above her head and pressing it into the bed. He kissed her deeply, letting his tongue invade her mouth as she kissed him back feverishly. He moved from her lips and placed kisses along her jawline. He smiled against her skin when he felt her back arch slightly under his touch.

He continued kissing and sucking down her neck, letting his tongue trace lines down her skin. Her soft moans made his dick throb uncontrollably. He kissed her neck harder and trailed his lips down to her breasts. Letting go of her wrist, he used both hands to massage and tease at her breasts while he sucked and nipped gently at her nipples. Her back arched against his onslaught and she let a long, low moan escape.

Hearing her made Nathan ache. "You. Are. Mine." He growled against her skin.

She ran her fingers through his hair as he continued to kiss down her stomach. She smiled as she rolled her hips against him causing a wanted friction. "Yours."

Nathan paused briefly at her response, looking into her eyes before continuing to place kisses down her front. He would show her how much he worships her body, how her body was made just for him.

She groaned softly as he slid further down the bed between her legs. He could feel her quiver under his touch as his finger slid gently between her wet, slick folds. Feeling how wet she was for him made him growl deep in his chest as he placed small kisses on her inner thighs, getting closer to her core.

She tugged on his hair causing a welcome ache as he smiled devilishly up at her. She closed her eyes and leaned her head back beckoning the ecstasy. He kissed the top of her slit before letting his tongue dip in and out of her folds, pressing in against her. She bucked at the sensation of his tongue penetrating her, his finger working in unison as he sank it deep into her. As he continued to suck and twirl her clit with his tongue, his finger thrust in and out of her, curling up and hitting her g-spot.

She couldn't help but grind her hips against his face, feeling herself nearing her orgasm. He could feel her body begin to tremble and tighten around his finger which made him only suck harder on the bundle of nerves of her clit.

"Don't stop baby." She forced out in breathy moans.

He thrust a second finger, pumping in and out of her faster as his tongue danced circles in her folds. He watched her body climb and fall under his touch and smiled wickedly as he continued to suck her juices dry as her orgasm withered out.

She grabbed his face pulling him up towards her. He smiled as he willingly obliged and kissed her deeply. She groaned into his mouth and he pulled back slightly.

"You taste mighty fine, Mrs. Suppan."

Tess smiled delicately as she let her fingers trace down his chest. She pressed her palm against his chest, asking him to roll onto his back. He rolled over, placing both hands behind his head as his eyes darkened and he smiled salaciously at her.

She shimmied down the bed, undoing his pants and pulling them down as she went. She smiled, taking a moment to savor her husband and the way he looked at her, like she was a drug he couldn't get enough of.

She moved in between his legs and gently grabbed the base of his shaft as she leaned forward and closed her lips around him. He closed his eyes and groaned deeply as Tess continued to suck and pump his dick, making him twitch under the pressure.

Tess took him deep into her mouth letting him hit her at the back of the throat. She loved the way she could torment him. He moaned again, goading her to lick the tip of his dick, swirling it around tasting the pre-cum. She trailed her tongue along his shaft and smiled when she felt him shudder.

"You are going to un-man me, woman." He growled seductively.

She giggled lightly. "We wouldn't want that." She rose from her position and crawled on top of him, hovering just above. He let his hands trail down her sides and settle on her hips. Grabbing them tightly, he thrust her down onto him.

She cried out as she closed her eyes, letting her head fall back at the fullness. He gripped her hips even tighter, directing them to rise and fall, pumping her on top of him. She moaned again as she reached forward placing her hands on his chest as she continued to ride him.

Nathan grunted as he reached up and palmed her breasts in his hands. He tugged softly at her nipples, watching her body buck back. She cried out again as she took him all the way in, letting her hips settle against his skin. He groaned as her hips began gyrating against him, and he could feel his eyes rolling in the back of his head. He knew he wouldn't last much longer if she continued to ride him this way.

He grabbed her back pulling her in close to him as he rolled them over while still inside of her. He laid there momentarily and stared deep into her forest, green eyes. He gently brushed a loose strand of hair away from her face and gave her a small grin. He knew then that sometimes love wasn't about fixing the broken parts of each other—it was about standing together despite them.

She was his, in every sense of the way. He had tied himself to her and would continue to do so any way he could. He could see their future falling out before him. She was his to love and protect—she was his soul. He would cherish and worship at her feet, and one day he would give her a baby. He would give her the world, as she had so willingly given him.

She grabbed his hand that had stilled by her face and turned it so she could plant a gentle kiss in the palm of his hand. She watched as his eyes darkened once more, and he trailed his hand down to her neck. He wrapped his hand around her throat as he leaned forward and kissed her. He let his tongue trace her bottom lip before her tongue invaded his mouth greedily.

His hand hardened gently on her throat as he began thrusting. He could feel her body begin to tremble under him, his thumb reached up and trailed along her bottom lip. He smiled as her eyes closed and her head tilted slightly back.

"Come for me baby." He demanded quietly.

He rammed into her harder, filling her all the way, letting her hips roll against his pelvis with every thrust.

"Nathan!" She screamed as her walls clenched around him and her body shook violently through the ripples of her orgasm.

He thrust into her again and again, and on the third pump, he stilled, letting his seed fill her. His mind blanked while his nerves snapped and reconnected themselves. He settled his face into the crook of her neck, planting a chaste kiss on her skin.

"I love you, husband." Her small voice sang up to him.

"I love you too—wife." He smirked, "Wife, hmmm. I do love the way that sounds."

She giggled at him making his now flaccid dick tickle her deep inside. She squirmed slightly as she scrunched her nose up at him. He smirked again as he leaned forward to kiss her as he gently pulled out of her.

He pulled her over to his chest, settling her down under his arm. With his other hand he tipped her chin to look up at him and gently caressed her red, swollen lips.

"Excuse my language Mrs. Suppan, but your lips look positively bruised and fuckable."

She immediately blushed at his remark before dipping her head back into his chest hiding her face. He could feel her face heat as she shook her head against his chest as she chided him, "Such a dirty man."

He smiled quite pleased with himself. "Only for you."

•••••

"Hi, pretty girl." Nathan cooed to her as he brushed the hair from her face.

She slowly opened her eyes. "Good morning, husband."

He smiled. "I really do like the sound of that." He said as he ran his nose along hers.

She leaned in giving him a small peck on the lips.

"I know it's early, but are you ready to go?" He asked her.

"I just need to get ready and pack a few last-minute things."

"I'll go put some of the bags in the car." He kissed her before getting out of bed.

She reached up and pulled him back onto the bed and kissed him once more. He groaned loudly as he deepened the kiss.

"Maybe we don't need to go. We could just stay here." He whispered against her lips.

She laughed and gently pushed his shoulder.

"Come on, get movin'." She playfully smacked his behind.

"Fine." He pouted.

"Tommy, you made it." Tess said as she stood up in the cockpit of the old sloop.

"I promised, didn't I?"

Nathan walked along the sloop's rim and jumped off in front of Tommy.

"Thanks for coming." He patted Tommy's back and hugged him.

"Come on, no mushy stuff. I'm here to send you on your way." Tommy huffed as he waved his arms, signaling Nathan to get back in the sailboat.

Nathan laughed as he climbed aboard. "Think you can handle the streets without me for a while?"

Tommy laughed as he untied the ropes. "I think I can hang in there."

"By the way Tommy, I heard from a very reliable source, you were quite the dance partner last night."

He stood straight up and stared with big eyes at Tess.

Tess chuckled playfully. "Don't worry, she said you were—charming."

Tommy cleared his throat and straightened his jacket. "Well, of course I was."

Nathan just rolled his eyes at his friend.

"Bye Tommy!" Tess called out to him as she blew a kiss in his direction.

"Bye Tess. I'll see you when you two get back."

"Bye Tommy." Nathan said as he took his place behind the wheel.

Tess smiled as she let the sun warm her face and the breeze flow through her hair. Nathan couldn't be happier in that moment. He was out there on the water, and suddenly the sea wasn't so immense and that was somehow okay. With Tess by his side, he could take on anything. He knew this was the woman he would love for the rest of his life—even longer than that if he could. He loved her beyond reason, beyond measure; but more importantly—she loved him just as much.

He twirled the wheel as they made their heading toward Oregon. They decided they would sail down the coastline to Oregon and back up. He was happy he was able to share this passion with Tess. Most women he knew would never agree to a honeymoon like this. But then again, Tess wasn't like most women. She would go where she wanted, when she wanted. She would say exactly what was on her mind, and she would love so deeply and unconditionally it hurt.

Chapter Fifteen

6 Years Later

"Mommy!" Parker screamed as he ran towards Tess.

She bent down to his level and held her arms out wide, catching him as he ran top speed towards her. She hugged him and kissed the top of his tousled, light, brown hair that mirrored Nathan's. "Hi Bub, how was your trip with Daddy?"

"We had so much fun! We went hiking, and swimming, and fishing, and made s'mores, and told ghost stories, and I learned how to make a fire!" Parker rattled off in sheer excitement.

"Really, you did all that? It sounds like you had a blast." She reflected her four-year-old son's excitement.

She stood up to face Nathan. "Ghost stories?" She hissed under her breath.

Nathan shrugged his shoulders to say sorry. She chortled as she rolled her eyes at him.

"Come on Parker, let's get you in the bath. Then, it's bedtime."

"Aw, but—"

"No butts Parker; now get your little patootie up those stairs." She playfully smacked his butt as he took off towards the stairs.

"Good trip?" She asked Nathan as he unpacked the cooler.

"Good trip." He leaned down to kiss her.

"Bedtime story or lullaby? Dealer's choice." Tess spoke softly as she laid down on the small bed next to Parker.

Parker squirmed underneath the covers trying to get comfortable until he laid his head on Tess's chest.

"Story." He yawned quietly.

Tess smoothed his hair and gently kissed the top of his forehead. "Once upon a time, there was a little boy, who traveled to a faraway place where villages floated on water, castles were houses, dragons lurked, and giants stood tall. This place was a place where anything you could imagine was real. The little boy imagined a queen and her court who showed him all the adventures he could dream of—"

Her voice faded out once she realized Parker was long asleep. She kissed him once more as she gently laid his head on his pillow before she quietly snuck out of his room. As she turned to leave his room she looked back down at him and whispered, "Sweet dreams, my baby boy. May you dream of Neverland."

Nathan slid his arms around Tess pulling her in close to him on the bed.

She smiled to herself. "I missed you this weekend."

He kissed between her shoulder and neck and whispered in her ear, "How much?"

His warm breath sent desire unfurling through her body.

She rolled over on top of him; smiling as she looked at him with her reddish-brown curls cascading down around her face. She began gently kissing his neck. She started on the right side and then kissed the left side, slowly kissing his throat. Nathan's body shuddered under her touch. He let out a low moan as he gently rubbed her sides feeling her lightweight nightshirt glide against her skin. He could feel heat from her core coming through her pajama shorts as her pelvis rubbed against his lower abdomen. Her balmy breath snarled against his skin, and her soft lips gently caressed him.

"I missed you that much."

"Good." He pulled her face in towards him and kissed her passionately. Their lips locked and moved in sync together, their warmth invading their lungs. Nathan pulled away, leaving Tess to catch her breath. He took the moment in her respite to roll her over. He used his knees to part her legs as he settled in between them.

He smiled salaciously as he brushed the hair from her face. He kissed her collarbone gently and let his left hand trail up and down the side of her body. His hand ran lightly against her skin causing goose bumps in its wake. He could feel her tremble under his touch. As he started to lift her shirt, they heard the faint sound of the doorknob turning.

Nathan grunted in frustration as he rolled off of her. Tess laughed pulling her nightshirt back into place and straightening her shorts that had become bunched at her apex. "Come in sweetie." She called out as she playfully nudged Nathan.

Parker peeked around the door and slowly walked in.

"What's wrong, baby?" Tess asked as she sat up in bed.

"I had a bad dream." Parker said in a soft voice as he wiped his eyes.

"Come on Bub, climb up." She patted the bed next to her.

Parker climbed up and crawled into his mother's lap. She held him in her arms and gently rocked him back and forth.

"Can you tell me what your dream was about?" She cooed softly.

"The ghost of Crescent Bay was after me."

Tess immediately shot Nathan a look. "Sorry." He whispered as he looked away like a dog caught doing something he wasn't supposed to.

She shook her head at him as she playfully rolled her eyes. "It's okay buddy. The ghost won't get you here."

Nathan turned back to watch Tess rock him in her arms as she began to sing to Parker his favorite lullaby, "Once Upon A December".

Nathan couldn't help but smile in awe. He adored watching her with their son, and her voice was something otherworldly. He laughed intrinsically knowing that her lullaby could ease anyone into the most peaceful of sleeps.

Once he had drifted off to sleep, Nathan helped her lay him on the bed in between them. Tess supported herself up on one elbow while her other hand gently rubbed Parker's belly as he slept. Nathan propped himself up so he could look at Tess.

"Sorry about the ghost stories. We were just having fun."

"I know you were." She said sincerely.

"How do you do that so well?" He asked her.

She looked up. "Do what?"

"Calm him down like that. It's so easy for you." Four years with Parker in their life and he was still in awe of how Tess so naturally assumed her role as Mom.

"He's easy to handle." She said smiling down at him.

"Yeah, he's a good kid."

"Nathan—" Tess began.

"Yeah, Tess?" He looked up at her waiting for her to speak.

"I uh—I'm, well—I'm pregnant Nathan." She stumbled getting the words out. She slowly peeked up at him looking for his reaction.

A calm washed through her when she looked up to see a smile spreading from ear to ear across his face. He gently leaned over Parker and kissed her deeply.

"Why didn't you tell me sooner?" He huffed out, slightly out of breath.

"You just got back and—" She trailed off when she was interrupted by his lips crashing into hers once more.

⸻ •◦●◦• ⸻

"Do we have any plans this weekend?" Nathan asked Tess from his seat at the table, watching her make Parker's lunch.

She looked over at him. "Not that I can think of. Why?"

"Good," he replied as he stood up.

"Good, why?" She eyed him warily as he walked towards her, gently wrapping his arms around her from behind. She smiled as she felt his hot breath on her neck. He tenderly kissed the nape of her neck before speaking.

"Because my dad is going to watch Parker for the weekend, and you and I are going to have some alone time."

"Really?" She turned towards him.

"All. Weekend. Long." He kissed her neck in between each word.

She wrapped her arms around his neck. "That sounds nice, but to what do I owe the pleasure?"

"I'll show you pleasure." He whispered nearly inaudibly as he gazed down at her breasts that were tightly pressed against him. He coughed, gently breaking him from his train of thought. "Because soon we will be caught up in getting ready for the baby, and then the baby will come, and we will have two kids we'll have to pawn off on my Dad." He joked, "so before that happens, I could really use some mommy-daddy time." He waved a finger back and forth between them and winked.

"I suppose you have a point." She whispered as she titled her head giving him access to her throat. He trailed kisses down her neck and across her jaw line. She shuddered again at his touch.

"Mhmmm." He murmured matter-of-factly as he continued to kiss her.

"Alright Bub, you got everything?" She asked Parker as he put his small backpack on, full of toys and blankets.

"Yup, I think so."

"Good. You and Grandpa Jack are going to have so much fun together." She took a moment to study his round, green eyes and kissed his nose before ruffling his hair and leading him out to Jack who was waiting by his car.

"Parker!" He called to his grandson.

"Grandpa Jack!" Parker yelled as he took off to hug him.

"Thanks again Pops. We'll pick him up Sunday." Nathan said.

His father eyed them once. "No problem, you kids err—have fun."

Tess blushed slightly. Nathan just put his arm around her shoulder and laughed smugly.

They waited until his car was out of sight before Nathan turned and immediately started kissing Tess.

He paused a moment. "Come on." He said with a scandalous grin as he took off into their house leading her by the hand.

"How's the book?" He asked as he stood up from tending to the fire.

Tess looked up from *Romeo and Juliet* and smiled at him. "It's good."

Nathan sat down beside her on the couch, lifting her legs on top of his. "I don't think I ever read it. Actually, I'm pretty sure I glanced at the first page, got so confused, that I closed the book and never opened it again." He laughed at the memory.

"You're missing out. It's a beautiful story." Tess said pointedly.

"Read something to me. Maybe this time I'll like it." He gently rubbed her legs as she looked down at the book.

"But soft, what light through yonder window breaks? It is the east, and Juliet is the sun. Arise, fair sun, and kill the envious moon, Who is already sick and pale with grief That thou, her maid, art far more fair than she…The brightness of her cheek would shame those stars As daylight doth a lamp; her eye in heaven Would through the airy region stream so bright That birds would sing and think it were not night." Tess smiled softly to herself as she put down the book.

"It's pretty."

Tess laughed softly; she knew Nathan hadn't understood what she read.

"Romeo is so amazed by Juliet's beauty, that even though it is late at night, he says Juliet is the sun, turning the night into day. It's very romantic."

He grinned knowing her uncanny ability to voice his unspoken questions was in full operation.

"Too bad I didn't have you as a tutor in high school. I probably would have been more willing to read this stuff." He motioned towards her book.

She laughed. "Well maybe one day you'll give it another shot."

"Maybe." He said as she leaned forward and placed her head on his chest.

They sat in comfortable silence for what seemed like hours, until Nathan noticed that she was listening intently to something.

"What are you listening for?" He whispered.

"I'm listening to the rain. Can't you hear it?"

He titled his head and listened quietly; she was right, it was raining. Actually, it sounded more like it was pouring. How had he not heard that?

Tess smiled in delight. "I love listening to the rain. I love everything about the rain."

Nathan started to get up. "Come on. Let's go for a walk."

"But it's cold and pouring." Tess exclaimed as she sat up on the couch alarmed by his request.

"Kind of the point." He mocked playfully and grinned as he reached his hand out towards her.

"Nathan, this is crazy!" She yelled over the sound of the pouring rain as they raced into the back yard.

He turned around and pulled her close. He started rocking her back and forth and spun her around. She laughed and lifted her face towards the sky. With her arms spread out wide, she embraced the rain. Nathan couldn't help but smile. Every day she amazed him. Every day he was falling deeper and deeper in love with her, even after all this time.

Once Tess noticed how he was staring at her, she looked him in the eye and, without hesitation, she stepped forward crashing her lips into his. He welcomed her kiss. He pulled her tighter to his chest and, with his hand, he held her face close to his forcing her to continue to kiss him.

The rain beat down on them. In uneven lurches and lulls, waves of water would blanket them. They thought the storm would never let up. He continued to kiss her, letting his tongue entangle hers. His hands pawed against her waist. She could feel heat seeping out from them onto her skin. She broke away and led him back into the house.

She led him silently to the fireplace where a blanket had been placed on the ground in front of the smoldering logs. She beckoned him to her as she slowly laid back on the blanket. He followed her lead and slowly sank back with her. He kissed down along her neck and down her sternum. He felt her chest rise up as he made his way down her torso. She tugged at his wet, black t-shirt that clung to him in all the right places, signaling for him to take it off. She smiled as she examined his bare chest. He was strong, but more than that, he looked damn good without a shirt. He took her momentary pause to appreciate how her light-weight, white tee was now see through. Her wet t-shirt clung tightly to her breasts, and he smiled wickedly. He lifted her shirt and slowly kissed along her stomach, allowing his tongue to lightly trace the lines she wore with honor from bearing their son. She closed her eyes and gently bit her bottom lip trying to keep from screaming out in ecstasy. Her gratification was intoxicating. Nathan felt his temperature rising and his ache for her was becoming unbearable. He helped her out of her shirt and smiled down at her with lascivious intent.

He thought by now he knew her body, and yet he could never get used to seeing her. He loved the way her body adjusted to motherhood, how her nipples were darker and swollen, and the smallest of bumps protruded from her belly. Just the mere sight of her was arousing, but to touch her—that had a libidinous effect that he found ravenous. He let his hands travel across her, caressing every inch of her. His touch had become so insatiable; she grabbed at his pants and undid the button and zipper. She helped ease his pants off as he pulled at the waistband of her leggings. He leaned back as he slowly pulled her form fitting leggings down and off.

He bent his neck down and kissed her as he let his body rock gently against hers. She gasped slightly as he pressed into her. She curled her arms up around his and pulled him in tight to her. He helped her roll them over so she was on top of him. She stared down at him for a moment as she pulled her hair to one side. He looked intently up into her eyes and brushed a loose strand of hair away from her face. She continued to pitch her body against his, swaying forward and back. As the pleasure increased, she threw her head back and sat up on him. He stared at her with beguiled, lust filled eyes as she continued to move, and he let his hands travel down her sides to her waist. He left his hands there feeling how her waist moved along his body. He groaned low in his throat as he watched her fall apart at the seams.

They spent the night in front of the fireplace, letting the rain beat down and the sounds of the crackling fire fill the room.

Tess smiled as she looked upon Nathan's face. There was something so comforting in the subtle grin that always lined his lips and the way his hair would stick straight up or get plastered to his face. She laughed silently at his messy hair. She placed her head against his chest. She loved to listen to his erratic heartbeat, one that would slow down or speed up for no reason at all. And she loved to watch the muscles in his arms tighten and tense as he dreamed. There in his arms—that was home.

Chapter Sixteen

Tess sat in the rocking chair, cradling her baby girl as she sang the same lullaby she always sings for Parker. She hesitated momentarily with a smile when she looked up at the door. She saw Parker's little, green eyes peering around the door watching her. She nodded for him to come in. He quietly took a seat on the ground next to the rocker and stared up at her as she sang them the lullaby. When the lullaby was finished, she looked down at Parker. "Do you want to hold your little sister?" She whispered.

"Okay." He whispered back enthusiastically.

She stood up and motioned for Parker to take a seat in the rocker. Once he was settled in, she gently tucked the baby in his arms. He looked so proud to be holding her, as he grinned from ear to ear.

"Mommy look, Henley's smiling." He exclaimed.

She grinned down. "Would you look at that. I'd say she likes you."

"There, how's that?" Tess asked as she finished tucking the blankets around Parker's body.

"Good." He giggled.

She tickled his stomach lightly. "Are you my hug-a-bug bear?"

"No!" He giggled. "I'm a snug-a-bug bear!"

She laughed with him. "Yes, you are." She tapped his nose with her finger. His nose crinkled up in response.

"Hey Mommy?"

"Yeah, Bub?"

"Are you gonna sing the lullaby to me every night still?"

"Of course, why wouldn't I?"

He lowered his eyes. "Because of the baby."

She sighed warmly. "Want to know something?"

He nodded his head yes.

She leaned in close to his face. "You will *always,* be my baby."

He laughed in delight. She kissed his head before getting up to leave. As she turned the light off, she faced him. "Goodnight snug-a-bug bear."

"Goodnight hug-a-bug bear." He whispered through the darkness.

"How about a picnic?"

"A what?"

"A picnic. You know, where we go to the park, pack a wicker basket, and eat on a blanket."

"I know what one is, but why do you bring it up?" Nathan eyed her as he poured his coffee.

"Well summer is short, and it's a beautiful day, and you've been working a lot lately. It might be nice for us to go on a picnic together. Besides, Parker would love the park, and Henley likes the outdoors."

"A picnic it is then." He said as he kissed the top of her head before sitting down.

"Parker, don't go too far." She yelled as he took off into the grassy area. He was running top speed with one of his toy airplanes in hand. Even from a distance she could hear his sound effects for the plane. She couldn't help but smile.

Tess leaned back as she watched her family. Parker was running in circles, tearing the plane through the air, completely content. The smile on his face was contagious. He looked like the happiest kid on the planet. He was so joyful and so free, something she hadn't felt for herself until she met Nathan. She turned her attention to Nathan who was lightly bouncing Henley up and down in his arms. Their baby girl giggled in delight and so did Nathan. He was a wonderful father; he enjoyed them just as much as they enjoyed him. She absolutely adored him for that.

She thought to herself, in this moment—here in the sunshine, with Parker running around, Henley smiling, and Nathan adoring his children—life couldn't be any better. Her kids were healthy and happy, and she loved Nathan more than life itself. What more could she possibly ever want?

Her attention snapped back into focus when Parker came running at her like a freight train. He giggled gleefully when he crash-landed into his mother's lap. She laughed with him as she took the opportunity to hold him there and tickle him. He wiggled and screamed under her touch. Nathan watched and laughed in adoration.

Tess stood up abruptly from the blanket and took off running from Parker. Parker chased her around in circles along the grassy hill. When he finally tagged Tess, she spread her arms out wide, beckoning Parker to do the same. Together they ran around the picnic blanket with their arms out wide, soaring through the air.

After a while, once Tess was finally tired, she fell down on the blanket next to Nathan. She perched her head against his thigh and stared over at Henley who was sitting on his other knee just looking around. Tess smiled and rubbed Nathan's leg with her hand and turned her attention back to Parker. Parker had just released a red kite and was letting it rise high above them.

He turned to his parents with a grin so wide, you could see a few teeth were missing. Nathan held a thumb up to his son and watched as Parker lifted his face to the sky, eyeing the red kite climb up above and soar among the clouds.

This was it. This is what it means to find happiness. Maybe she didn't know a lot about a lot of things, and maybe she wasn't wise enough to know any better, but right there in that moment she knew—the key to happiness is getting the thing you want most and never letting go.

Chapter Seventeen

3 Years Later

These violent delights have violent ends,
And in their triumph die,
Like fire and powder.
Which as they kiss,
Consume.
Romeo and Juliet Act II, Scene VI

"Date night?" Hadley asked as she picked Henley up in her arms.

"Yeah, thank you again so much for babysitting and on such short notice."

"My pleasure, I love these munchkins." Hadley smiled as she spun Henley around in her arms making the little girl giggle. "What are you doing anyway?" She asked as she set Henley back down.

"Nathan was able to get last minute tickets to see Romeo and Juliet for our anniversary. It's my favorite play." She smiled as she clasped on her teal sapphire, dangle earrings.

She stepped back from the mirror and twirled around to show Hadley her outfit. She was wearing a wispy, medium length, peach color, tulle dress. It flowed in the wind she created and hung low off her left shoulder.

"Wow Tess, you look amazing. No wonder Nathan still has to have date nights with you."

Parker turned his attention to Tess. "You look pretty."

Tess blushed slightly as she thanked both of them. "We should be back by eleven, if that's okay?"

"Of course, you two go have some fun." Hadley said as Nathan walked in.

"Wow baby, you look amazing." He kissed Tess quickly trying not to linger on her body for too long in front of someone else before turning his attention to Hadley. "Thanks again, we really appreciate it."

He kissed her cheek in gratitude and kissed Henley's little nose, which made her giggle. "Bye pumpkin, bye squirt." He looked down at Parker who was content building his toy model car on the ground.

"Bye Dad." He quickly focused back in on his toys.

"Buh bye Daddy." Henley said as she focused on getting Parker's attention.

Tess laughed softly. "Parker, you behave, and help Auntie Hadley with your sister. It's your job to take care of her when we're not around."

He looked up at his mother in earnest. "I will."

She smiled down at him. "Good boy. Love you, Bub."

"Love you too."

Tess crouched down in front of Henley giving her an Eskimo kiss as Henley giggled wildly in response.

As Nathan led Tess towards the front door she quickly turned around and blew a kiss to Parker and Henley before they slipped out.

———————•••••———————

"That was so romantically beautiful." She exclaimed as she walked out of the theatre.

Nathan shook his head and arched an inquisitive brow. "You cried almost the whole time?"

Tess laughed. "I cried at the beauty of it. I mean, yes, of course it's sad, but their love is so strong."

He wrapped his arm around her and kissed her hair. "I guess I can see what you mean."

"Did you not like it?"

He just smiled. "If you like it, then I like it."

There it was again, that blind faith he always had in her. To this day it still surprised her.

She laughed with him as they climbed in the truck. Once Nathan got in, he looked over at his wife.

She was fixing her make up in the small mirror. Even with black streaks of mascara running down her cheeks, she still looked beautiful. After nearly 10 years of marriage, he would find himself still staring at her—completely entranced by her. She knew exactly how to captivate his attention. Maybe it was her undying gorgeousness, the way that even after she left a room, he could still see her because her beauty pulsed out around her. She was more beautiful than anyone had the right to be. Or maybe, it was the way she loved him back so unconditionally and irrevocably even after all they had been through.

She smiled as she caught him watching her. She sighed softly and cocked her head a little to the left. "Let's go home."

—••◆•◆••—

Tess.

Everything suddenly blurred into view. Water was crashing in through the windshield. There was a pounding pain in his head. Warm liquid cascaded down his forehead. Out of instinct, he touched his forehead and winced in pain as his fingertips caressed the large open wound. It only took Nathan a moment to realize where he was. He immediately looked to his right and his body went rigid with unforgiving dread.

The passenger seat was completely submerged under water; he could see her reddish-brown hair lying on the surface of the water.

Panic laced threw him and he rushed to unfasten his seat belt. Thoughts swirled raggedly through his mind, too fast for him to clutch onto any of them except for one: *How long had she been under?*

He struggled with the seatbelt. "Tess, hang on baby!" He cried.

Finally, he was able to break free and reach over to her. He tried to lift her head above water, but with every passing moment the truck was taking on more and more water. He knew he had to move fast as he tugged at her seatbelt, struggling to get it free. He cried in frustration as he used all of his strength to loosen the seatbelt. It wouldn't budge; he took a large breath of air before submerging himself under water to look at the seatbelt. He yanked and pulled, but it was no use, it was locked in place.

He came up and gasped for air as he looked around the truck for anything he could use. He found Tess's purse floating in the back seat, and he quickly searched through it to find her house keys. With the keys in hand, he submerged again using one to tear through the seatbelt. He was able to then rip the material apart, freeing Tess from the constraints that were holding her under.

He kicked the windshield out, and with as much momentum as he could, he quickly pulled Tess's body out through the windshield.

Nathan swam with Tess under his arm to the riverbank. He carried Tess out of the water, her arms dangling out beside her—limp. He tried not to look at how pale her body was; she was under for too long. Instead he focused his attention dead ahead on getting her up to the bridge away from the water.

He silently thought a prayer or command he wasn't quite sure. *Don't do this to me Tess.*

Once he got her up to the bridge he gently laid her body down on the wet pavement and quickly started CPR.

Mentally he counted to himself, *one, two, three, four*. "Breathe. Come on!"

He pumped her chest repeatedly stopping only to fill her lungs with air. "Breathe, Tess!"

He started to scream out in frustration as he continued to pump her chest, but nothing was happening.

He continued with the compressions, but his strength slowly vanished as he looked upon her face. She was ashen, white as a ghost—her lips were blue and her smile was gone. He could see blood steadily streaming down her temple and he began to cry.

"You can't do this to me Tess. You can't leave me."

An ambulance pulled up behind him. He heard the rushed noises of paramedics jumping out of the rig and running to his side. That's what they were trained to do, run to their aid, assess the situation, and do everything they could to make things better. She would be okay now that they were here, right?

Nathan watched silently as a paramedic took over Tess's compressions. "Sir, I'm going to need you to give me some room."

"She's my wife." He stuttered.

"I know sir, but I'm gonna need you to move so I can help her."

"Okay." He stifled his cry as he fell back onto the ground.

Again, he quietly prayed, "Tess, you can't leave me. I can't do this without you. Please baby, just breathe."

<hr />

Hadley raced through the hospital wing. When she turned the corner, she saw him sitting there on the ground with his head in his hands. He was completely drenched. His white dress shirt that was now stained brown and red, clung to his torso, and his soft, brown hair was plastered to the bandage that took up space on his forehead.

"Nathan?" Hadley crumpled down next to him.

He looked up at her, tears welling up. "She's gone Hadley."

Hadley started to sob with Nathan as she wrapped her arms around him. He leaned into her arm and let the sobs come in waves.

It took Nathan minutes before he could stop crying long enough to ask Hadley about the kids.

"Jack has them, he's staying at the house." She tried to reassure him.

Their attention was turned when they heard someone break through the waiting room doors.

Tommy burst through the hospital doors. He skidded to a stop and bent over as he started to cry horrible heart-wrenching sobs when he saw Nathan sitting there with Hadley. It took all of Nathan's strength to stand up to face Tommy.

Tommy righted himself and walked over to Nathan and hugged him tightly. "I'm so, so, sorry Nate."

Tommy and Hadley sat in the waiting room with Nathan for over two hours; patiently waiting for the moment when Nathan would finally speak.

"This has to be a dream." He finally said aloud trying to convince himself.

Hadley fought back tears again and looked at Tommy. He cleared his throat and in a low hushed voice asked, "Nate, what happened?"

Nathan started getting choked up again. "I don't know, it all happened so fast."

They quietly waited for Nathan to continue.

"We were on our way home from the play, and it started to rain—"

His voice drifted off as something floated in his mind. Tess talked about the beauty in the tragedy of the story of Romeo and Juliet; she used the word 'romantic'. The word tasted bitter in his mind; there was *nothing* romantic about death.

"Nathan?" Tommy pressed after a long moment of silence.

Nathan jumped subtly as Tommy broke him out of his reverie. "Tess screamed because there was something in our lane. Something, I don't know what, but I didn't see before it was too late. I tried to swerve out of the way, but the roads were so slick that we went right into the side railing of the bridge, and—and we just drove right over the edge into the water."

Both Tommy and Hadley blanched as they pictured the horrific scene.

"I—I don't know how long she was under there before I woke up." Nathan cried as his chest heaved in and out.

Tommy grabbed Nathan's shoulder and gripped him tight, while Hadley reached over and held his hand desperately hard. Nathan peered up at Tommy as he choked on his words, "You know, I was sitting there at the play watching her study the performers, and all I could think about was how happy she made me. How lucky I am to even know her. I thought about how she changed everything I ever knew about myself. She's the most amazing mother to our children and I loved her with every fiber of my being. I was going to tell her all of this, but I thought I'd wait until tomorrow. You're supposed to get a tomorrow."

Tommy continued to stare at his best friend. What do you say to the man who lost everything?

"Dad's home!" Parker cried as he jumped off the couch next to his grandfather and bounded towards the door.

Nathan opened the door and bent down to hug Parker. It was well past one in the morning and he had been desperately hoping Parker was asleep so he could prolong this moment. "Hey buddy."

Jack looked at Nathan as he fought back tears. He closed the gap between them and hugged Nathan when he stood up. "I'm so sorry, son."

Nathan couldn't find any words to say, he just nodded and looked down at his son who was staring up at him with those big, round, beautiful, green eyes that looked just like Tess's.

"Dad, where's Mom?"

If Nathan's heart hadn't already broken, it would have, right then and there.

"Come on buddy, I need to tell you something." He led Parker over to the couch and had him sit down next to him.

"Dad, why are your clothes so dirty? What's on your forehead?"

Nathan looked down at his dress shirt. It was torn and some of the buttons were missing in sections, and dirt and blood stained it.

"I hadn't even noticed." He said absentmindedly as he gently caressed the bandage on his head.

Jack crossed his arms trying to keep from falling apart in front of his son and grandson. He remembered this moment all too well.

"Parker, do you know what the phrase 'life isn't fair' means?"

Parker took a moment to consider the question. "Yeah, I think so, why?"

Nathan hugged Parker close. "Cause buddy, life isn't fair—there was an accident."

"What kind of accident?" Parker asked looking up at Nathan.

"Your mom and I were in a car accident."

"Is she okay?"

Nathan could feel the tears coming back, burning behind his lids. "No buddy, she isn't."

"Parker, buddy, what is it?" Nathan crept into the dark room to see Parker sitting up in bed screaming and crying.

"I had a bad dream. I want Mommy." He cried into his father's chest. Nathan knew it was bad; he hadn't called Tess 'Mommy' in years.

Nathan's throat constricted. He didn't know what he was supposed to do. Tess was always the one to calm him back to bed, and no matter how hard he wished it, he couldn't give Tess to Parker.

He rocked Parker back and forth on the bed and did the only thing he could think of, he tried to sing the lullaby.

"Nathan, have you slept at all?" Tommy asked as he unpacked grocery bags into Nathan's fridge.

"Parker had another bad dream." He brushed his face, trying to wake up.

"Again?"

"Every night since—every night since the accident." Nathan flinched at the words.

"I can take the kids today so you can get some sleep." Tommy offered.

"No." Nathan snapped.

"It was just an offer." Tommy spoke quietly.

Nathan sighed letting his shoulders shrug. "I know. I didn't mean to snap, I—I just couldn't imagine not having them around. They're the only thing holding me together right now Tommy." Nathan confessed.

Tommy sighed. "I know Nathan, I know. But Nate, you're running on empty. I don't mind hanging out here for the day, but you have to at least try to sleep."

Nathan knew he was right. He hadn't slept well in over a week. With Parker's nightmares, and Henley starting to ask questions—he just couldn't find the time to close his eyes. Truth be told, he didn't know if he wanted to. Not when all he could picture was that night out on the bridge.

"Alright Tommy. I'll try." Nathan said as he bowed his head and slowly walked back towards his room.

Tommy shook his head sadly. He couldn't begin to understand the pain Nathan was in, but Tess was Tommy's family just as much as Nathan is. He missed her too. It broke his heart to come over and not hear her laughter, or see her with those kids. She was such an amazing mom, it was devastating to know those kids would grow up without her. And to see his best friend so broken, without the love of his life, was unbearable. But selfishly, most of all, Tess was always there for Tommy. What was he going to do without her presence in his life anymore? He too felt lost and incomplete without her.

He tried to shake away his grief when he saw Parker chasing Henley up to the back door from the backyard. He smiled gratefully; at least the kids were able to smile still.

"Hey kids!" Tommy hollered as they ran in through the door.

"Hi Uncle Tommy." Parker said as he sat down at the kitchen table.

"Hi Henley." Tommy said coyly to the little girl.

"Hi Uncle Thommy." He chuckled softly; she had struggled with her T's for so long, that 'Thommy' had become his name ever since.

He bent down to the table. "Well guys, looks like it's going to be you and me today, wanna watch a movie or play a game?"

Nathan closed the bedroom door and stood there for a moment without facing his room. He took a deep breath and slowly turned around. The light from the windows was shining down on their bed. Suddenly, visions of Tess lying on the bed in her tank top and panties, basking in the sunlight reading a magazine, came to mind. She would look up when he walked in the room and smile at him, and she would smile that brilliant smile. God, how he missed it.

He tried to shake the memory from his mind as he walked over to the dresser and pulled off his shirt and tossed it into the bin. He began taking off his watch when her ring caught his eye. The doctors gave it to him after the accident. He held it between his fingers, remembering the night in the lighthouse, the night she agreed to marry him. She was such a mess then. She had gone through hell and back with her mom, with Bobby, and with him, but somehow, she found it in her heart to open up to love. To open up to the idea of a life with him, a life she would never get to live fully. Tears started welling in his eyes. He squeezed the ring in his fist and looked around for a chain. He shuffled around a few of Tess's necklaces until he found a long silver chain with a small pendant on it. He pulled the pendant off and replaced it with her ring. He carefully clasped the chain around his neck and let the ring hang there, heavy against his chest.

He slowly sauntered towards his bed and sat down. It was too quiet in here, he didn't think he could ever get used to it. He swiveled his legs onto the bed and rolled on his side. There she was, lying next to him. She smiled at him, her reddish-brown hair lying wildly around her face. Her eyes were bright and doe eyed. She could make him do anything with that look of hers. He smiled at the memory, and just as quickly as she appeared, she was gone.

The room was then grey; everything felt cold and distant. This was no longer the warm room it was when Tess was there. It was empty, quiet, and sad. He shut his eyes tightly, trying to bring Tess back. When he opened them again, she was sitting in the chair next to the window with a book on her lap. He could see the focus in her eyes and her brow furrowed in concentration. She glanced up and her expression softened as she smiled at him. When he smiled back, she got up and started to walk towards him. As she got closer, she started fading away. When she leaned in to kiss him, she disappeared completely.

He swore there were times he could still feel the warmth of her breath against his skin, or the gentle imprint of her lips against his. He started to cry; he was so lost without her here.

"Hey Nate, did you get any sleep?" Tommy asked quietly as Nathan walked into the living room.

Nathan looked at Tommy with both of his arms wrapped around Parker and Henley, one on each side.

He managed a small smile. "Yeah, I did. Thanks." He lied.

Chapter Eighteen

Grief is like the ocean, it's deep and dark, and bigger than all of us. And pain is like a thief in the night. Quiet. Persistent. Unfair. Diminished by time and faith and love.

"You know, Nathan, I'm proud of you." Jack said as he sat down on the back deck next to Nathan.

"For what?"

"For staying as strong as you have."

Nathan sagged his shoulders. "I haven't been strong at all."

Jack put a hand on his shoulder. "Nathan, just because you don't feel strong, doesn't mean you aren't. The fact that you feel weak, and manage not to show your kids what you're *really* feeling—well that right there is strength."

"They're just kids, Pop. They shouldn't have to know how this feels."

"You forget that you were just a kid too, Nathan. That didn't stop me from showing how I was really feeling." He paused for a moment as he gazed out into the forest. "Nate, you will always be twice the man I ever was. I want you to know how sorry I am for what you lost, but I am so proud of how you are still taking care of those two beautiful kids in there. They deserve a dad as good as you."

"Thanks, Pops." Nathan said sincerely.

Jack hesitated to look in his eyes. "Is it getting any easier?"

Nathan half-heartedly laughed. "No. I didn't think it was possible, but it's getting worse."

Jack waited for him to explain.

"I don't know how to raise these two kids on my own."

"You start by loving them, the rest will follow."

"Will it though?" He looked to his father as he spoke.

"Be the man she taught you to be, and that will be enough. You give those children anything less and it will make this a much greater tragedy than it already is."

"With each day that she's gone, it's just getting more impossible. Just the other day Henley came home from preschool and asked why she didn't have a mommy do her hair like all the other mothers did. It was heart breaking. I mean I try, but what do I know about hair or clothes or anything?" Nathan hung his head low. "And Parker, that kid is trying so hard to be brave. I hear him get up in the middle of the night and go in Henley's room, so I followed him one night. He sat by her bed and sang her the lullaby Tess used to sing. When I asked him about it, he said he didn't want Henley to forget her."

Jack rubbed his shoulder in comfort trying to stifle a sob working its way to the surface.

"Pops, it's like no matter what I do, I'll never be enough for them. I can't give them the things they need like a mother could. And how is it possible to miss her more and more every day? I thought the hurt was supposed to go away?" He wiped at his eyes.

"I'm sorry Nate, but whoever told you that was lying to you."

Nathan looked up at his father with a pleading look in his eyes.

"The hurt never goes away. And when you meet someone as special as Tess, the love never goes away. That's what makes it so hard. The hardest day of loving someone, is the day that you lose them."

"I just don't understand. That's her whole life? That's all she gets?" Nathan couldn't fight his emotions any longer. He could feel the tears welling at the brim.

Jack took a moment to figure out what to say. "Nate, I know you want answers, but you are never going to get them. There will never be a right answer, there is only life. As horrible and tragic as it is, it's just that—life."

Nathan stood in the corner of the living room nursing a beer. Another deputy walked over to him. "Nathan, how are you?"

Nathan shook his head as he loosened his tie, feeling suffocated. "Honestly? I am so fucking uninterested in a life without my wife."

The deputy didn't know what to say so he gently clapped a hand on his shoulder, nodded, and walked back to join the others. Tommy watched the exchange and as the deputy walked away, he went over to join Nathan.

"Hey Nate, do you want to maybe talk to the guests? I can't imagine what you're feeling, but—they are all here for you—for her."

Nathan looked up at the room full of people. They all wore black and all had the faintest traces of tears in their eyes. Everyone in that room loved Tess. Everyone in that room was there because they missed her. Everyone was there to say goodbye to her. He shut his eyes tightly trying not to cry. He took another sip of his beer, sat down on the arm of the couch and looked up at Tommy.

"It's my fault." He sniffled a little as he wiped his nose. "I was distracted, thinking about everything other than the road in front of me. It was raining, and that bridge is nasty on a good day—and I just didn't see the damn debris in our lane. I should have been paying better attention, I should have reacted faster."

Tommy looked shocked at his friend's admission. "Is that what you think? That you caused this?"

"I did cause it."

Tommy stared at Nathan; how wrong he was, and how he couldn't even see it. "Nathan, it was an accident. A terrible and tragic *accident*."

Nathan stared back at Tommy and hissed, "One that could have been avoided."

Tommy was almost to the point of anger. "Nate, think about what an accident is: anything that happens suddenly or by chance, without any apparent cause. That is what happened. Not you, there was *nothing* you could have done."

Nathan shrugged as he stood up and sauntered off to the back yard to be alone.

Jack had overheard their conversation and made his way over to Tommy.

"He's going to be fine. He's going to be fine, because she is always going to be with him. Standing in the shadows, ready to protect him, laughing with him in the light, watching through his eyes all that get close. She will always be there, and he will be fine. But my son, my grandbabies, they will have learned the toughest lesson of all: love invites loss."

•••••••

He woke up in the truck. He felt a hot liquid streaming down his face; he touched his forehead gingerly and cringed in pain as his fingers touched a wound on his face. He tried to shake the confusion away and looked to his right. Tess was sitting in the passenger seat. Water was up to her chest now, and she looked over at him. He could see how scared she was, but she was trying to be brave. A steady stream of blood trickled down the side of her face as she looked at him in forlorn longing before she spoke.

"Nathan, I love you."

Nathan squirmed in his seat as he unclipped his seatbelt. He turned and tried to undo her seatbelt. "No. Don't say it. Tess, I am going to get you out of here. I promise." He pulled and pulled on the seatbelt, but it wasn't budging.

"Damn it!" He cursed as he continued to fight with the belt.

"Nathan, tell Parker and Henley—"

Nathan cut her off. "No. This isn't happening. You and I are going to live a long life, right here in Sitka, until we are grey and old. We're going to take Parker to a baseball game, and we're going to watch Henley at her first ballet recital—*together*."

She nodded to him as he continued to work. He took a big gulp of air before submerging under the water to get closer to her seatbelt. Water was surrounding her by the second, and as Nathan worked hard to break the seatbelt, she felt the water closing up around her face.

With her last moment above water she said, "Nathan—I love you."

"No!" Nathan screamed violently as he woke up from his nightmare. He panted in the darkness, trying desperately to catch his breath. He wondered when this torment would end. He couldn't bear to watch the worst day of his life on repeat every time he shut his eyes. He was placed on Ixion's wheel with no hope of ever coming off of it.

Chapter Nineteen

Gone. The saddest word in the language. In any language.
Mark Slouka

It had been three months since Tess had passed. Three of the longest months Nathan had ever experienced. He tried to do the best he could with the kids, but it was bad, for all of them. More and more he found Henley being the one to try and make Parker and himself smile or laugh. He found Parker crying in his bed almost nightly, and he, himself, hadn't slept much. The nightmares were overwhelming. He thought going back to work would help; maybe it would help him find some sort of normalcy in his life. But the truth was, work didn't help; nothing did. He only kept going to work because he thought it was what Tess would have wanted him to do. She would have wanted her family to get on with their lives, even though he knew that would be impossible. How does someone just get on with his or her life? How does someone move on, knowing everything they lost? The idea was unfathomable.

He pulled up a seat at the bar and nodded to Frank, one of the deputies he worked with. Frank sat down next to Nathan and motioned to the bartender for two beers.

"Hey Nate, how's it going?"

Nathan stared down at the bar and then looked over at Frank. "It's been a long day."

Frank nodded and shrugged his shoulders slightly. "I just wanted to say how sorry I am, and wanted to let you know if you ever need anything, just let me know."

Nathan snickered softly. "Did your wife put you up to that?"

Frank laughed as he picked at the label on his beer. "She may have said something to the effect of me needing to be more—sensitive."

Nathan laughed as he took a sip of his beer. "I guess that's what sweethearts are for, to be heavy on the sweet and hard on the heart."

Frank chuckled in agreement. "Regardless of my wife though, I am sorry. I couldn't imagine what you're going through. I guess you just have to be grateful for the time you did spend with her."

Nathan immediately clenched his mouth shut. He tried to calm himself but unfortunately for Frank, anger was an easy emotion to succumb to these days. He looked over at Frank and narrowed his eyes at him. "Don't."

Frank looked contrite and slightly flummoxed. "Don't what?"

"Don't you dare say at least you had ten years with her. Tell me, what year would *you* choose for your wife to die?"

"Nate, I didn't mean—" Frank trailed off.

Nathan stared back down at his beer, unable to look at Frank. Frank sighed heavily and patted Nathan once on the back before he left.

A man at the end of the bar huffed and laughed slightly into his beer. "Some men just don't have the fortitude."

That caught Nathan's attention. He looked over at the stranger. The man was wearing a suit and was folding up papers. From the looks of it, he had just finished up a business meeting.

"Excuse me?"

The man shuffled his papers more and then walked closer to Nathan dragging his briefcase along the bar top.

"I said, 'some men don't have the fortitude'. You're here sucking on a bottle instead of dealing with your problem, whatever it is. I can guarantee the answer isn't at the bottom of that bottle." He said accusingly smug as he took a seat next to Nathan.

Nathan slammed his beer down and looked the guy straight in the eye. His own eyes glazed over with an impassive expression. "My wife died. Suddenly and unfairly. She died, and now she will never get to really know her two kids. She died, but she believed in me, and she believed that I would continue to do the best for our children. So, I buried her. I picked out a headstone, and then I went to work, and I go home each night to tuck in my kids. So don't lecture me about fortitude, or dark days and problems, because this is far from my darkest or worst day."

He stood up, paid the bartender, and stole out of the bar. He didn't give the stranger a chance to respond. He didn't need to.

He slammed the Impala into park. He sat in the car silently for a few minutes as he examined the steering wheel. How many times had he and Tess gotten into the car to drive off to nowhere. He swears there were times she was attracted more to the car than to him.

He remembered the very first time he ever saw Tess. Often times he would leave his car in the Spar parking lot so he didn't take up a spot at the marina. One day, after a long morning out on the water, he was walking up to the lot when he saw her. She must have just gone on a break. She was leaning up against the building with her arms crossed and her brow furrowed. He laughed to himself; this girl was concentrating on something fierce. He wasn't sure he'd ever seen someone focus so hard on something. If she looked any harder, she would surely drill a hole right through whatever it was. He paused and took a minute to examine her. She was beautiful; that was for certain. She had wild, reddish-brown hair that looked as if it had a mind of its own, all Medusa-y, and her eyes sparkled in the sun. They were the brightest shade of green he had ever seen, like fresh budding leaves in a damp forest. She had long legs that went on for days and looked as though they had seen their fair share of the sun. He realized then she must have recently moved to town.

He jumped when she straightened herself up from the wall and began sashaying towards him. He felt his hands start to sweat with nerves and his heart began to race. He sighed in relief when he saw her stop short of him. She hadn't even noticed him standing there. He walked around a car to get a better view of what she was looking at. He bowed his head and chuckled to himself; the girl had great taste. She was walking around his Impala, letting her hand lightly trail along its body as she admired it.

He took a deep steadying breath, willing himself to have a little courage. As he exhaled he took her silent admiration as the opportunity to approach her. "You like it?"

She yelped softly at the sound of his voice. "Oh gosh. Sorry. You startled me."

Nathan held his hands out in front as a friendly gesture. She looked back down at the car and then back up at him and pointed. "Yours?"

He shrugged his shoulders as if to say 'guilty'.

She smiled as she walked around it once more and then she locked eyes with him. "'sixty-seven, right?"

Nathan smiled as he shoved his hands in his pockets. "A girl who knows her cars, that's impressive."

She chided gleefully, "This isn't just any car though, is it?"

He couldn't help but just stare back at her. Who was this girl?

She took his silence to step forward, and she stuck her hand out in front of her. "Hi, I'm Tess."

He balked to himself; she was telepathic surely.

"Nathan."

Nathan stood there gawking slightly at her. He had dated beautiful women before, but no one ever made his heart stutter in his chest the way she did. But even so, he had never been shy around women. So why was she any different? He had no idea why it was so damn hard to spit out a couple words, but for the life of him, he didn't know how to pronounce a single one.

Tess dropped her eyes, slightly embarrassed when Nathan didn't say anything more. She took a step back and signaled over her shoulder. "Well, I should be getting back to work."

Nathan shuffled where he stood, finally getting the power of language back in his arsenal. "Oh, of course. Maybe I'll—well maybe I'll see you around."

He cursed to himself mentally, so much for having the power of language when that was really the best he could do.

She stopped walking and smiled at him. "Sitka doesn't seem too big, I'm sure you will."

At that, he smiled that face-splitting grin at her. She laughed effortlessly and walked back into the diner.

Nathan shook the memory away. This car had been there for so many big moments in their lives. From first dates, to driving Parker home from the hospital. This car had seen so much with him. He was sad to stop driving it when they got the truck, but now, being back in the car—it was almost as if he could drive home and see Tess sitting there on the front porch waiting for him. His eyes dropped as he realized that would never happen again.

He sighed once before throwing open the car door and slamming it shut behind him. He breathed heavily as he looked up in the night sky. He could see his breath in the cool air coil up around him. He shook his head once and then made his way through the cemetery. It had started to rain as he walked towards her headstone. He tried to smile knowing how much she loved the rain, but he just couldn't bring himself to do it.

He stood silently at her grave for over an hour. He stood there staring at the name carved in the stone with his hands in his pockets. He memorized every imperfection in the stone and studied the small vines that had begun to crawl their way up it.

Lost in his thoughts, he heard twigs crack in the distance. When he glanced up, there she was. Not just some mental image he conjured up. No, it was the real her. She seemed to notice him, but when their eyes met, she turned on her heel and took off running into the woods.

"Tess?" He yelled to her as she disappeared into the woods. He took off in a full-on sprint trying to catch up to her.

He chased after her, but then, she suddenly stopped in a small clearing and stood eerily still. "Tess?"

He started to approach her slowly with his hand held out in front of him to show he meant no harm. He could feel the blood slowly draining from his face, and his body started to quiver as he inched his way closer to her.

He watched as she slowly turned around to face him. "Nathan?"

Nathan froze and stared blankly back at her. There she was, standing not five feet in front of him. There was his Tess. She stood before him in her favorite pair of blue jeans, a black, V-neck tee, and a canvas, army green jacket. Her long, wild hair lay limp and wet from the rain with a small strand plastered to her cheek from running. How was this possible? Had he finally gone mad from grief?

"Nathan?" Her voice seemed to draw him out of his reverie. He blinked his eyes, forcing himself to test if he was dreaming.

"How—? How are you standing in front of me?" He tried to spit the words out.

She looked around them at the woods and then up into the night sky shrouded with dark trees and heavy clouds. Her mouth twisted into a slight frown. "I've been here before."

Before he could say anything else, she took off running back to the cemetery. He trailed behind her screaming, "Tess! Wait!"

She ran through the pouring rain, weaving her way through the headstones. She could hear his footsteps trailing her, but she couldn't stop until she found it. She suddenly stopped running; she looked down and started panting and sobbing as she doubled over.

Nathan tried to steady his breath as he finally caught up to her. When he saw where she was he felt his throat constrict. "Tess." Her name was a mournful prayer.

Her face was streaked with tears and rain. Her eyes were wide as she looked up at him. "I—I—I remember now. We were driving home from the theatre and it was raining. It was raining so hard and we were coming up on the bridge, and I remember, you looked over at me and smiled. I remember thinking how lucky I was to have a smile that still made the butterflies dance in my belly." She hesitated catching her breath. "But then, I looked back at the road and I was too late. I tried—I tried so hard to warn you, but I just wasn't quick enough. And—and it just all happened so fast." She put a hand up to her forehead trying to recall the memory. Her fingers delicately traced the spot where she had hit her head on the dash.

Nathan stood there staring at her. His eyes ached and burned from the tears, and he felt as if his heart was being squeezed inside the confines of his chest.

"It happened so fast, and we were in the water. The water I remember. I remember trying to scream because it kept pressing me down, but when I screamed my lungs filled with water and I couldn't—I couldn't scream anymore. I felt my body shut down." She paused again and looked up at him as she spoke slowly, "I *died,* didn't I?"

Nathan's face contorted in pain. Every nightmare, every dream, every memory—this is what he feared. More than anything, he hoped and prayed she hadn't suffered, and now standing in front of him—he could see she had.

He sobbed, "Tess, I am so, so sorry. I'm sorry I—"

Tess's head snapped up, and she looked him square in the eye. She looked scared and repentant as she cut him off. "But you didn't—did you?"

"I didn't what?"

"Die?" She asked as she took a step closer to him.

His head dropped. "No," he tried to clear his throat, "no, I didn't." Although, at this point, he was no longer sure. Maybe he had been the one to die that night. Maybe he was the ghost visiting Tess after having stayed in purgatory for so long.

She took another step closer to him, and when he raised his eyes to meet hers, something had changed. She was smiling and her eyes were glowing, just like he had remembered.

"Then, I'm going to be okay." Her voice no longer shook as she stared at him resolutely.

"No Tess. If we had left even five minutes sooner or five minutes later, I may never have swerved and driven us over that bridge. If I had just been faster, you wouldn't have died."

Tess moved slightly, and she looked at Nathan with remorse for him in her eyes. He wanted so badly to tell her not to look at him that way, that he didn't deserve it.

"But I want you to know—I did save you." He whispered out with tortured breath. "Every night in my dreams, after I've awoken from the nightmare, I dream that I save you. Of course, I didn't when it counted, but I did save you. I replay it all again, see it all again, and I'd change it. I'd be faster. I'd be cleverer. I'd save you a million different ways. Each time, I did save you."

The faintest smile crept across her face in recognition. "I know why I'm here now."

"What do you mean?"

"I'm here, because you still can't see it."

Nathan threw up his arms as he looked around the cemetery. "What can't I see Tess? What do you mean?"

"That you did save me."

Nathan dropped his arms and shook his head. "I didn't Tess. God, I wish I had. I wish every day that I had, but I didn't."

"That night on the bridge, that night was an accident. That night was the end of my story. But you, you saved me when it counted. You saved me and gave me the greatest life I could have ever imagined. You saved me and because of it, I have two beautiful children and a husband I know will continue to love them for me."

"Tess, that's not enough. I need you." Unbidden tears began to stream down his face.

She smiled sweetly at him. "I won't leave until you're ready."

He looked down at the ground and spoke quietly, "But what if I'm never ready?"

When he looked back up, she was gone. He spun in circles looking for her, but he was standing alone in the cemetery. Utterly alone.

———•••••———

It was late when he arrived home. He walked inside and set the keys on the counter. He stood there staring at the keys for a minute, and then he stalked off through the back door. He walked down onto the soggy grass and looked up into the sky. The rain had yet to let up, but he continued to stand there; quietly at first, just staring up at the sky letting the rain pound down on him.

"You bastard. How could you take her away from me? How could you take my Tess?" He screamed up at the heavens, his voice hoarse with more unbidden and unshed tears. "How could you do that? You turned your back on me. You let me down! You and I both know she wasn't supposed to die! She was supposed to live a long and healthy life; and you took that from her! And then tonight—you let me see her, and then what? You just take her away again? What, is it fun for you to pour salt into the gaping wound that is my life? You son of a bitch, you bring her back. Give her back to me!" He yelled into the night sky.

He stood with his arms spread wide as he stared up into the night. He waited for a response, but after a while he dropped his arms and bowed his head.

"Nathan."

His head shot up at the sound of her voice. She was standing on the deck looking down at him on the grass.

"Tess?"

"Come inside, you'll freeze out here."

"Will you stay tonight?" He adjusted the comforter as he climbed into bed and watched as she turned from the window and walked towards the bed.

She sat down next to him. "Do you want me to?"

He stared at her; she truly was his Tess, the chance to see her again to have her near him—

"More than anything."

She took a moment to consider it, and then she laid down next to him on her side and stared at him. "I've missed you."

He turned on his side to face her fully. "Tess, I miss you so damn much."

She smiled softly as she adjusted her arms. "You can sleep now."

"I'm scared that I'll wake up and this will have been a dream."

"You're just going to have to trust me."

He gazed upon her one last time and sighed heavily as he closed his eyes and whispered, "'til kingdom come?"

"'til kingdom come."

He leaned backwards thrusting his legs forward as he kicked the windshield out. He watched as it broke off from the truck and slowly slid down the hood and off into the bottom of the basin. He took a deep breath and grabbed Tess by the waist, maneuvering her out through the opening. He focused his energy on kicking his way to the surface, and when he could see the faint streetlights, he pushed them up. He burst through the surface, gasping for air as he pulled Tess's head from the water. He pulled her by her waist until he made it to the riverbank.

His lips formed a straight line across his face, and his brows furrowed as he mustered the strength to pull her limp body from the water. As he held her in his arms, water fell from her body in waves and her arm dangled by his side, lifeless. He carried her to the road and laid her on the pavement as the rain beat down on them. Her skin was pale and her lips were a bluish-purple.

He pumped her chest. "Come on baby, breathe!"

He blew air into her mouth trying to breathe life back into her. Each time he would look for some sign of life, and each time her pale face showed no reply.

He hit the ground next to her. "Damn it, baby, don't leave me!"

He beat the pavement with his hand until it was bloody and bruised. He rocked himself forward and gently kissed her cold lips. "I still need you baby."

Chapter Twenty

He felt his eyelids spring open as he woke from the nightmare, but he quickly forced them shut, trying to keep the other memories or dreams from last night from escaping. He wanted to hold on to them for as long as he could, because he knew there was no guarantee she would still be here. It wasn't fair how fleeting the good memories were, when the bad memories lingered, unwanted. Those memories were the ones you can't outrun, no matter how far you go. They live in the spaces between heartbeats, in the silence just before you sleep.

He sighed softly and slowly opened his eyes; there she was sitting in the chair next to the bed. She was wearing the same outfit she wore the day she agreed to go on a date with him. Dressed in a pale-yellow blouse and white shorts, she looked so vibrant and beautiful.

She had her legs pulled to her chest and her wild hair cascaded down her shoulders. She sat there staring at him with her big, green eyes and that smile that he missed so much.

"Hi."

"You're still here?" His voice sounded surprised and light.

She slowly let her legs drops down; she walked to the bed and sat down beside him once more. "I made you a promise."

He sat up in bed noticing how the bed did not dip under her weight; she really was a ghost. "Tess, how do I do this? How do I do this without you?"

She smiled and gave a light carefree laugh. "How about you start with something easier? Tell me about the kids."

He chuckled softly as he tousled his soft brown hair.

"It's hard. Parker misses you. He tried so hard to be brave, and he continues to try so hard to make sure Henley knows how much you loved them both."

"And Henley?"

"She's smart. Really smart, and funny." He smiled thinking of the little girl just two doors down. "But, it's hard for her too. She doesn't understand—she sees other kids with their mothers and she doesn't understand why she can't be with you."

Tess rubbed her legs. "I wish I could be there for her, for the both of them, but I can't; so, I need you to be."

"Tess, I'm trying—"

She cut him off. "Nathan, I know you are. My faith in you has never wavered, but with Henley, especially Henley, you need to do the things I was supposed to do for her."

Nathan shook his head resolutely. "I promise."

He jumped when he heard a soft knock at the door, and Henley slowly pushed the door open. She stared at him still in bed.

Nathan looked from her back to Tess, but she was gone. He shook his head trying to clear his mind. "Henley, baby, are you okay?"

"Are you going to take us to school?"

He nodded his head. He hadn't realized what time it was. "Yeah, sweetie, I am. Give me a couple minutes and I'll come help you get ready."

"I'm already dressed."

"Okay, then ask Parker to help you with your cereal."

"Okay." She smiled as she closed the door after her.

Nathan felt himself smile genuinely for the first time in a long while. His baby was growing up so fast. He got up and got dressed. Seeing Tess, hearing her voice, was enough to make him want to get up. It was enough to show him he needed to try harder. But most of all, seeing her gave him hope that he had long forgotten.

"Henley, can you come in here please?" Nathan called out from the bathroom.

He watched as his little girl walked in the bathroom, her wild, brown hair was just like Tess's, never tame, ferocious—beautiful. And her big, round, blue eyes were as blue as the sea that used to call to him so many times. He smiled down at her.

She walked in and climbed onto the toilet and looked at the counter that was covered in hair supplies: hairbrushes, clips, barrettes, and hair ties.

"What's all that?" She asked.

"Well pumpkin, your mom isn't here to help you with your hair, but maybe I could try?"

The little girl smiled in unadulterated delight as she took a seat in front of the mirror.

"Okay, well first let me try this—" He trailed off as he tried concentrating on dividing her hair.

"Okay, I think I'm on the right track." He looked up to see how he had done so far. Henley giggled as she turned her face side-to-side looking at the lopsided pigtails on her head.

Nathan laughed and shook his head as he took a seat on the edge of the tub.

"Henley, am I doing anything right?"

She took a moment to think about it. "You're much more handsomer than the other dads. They don't have hair, and they have big bellies."

Nathan laughed freely. He could always count on Henley to make him feel better; she was just like her mother in that sense.

Maybe that's why it hurt so much. Because in so many ways, Tess was always right here with him. In his son's kindness and eyes, and in his daughter's looks and ability to make the best of any situation.

All day he waited to see her. He thought maybe she would come to him when he was alone in the locker room at work, or when he sat by himself in his patrol unit, but each time he thought she would have come, she hadn't. He tried to stay hopeful though; he wanted to show her he could do this. When he got off duty he went home and went straight to work on cooking dinner.

Parker walked in holding Henley's hand forty-five minutes later. He stood there at the kitchen entrance staring at his father with a bemused expression.

"Dad?"

Nathan looked up and smiled at his kids. He slowly put the spoon down in front of him and smiled. "Hi. Why don't you take a seat?"

Both kids immediately dropped their small backpacks and ran for the table. Parker helped lift Henley up onto the chair and then he took a seat beside her. He watched as their father started plating their dishes with spaghetti and broccoli. Parker smiled. It was the first non-frozen or refrigerated meal they had in months.

After he was done, Nathan took a seat across from Henley and Parker. He smiled at both of them and sighed softly. "I'm sorry. I'm a bit rusty."

Both Parker and Henley looked up at him with their mouths full. Parker smiled as he tried to talk, "It's delicious."

Henley nodded with exaggerated movements in agreement with her brother. Nathan laughed gleefully as he shook his head to himself.

After dinner was finished, dishes had been put away, and the kids were content, Nathan excused himself and took a seat on the back steps as he watched the sunset. He jumped slightly when she quietly sat down beside him on the steps.

He looked over at her and smiled. She sat there so peacefully, staring out, watching the sun slowly sink behind the mountains in the distance. After a few minutes of silence, she finally looked over at Nathan. "Henley's hair looked good today."

He laughed freely. Tess was always much too kind to him. He looked down at his hands as he spoke, "I tried."

He picked his head back up and watched the last rays of light finally set. They sat there silently together for what felt like hours until he turned to her.

"Tess?"

"Yeah?"

"Can we just stay here? In this place, just the two of us. Would that be okay?"

She cocked her head to the side looking at him. "I'd like that."

Nathan jumped out of bed and bolted down the hallway, bursting into Parker's room where he was thrashing around in his bed screaming. Nathan fell to the floor next to the bed and tried pining Parker down to stop him from hurting himself.

"Parker, come on buddy, wake up."

Parker finally woke up. His eyes opened wide, and he looked at his father and started crying. Nathan pulled Parker forward and hugged his son tightly.

"Another nightmare? Buddy, I thought we were past this." His voice was despondent as he got up and took a seat on the bed next to Parker.

Parker wiped his nose with the back of his hand as he spoke, "I thought so too."

"Wanna tell me about it?"

Parker looked up at him with his big, round, green eyes. "It was the lullaby one."

Nathan shook his head and gently rubbed Parker's back. If Parker's dream was half as vivid as he was imagining it, the poor kid was living in a Hitchcock film. This particular nightmare started after Parker begged him to tell what happened. Nathan never wanted to tell his son the details of that night, but he also knew he couldn't keep avoiding it forever. He tried to tell Parker about that night with as little visual aid as he could, but the kid had more imagination than he could control.

He told Parker he had swerved and the truck went over the bridge and landed in the water. He tried to explain how cars sink slowly because it takes a while for water to get in. He then had to tell his son that his mother had fallen asleep under water and never woke up. Parker seemed to take it okay—as okay as any almost eleven-year old could.

But that night, he heard Parker screaming in his sleep. When he woke him up, Parker told him he had a nightmare.

Parker gently pushed open his bedroom door and smiled an all-teeth-showing smile when he saw Tess sitting on the edge of his bed.

"Mom!" He screamed as he raced into her arms, throwing himself onto her lap.

She giggled softly as she stroked Parker's back and held him close. Parker began to weep into his mother's arms as she rocked him back and forth. She held him until he had finally stopped crying, and then she gently laid him in his bed. His eyes stayed fixed on her as she pulled his covers up to his neck and gently tucked him in.

She leaned in and gently pressed her lips to his forehead before she backed up to the foot of his bed.

"Mom?" Parker questioned as he tilted his head to the side, wondering what she was doing.

She held her finger up to her lips, hushing him as she started to sing 'Hush, Little Baby'.

Parker bolted up in his bed. The lullaby was all wrong. Something was terribly, terribly wrong; and that's when he heard it.

A loud hissing noise ripped through his room as the walls started to burst with large cracks, spewing out water.

"Mom!" He screamed and reached his hand out her for her to grab.

She continued singing as water ripped through his room. She raised her hand out towards him and before Parker could cry for help, the water rushed up around her and swallowed her whole.

Nathan shook the memory and focused back on Parker staring up at him. "I really miss her, Dad."

Nathan grabbed Parker, pulled him to his chest, and kissed his head as he rocked his son back and forth. "I know buddy, so do I."

After an hour of sitting with Parker, Nathan finally sauntered back into his room. He rubbed his eyes from exhaustion and looked up when he noticed her sitting by the window. She was staring out into the darkness. With the light from the moon, she turned to look at him as he sat on the edge of the bed.

"Does he have nightmares often?"

Nathan scratched his head and then leaned forward. "It's gotten better. He used to get them a lot. Now it's only once in a while."

She nodded in understanding. She waited for Nathan to speak, but when he didn't, she quietly asked, "And you?"

Nathan looked up at her and studied her face. After a brief moment, he shrugged his shoulders and tried to force a little smile.

Chapter Twenty-One

When he woke up she was waiting for him. She sat beside him and smiled that radiant-you-will-never-ever-recover-from-this smile as he opened his eyes.

"Hi."

He groggily stirred and beamed up at her. "Hey beautiful."

She reached her hand out to caress his face, but as she got close she drew her hand back shakily and turned her gaze out the window.

Nathan sat up suddenly unsettled by her reaction. "Tess, what's wrong?"

She turned and gave him a half smile. "Nothing. I just, I need to go away for a while."

His eyes widened and he began to panic. "No Tess. No, you can't leave me."

"Shh—it's okay. It's not forever."

He tried to calm his breathing, but it felt as if his insides were collapsing in. "For how long?"

Her shoulders shrugged. "I don't know, but I need you to do something for me."

"Tess, I can't—"

"Please Nathan?" She stared at him with those big, beautiful eyes of hers.

He sighed in defeat. "Okay Tess."

"Take care of my babies. Try to live as normal of a life as you can. I promise I will always be with you."

"But I won't be able to see you?"

"I need you to try to move on."

"Tess, I can't do that. That *is* too much to ask of me."

She closed her eyes and when she opened them he could see the heady resolve in them. "Try, that's all I ask."

He gazed at her trying to memorize every inch of her. She cocked her head slightly and smiled at him as he bowed his head. "'til kingdom come."

After sitting silently for a few minutes, he finally looked up, but when he had, she was already gone.

Tommy walked into the garage and kicked Nathan's boot that was sticking out from under the Impala. Nathan slid out from under the car and looked up at Tommy.

"Give me a hand?" Nathan reached his arm out to Tommy who helped pull him up to his feet.

"How's it going?"

Nathan took a rag and wiped the grease from his hands as he examined his car.

"The kids are at school and I thought I would upgrade the suspension."

"So, this is what you do on one of your only days off and when the kids are at school?"

Nathan eyed Tommy with scrutiny. "What else should I be doing?" He asked as he handed Tommy a beer.

Tommy took the beer and leaned back on the tool bench.

"Look Nate, I don't say this lightly, but have you considered—well have you considered dating again? It's been almost six months now."

Six months seemed like an arbitrary time frame to Nathan. It couldn't matter any more or any less to him had it been one day or ten years. No measure of time would ever make her absence be okay. The only meaning six months had to Nathan was the fact it had been three months since he had seen her last, and those three months had been *very* long. Nathan walked over to the small, black boom box and hit pause on *Knockin' On Heaven's Door*.

"Back to the classics I guess?" Tommy broke Nathan out of his reverie making him realize he never answered Tommy's original question. He wasn't sure how to even answer Tommy's first question, so he focused back on the black boom box instead.

Nathan shrugged. He hadn't even noticed he hadn't played *Do You Love Me?* since Tess died. He could never find the right time or the right mood to listen to that song, not when so many memories were attached to it.

He took a swig of his beer before he turned around to face Tommy with an impassive expression. "It's not that I haven't considered it, it's that I never will."

"C'mon Nate, she wouldn't have wanted that."

Nathan smiled contritely at first and nodded, but then he took another swig of his beer and set his eyes on something in the distance. He wasn't sure how to explain to Tommy that he would never want someone the way he wanted Tess. Tess would always be the only woman for him, and he knew dating anyone would only push him further into denial that the love of his life really wasn't with him anymore.

"The thought of kissing another woman, it's unbearable because it means I will have killed Tess."

Tommy turned and faced Nathan straight on. "Nate, you can't think like that. You know Tess wouldn't see it that way."

"But it's true Tommy. I will have killed her, because if I kiss another woman, even for just a moment, it means I will have let her be dead."

Tommy walked over and put a hand on Nathan's shoulder. "Look Nate, I can't tell you what it feels like to lose the woman you love. I mean look at me."

Nathan had to laugh. "Yeah, you kind of are a man-whore."

Tommy considered it for a minute and then shook his head in agreement. "Yeah, but it's fun to be me." He wiggled his brows at Nathan which made him chuckle again.

"All I'm saying is that I don't think Tess would have wanted this. Tess was the most amazing person in this world; she, you, those kids—you are my family. She is someone I will never forget, and she is someone I promise to always tell your kids about and remind them on the days they just don't remember too well. But man, she left me to take care of you, and Nate, I gotta tell you—I feel like I'm failing her."

Nathan looked up at his friend and sighed. "I know Tommy, but can you really not understand what it's like to have been plucked from obscurity and chosen to be loved so fiercely, without limitations, and then have that ripped from your world?"

Tommy bowed his head and shrugged his shoulders.

"Maybe it's because you haven't found the right girl to experience it with, but I'm telling you, if you knew what that was like—if you understood, then you would see exactly why there will never be anyone else for me."

⸻ ••●◆●•• ⸻

Nathan rolled over and wrapped his arm around her as he gently kissed her exposed shoulder. She smiled widely to herself and pressed her back in close to his chest. She loved the feel of his soft, warm skin and the fluid thumping of his heartbeat against her skin.

"Good morning, beautiful."

"Good morning, husband." She spoke softly as she turned in his arms to face him.

She smiled up at him as she gently caressed his face with the back of her knuckles. With his fingers, he lightly brushed her hair, smoothing it down on the pillow.

"Do we really have to head home tomorrow?"

He chuckled softly and pressed his lips against hers. Once he pulled back, she sighed quietly and stared up into his warm, grey eyes. He let his fingers travel down to her hand and pulled her hand up, intertwining their fingers.

She looked down at their locked hands where his fingertip lightly caressed her wedding band. "It's just, everything is better with you. Everything is safe."

He pulled his hand from hers, gently nudged her chin towards him, and kissed her deeply. As his lips moved against hers, she let her hands trail up along his arms and run across the muscles in his back. His response signaled he felt the same and she couldn't help but feel smugly giddy inside.

He tore his lips from her hers and trailed heated kisses down her throat smiling into her neck when he heard a soft whimper escape her. He pushed his leg between hers, forcing her legs to part for him as he nestled himself in between them.

She ran her fingers through his hair, tugging and pulling slightly with a mischievous grin. Nathan smirked back in response. "Is that so, Mrs. Suppan?"

She grinned widely and nodded.

He continued trailing kisses down her sternum and danced delicate circles around her nipple with his tongue before taking the small bud gently between his teeth. His hand trailed down her side and dipped in between her legs. He slid his fingers between her folds and thrust a finger into her forcefully.

"What was that, Mrs. Suppan?" He spoke seductively as his finger continued to pump in and out of her, curling up inside her to hit her g-spot.

"Yes, sir." She moaned out breathily.

Nathan grinned from one ear to the other before he went back to sucking on her breast as he inserted a second finger. Tess moaned as her arousal flooded around his fingers.

"Baby, don't stop." She breathed out as she rolled her hips to the rhythm of his fingers thrusting in and out.

Nathan smirked as he continued his onslaught, loving the way he could feel her start to constrict around him. Her body started to tremble and just as she was reaching the edge, he quickly pulled his fingers out and kneeled up between her legs. Grabbing her hips, he moved the tip of his dick to her entrance and slammed into her.

She cried out as he continued to pump into her at a punishing rate. He leaned forward gently grabbing her throat as he kissed her roughly. She whimpered into his mouth as he thrust into her.

He pulled out of her and gently tapped her hips. "Roll over, baby."

She did as he asked and rolled onto her stomach. He grabbed her hips and forced her up onto her knees. She could feel her face heat at his actions. He playfully smacked her butt. "Ass up, baby doll."

Her stomach clenched and she could feel a pool of wetness forming under his touch. He grabbed her hips again as he positioned himself behind her and with strained force, thrust into her.

She mewled and moaned as he rammed into her again and again. He leaned forward placing kisses down her back as he continued to pump into her. Digging his fingers into her hips, he slammed into her once more before he reached forward to grab her by the throat. With his hand wrapped around her neck, he pulled her back to him so they were both upright.

He moved her hair from her neck and placed a hot, wet kiss on her neck as he slowly began moving inside her again. Her eyes closed and he could see her bite her bottom lip as her body trembled under his touch.

Continuing to move inside her, he began massaging one breast with his hand while the other hand reached forward into her folds. She gasped as he began rubbing circles around her clit.

Feeling herself beginning to quick, she moaned out, "God, that feels so good, baby."

He smiled into her neck as he continued to tug at her nipple with one hand and rub her clit with the other. He could feel her insides begin to clench, pounding into her as she screamed out, and finally stilling as they both reached their climax.

Nathan gently kissed her shoulder as he pulled out of her. He smiled to himself seeing her limp body fold. If it weren't for him holding her up, she would surely collapse.

He carefully laid her down on the bed before lying beside her and pulling her onto his chest. He leaned down to kiss the top of her head and listened to her sigh blissfully. He smiled to himself again. "I will never get enough of you. You are truly a vixen."

She giggled lightly as she trailed circles on his chest. "You sir, know how to make me feel like a lady of the night."

Nathan smirked. "As long as I am the only one who gets to enjoy your services."

Tess laughed playfully as she turned her face in to kiss the middle of his chest. He reached down to pull her up to him and crashed his lips into hers. The warmth of their breaths flitting into one another, their lips molding together, and their tongues playing passionately.

She pulled her lips away from him and groaned slightly as she pulled his body in close to hers and hugged him tight.

"I don't want to leave this bed, but I'm thinking we shouldn't stay anchored here for too much longer."

He grunted once at her comment and kissed her neck before he rolled over and turned his mouth down into a pout. "I guess you're right."

She playfully pushed his chest and then rose from the bed letting the sheet billow down around her. She smiled bashfully at the way his eyes caressed her body in carnal appreciation. She dipped her head slightly and peeked up at him under her full lashes, and with a faint smile and a wink, she flitted off towards the bathroom.

He took a moment to lie back in bed and smile to himself. After his brief moment of contented euphoria, he started getting dressed for the day. As he sat on the edge of the bed lacing up his boot he looked up and at the entrance of the stairwell, there she was watching him. Her wild curls framing her beautiful face, and her bright, green eyes staring straight at him. She stood there smiling in that peach colored dress she wore the night of their anniversary.

The blood from Nathan's face drained instantly. "I'm dreaming, aren't I?"

She looked down at her dress and pulled the material out with her fingertips before letting it gently fall back down to her side. "I'm sorry. Do you not like it? I thought you enjoyed this dress."

Pain filled his eyes. "It's not that, it's just—"

She cocked her head slightly to the left and frowned faintly. "It's this memory that pains you. The memory of our honeymoon?"

He shut his eyes tightly to take a moment to think about all the things he wanted to say, and then he opened them slowly. "Tess, I just miss you so much. It's been almost three months. Why won't you let me see you anymore?"

She took a step backward and gracefully took a seat on the last step.

"I shouldn't have even come, but—well truthfully, I was being selfish."

He scratched his head once before he spoke softly with a stern command, "Be selfish. Stay with me."

She looked up at him and gently shook her head, even though he could see she was trying desperately to deny surface of her true feelings. "I can't do that. You deserve better than that."

His eyes shot up and met hers. "And what about you? You deserve better than this. Tess, I can't move on. I can't get to just move on, to continue living, to watch our kids grow. How is it fair that I get all those opportunities and you don't? That's selfish of me."

She stuck her hand under a shaft of light coming from the stairwell window. She watched as her hand danced in the turning light, and she smiled. She looked back at Nathan. "Every time I get to hear Parker's laugh, it's a dream come true. Every time I see Henley's smile, it's a dream come true. They are my life, as they are yours. You owe it to them to be the very best version of yourself. The version where you fight for what you want. The version where you're not afraid to be great. You're better for them when you're living your dreams, and there is nothing selfish about that."

"But Tess, my dreams, what I want to fight for, it's you. Give me something I can fight for. Give me that purpose, because without it, without you—"

"You feel like you're swinging at shadows." She finished for him.

He bowed his head down as he spoke, "Yeah, I suppose I do."

She took a moment to consider it. "Would you settle then for knowing that I'm happy?"

He eyed her carefully. "Are you though? Are you happy?"

She stood up and straightened her dress. "There are times that I am sad. I'm sad I'm not there with you and the kids, but I know in my heart that the three of you can take care of each other. I believe in my heart that you three will find happiness. And that—well that is more than anything I could have ever hoped for, dead or alive. So, am I happy?" She paused and a small smile spread across her face as she spoke, "Yes Nathan, I am."

He swallowed the lump in his throat. "Then, I will try."

She smiled and nodded a thank you. "'til kingdom come."

She spoke so softly as he watched her slowly fade away into the sunlight. He bowed his head once more before the dream before him vanished completely, and he woke up alone in his bed once more.

He rubbed his eyes and rolled over in his bed to face the small picture on his nightstand. He stared at a picture of Tess and quietly whispered, "'til kingdom come."

Chapter Twenty-Two

Nathan stared into the review mirror, studying Parker's face. He could see a bruise forming under his left eye. Never in a million years did he think he would get a call saying Parker had gotten in a fight. Parker was such a gentle soul, so much like his mother. Nathan never even considered Parker would take after him. He wanted to be angry, and he was. Not because it happened, but because Parker could have been hurt. As he studied his son's face in the backseat, he felt the anger vanish and his shoulders sagged as he let out a heavy sigh.

He pulled the car over on the shoulder of the road, got out, and took a seat on the hood of the car. He was only there a moment before he heard the back door open and Parker slowly walked up next to him.

Nathan eyed his son and then patted the hood next to him. "Hop up."

Parker hopped up on the hood and quietly stared down at his hands knotted in his lap.

Nathan stared out in front of them as he spoke, "I'm not going to ask what happened. I understand what it's like to be angry. I was an angry kid and I carried that anger with me well into adulthood. I was always looking for trouble, putting myself in bad situations. I don't know if I thought it would help or what. Turns out all it did was hurt the people around me."

Parker looked over at his father. Nathan turned to smile softly once at him before returning his attention off into the distance with a deadpan expression.

"It was your mom who made me see the damage I was doing. She made me realize that no matter how good it felt to fight, it wasn't worth it; not when I had someone like her, who cared for me and worried about me, waiting at home." He paused looking down at his hands. "I know your mom isn't here to do the same for you, and buddy, I wish she was. She would know what to say. She always knew what to say, sometimes without even saying anything at all." He chuckled softly to himself before continuing with a voice that cracked as he spoke, "But all I can tell you is your sister and me, we need you, and we need you in one piece."

Nathan softly grabbed Parker's shoulder and watched as he nodded in agreement making a silent vow. He smiled and then resumed sitting in silence giving his son a minute to himself.

"He teased Henley."

Nathan looked over surprised to hear Parker. "What?"

"I walked her into preschool like I do every morning, and Trevor from fourth grade was walking by us and he started teasing Henley about her hair. I—I told her just to ignore him, and I walked her into school, and that was it."

Parker hung his head low as he spoke, "But at lunch I heard him telling other fourth graders about Henley. He told them her hair looked the way it did because she doesn't have a mother."

Nathan swallowed hard. He had forgotten how cruel some children could be. "So, what did you do?"

"I pushed him down to the ground and hit him."

Nathan sighed. "Buddy, I know you were trying to stand up for your sister, and she's lucky to have a brother like you, but—"

At that, Parker jumped off the hood of the car and turned to face Nathan. "I wouldn't have to stand up for her if mom was here! If mom wasn't dead, this never would have happened!"

Nathan stared blankly at Parker. The power of speech completely evaded him. When Nathan didn't respond, Parker stomped off and climbed back in the car slamming the door behind him.

Nathan rubbed his forehead. He hadn't even realized how angry Parker had become. He knew Parker was sad, he knew he missed his mother, but angry? How had he missed that one?

Nathan drove them home in silence. When they pulled up, Parker made a run for it, straight passed his grandfather on the front porch and into the house.

Jack watched Parker and then looked over at Nathan who slowly climbed out of the car and forced the door shut with a heavy sigh. Jack walked down towards

Nathan. He clapped Nathan's shoulder and then leaned up against the Impala next to his son.

"Rough day I take it?"

Nathan rubbed his eyes. "Henley inside?"

"Oh yeah, she's inside coloring."

"Good." Nathan said as he forced his hands into his jacket pockets. Jack stood there silently waiting for Nathan to speak.

"Parker is angry."

Jack crossed his arms and nodded. "Losing someone will do that to you."

"Pops—I hadn't even noticed he was angry before today."

"You've had a lot on your mind."

Nathan shook his head. "That's no excuse."

Jack chuckled softly. "No, I suppose it isn't. But Nate, I say this with love in my heart for Tess, the truth is you're clutching so tightly to the past, that maybe—maybe you're missing out on what's happening in the present." Jack knew in his heart that the weight of the past wasn't something you could simply let go of. It clung to you, whispered in the quiet, and reminded you of everything you had lost. He didn't want this fate for his son.

Nathan cleared his throat. "I know, but I can't let her go."

Jack turned to face Nathan. "She's in God's hands now son, let her be."

Nathan felt anger boiling beneath his skin. He straightened himself up to face his father. He set his jaw tight and hissed out, "She's in God's hands? Is that supposed to be a comfort? Some kind of security? God has nothing to do with this equation. He turned his back on me and mine a long time ago."

Jack watched with bewildered eyes as his son stormed off towards the house. "Nate!" He called out, but Nathan motioned for him to leave him alone.

Nathan stormed upstairs to his bedroom and closed the door. He sighed heavily as he sat down on the edge of the bed and put his head down between his knees. He tried to get control of his breathing, but he couldn't shake the resentment. He was angry at his father, angry at the kid Parker fought with, angry at God, angry at Tess, and most of all angry at himself. He was letting Tess down, and he didn't know what to do about it. Tess was the one who got through to him, so how was *he* supposed to suddenly know how to get through to Parker?

After a few moments, he gently raised his head and pleaded, "Tess? Please talk to me. I need your help."

He waited for over ten minutes hoping that she would show. When she didn't, he shook his head, and slowly got up from the bed, and headed downstairs in defeat.

••●●••

"Daddy, will you tell me a bedtime story tonight?" Henley asked as she quickly got under the covers.

Nathan smiled as he walked over and sat down on the bed beside her. "Sure pumpkin, which one?"

"The one about the angels."

Nathan gulped. He remembered listening to Tess tell this story a thousand times, but now the words seemed to stick in his throat. Tess believed in this kind of thing. She believed in magic, and hope, and faith; but he—well, he wasn't so sure anymore.

He looked over at the angel that hung above her door and turned back to look down at Henley with her big, blue eyes staring up at him. He smiled and brushed the hair away from her face.

"Okay." He said as he shifted on the bed next to her so she could curl up next to him. He softly stroked her hair as he spoke.

"They say that every time a bell rings an angel receives their wings. Adeline was walking by St. Louis Cathedral, an old church, when she heard the bells begin to ring. She looked at the clock upon the cathedral and saw that the bells should not have sounded. Why are the bells ringing, she wondered, but then a ray of light burst down from heaven and cast over her. She felt herself being lifted up by the light. She looked down below her and watched as the busy town grew smaller and smaller. She was not afraid, however, for the light was warm and peaceful. She smiled as she rose up into the sky. Once she was high up in the clouds, she noticed something wonderful. Giant, white wings appeared and wrapped around her like a warm blanket. Where have these wings come from, she wondered, and then she heard someone answer her, 'They are yours now, Adeline.' She looked ahead and saw an angel floating there. He smiled at her. 'How are they mine?' She asked. 'You are an angel.' He answered. She looked at the wings around her and watched as they slowly unraveled and spread out next to her. She smiled as she felt them flapping in the wind; she had never known what it felt like to fly before. 'Are you an angel too?' She asked. He smiled again and nodded, 'I am Michael, the archangel.' He nodded for her to follow him, and together they took off gliding through the clouds. She felt the rush of wind in her hair and smiled in excitement as Michael led her through the clouds and soared over towns. She watched as everything below her rushed passed them: cities, towns, forests, mountains, lakes. She saw all of Earth's beauty. Michael slowed down and stopped, hovering above a young girl on her way to school. He looked over at Adeline and told her, 'Do not worry. She cannot see us.' 'Who is she?' Adeline asked. 'Her name is Katarina and she is your charge.' He told her. 'My charge?' She asked. Michael nodded and smiled at her. 'You are her guardian angel now. It is your duty to watch over her— to guide her, to protect her. You will be there for her when no one else can. And you will love her with all of your heart.' He told her. 'But, how will I know what to do?' She asked him. He laughed and told her, 'You will know when the time comes, but for now, watch over her. She is yours to protect.' Years passed and Adeline watched little Katarina grow into a beautiful woman. Michael was right; Adeline loved Katarina with all of her heart. She watched over Katarina, protected her from the shadows and illuminated the way when it was dark. Adeline stayed with Katarina her whole life, always being there when she needed her, and when it was Katarina's time, Adeline wrapped Katarina in her wings and flew her into Heaven."

Nathan looked down and smiled at Henley who was fast asleep. She, like her mother, always had the faint trace of a smile on her lips when she slept. Her breathing was even and light as he gently moved her while getting off the bed. He adjusted the sheets around her and kissed her hair once before leaving the room.

⚬⚫⚫⚬⚬

Nathan banged against the truck window, using all of his strength to try to break the glass, but it wasn't budging. He could feel the palpable panic rising in him as he peered inside the cab of the truck from the outside. She was sitting there in the truck, crying as she watched water slowly surround her. She tried screaming for help and tried to tug on the seatbelt, but it was stuck. He watched as the water gradually took Tess under. He stared in horror as she struggled and squirmed, locked down by her seatbelt. He watched her try to fight it. His guttural scream was muffled by the water as he continued to bang his hands against the window, but no matter how hard he tried, the glass wouldn't break. He was trapped outside, forced to watch as Tess slowly drowned. He banged, prodded, and pushed as a ball of light emanating from Tess's chest slowly faded until it was gone completely.

"No!" Nathan screamed as he woke up in a panic. His breathing was aggravated as he wiped the sweat from his face and turned to look at the clock. It was just a little after two in the morning. He knew he wouldn't be able to fall back asleep. He swung his legs off the side of the bed and groaned into his hands. After a moment of sitting, he got up and got dressed. He headed downstairs, past his father asleep on the couch, and headed out front.

It didn't take long for him to get to the cemetery. He weaved his way through the headstones and stopped abruptly once he reached it. He looked down at her name carved into the stone and sniffled slightly in the cold air.

"Tess, I need you. I need you to talk to me."

He waited patiently looking around him to see if she showed up. After a few minutes he huffed into the cold air, "You know it's not fair to haunt my dreams and then not talk to me when I need you most. Talk to me Tess. Tell me what to do. I'm out of my league here." He held his arms out wide as he spoke.

He bowed his head down. "Tess, I don't know what to do. Parker, he's just so *angry* and I hadn't even noticed." He hesitated before continuing, "But what do I do? I'm not a role model. I mean look at my track record. You were the one to fix me. So, now what am I supposed to do? And Henley? Baby, she needs you. I need you."

He waited at the cemetery for over an hour, but when she still hadn't shown he left with his head hung low. It was still dark when he got home, and his father was still peacefully asleep on the couch. Nathan quietly made his way upstairs, but as he looked into his room, he just couldn't find the strength to go in knowing she wouldn't be there.

He sighed to himself, walked back down the hall, and quietly crept into Parker's room. He sat down on the bed next to him and gently brushed the hair from his face. He smirked subtly to himself in the darkness; his son was so like himself, and he had never even noticed. His hair was over grown and he had quite the shiner. If Nathan had a crystal ball to look back in time, he imagined seeing his father looking down on his sleeping son who looked exactly the same as Parker.

After a while of watching Parker, he exhaled deeply and climbed onto the bed lying next to him. He watched as his son moved slightly in his sleep, but he was happy to see he hadn't woken him.

Nathan had just started to doze off when he heard Parker's bedroom door creak open. He watched as Henley quietly entered the room and crawled up on the bed inching up in between Parker and Nathan. Nathan smiled and hugged her in close to his body as he drifted off to sleep.

When Jack woke up the house was quiet. He rubbed his face trying to rid the sleep from his eyes. He made it upstairs, but when he opened Henley's door to check on her, she was gone. He then walked down to Parker's room and gently pushed open the door. He smiled to himself when he saw the bed: Nathan with his arm around Parker and Henley nestled in between them. They were sound asleep, and for the first time, Jack knew for certain that his family would be okay.

Chapter Twenty-Three

"Daddy, will you play with me?" Henley stood in the doorway of the garage.

Nathan was busy setting up his investigation board. He continued to line up strings and pinned them, connecting one photo to another as he spoke, "Why don't you ask Parker to play?"

Henley looked down at her feet and spoke in a quiet, resigned voice, "He said no."

Nathan stopped what he was doing and sighed as he looked down at his little girl.

"I'm sorry pumpkin, but I just can't right now."

She kept her head bowed as she turned to leave. "Alright Daddy."

Nathan rubbed his forehead as she left. He didn't know what he was doing anymore.

Jack came out into the garage a few minutes later. He stood quietly for a moment, and then he crossed his arms and looked at Nathan. With contempt edging his voice he snipped, "You know that's the fourth time this week she's asked you to play and you've said no."

"What?" Nathan turned around to his father before shaking his head, "Not now Pops. I've got a lot on my plate."

Jack stared back at his son for a minute and then stalked off back into the house. A month ago, he thought maybe, just maybe, his son was going to be okay; but now—now, he wasn't so sure.

———————••◆••———————

"Daddy, wake up." Henley pushed and pulled on Nathan trying to get him to wake up.

"What? What is it sweetie?"

"You have to come downstairs and take us to school."

Nathan rubbed his eyes. "Sweetie, can you ask Grandpa Jack to drive you two today? Daddy's not feeling so well."

Henley stared at her father and shook her head adamantly. "No, it has to be you."

Nathan exhaled deeply, nodded, and watched as she flitted out of the room. He rubbed his face again trying to wake up; he hadn't realized how much he drank last night.

When he finally made it downstairs, he heard the fire alarm go off. He darted into the kitchen and saw smoke rising from the waffle machine. He quickly unplugged the machine and started swinging a rag around to get the smoke to leave.

He looked down at Henley and saw her hands covered in batter and flour was plastered against her cheek. "Henley, what were you doing?"

Her eyes dropped to the floor immediately. "I was trying to make waffles."

He knelt down to her and in an exasperated voice ushered, "Henley, you know you're not allowed to touch this without me in here. What's gotten into you?"

He heard a bag drop to the ground. He looked up and saw Parker standing there with his eyes narrowed and his face taut.

"She was trying to make me waffles because that's what *you* used to do on our birthdays." Parker strolled in right passed Nathan, grabbed Henley's hand, and led her out of the kitchen.

Nathan collapsed back. He sank down on his backside and leaned his head against the lower cabinets. How could he have messed up so royally? This was way beyond any other screw up he had so far. He wrapped his hands around the back of his neck and sat with his head down for ten minutes before he heard his father walk in.

Jack stood there silently for a minute, and then he picked up Parker's backpack. "I'm taking them to school today, but when they get home this afternoon—Nathan, you better make this right, you hear me?"

Nathan downed a bottle of water as he walked into the precinct. He walked towards Tommy and threw his keys down on his desk.

Tommy walked around to Nathan's side. "Hey, shouldn't you be—"

Nathan's head shot up and he barked back at Tommy, "How about you mind your own damn business and hand me the file?"

Tommy held his arms up at his sides. "Chill man. Debrief in twenty." He threw the file down on Nathan's desk as he turned back to his own desk.

Nathan quickly skimmed through the file. He knew the details on the case already, but he couldn't tame his thoughts long enough to truly focus. If Tess could see the mess he made of himself, she would be so disappointed—ashamed even. Nathan leaned back in his chair and sighed heavily.

Tommy was waiting outside of the briefing room. "You ready now?"

Nathan shook his head as he walked in past Tommy. "I guess."

Another deputy who was nearby and listening chimed in, "Always late to the party, huh Suppan?"

"Oh suck me." Nathan snapped back.

The deputy laughed as Tommy grabbed Nathan's shoulder and pushed him further into the room. Once they were out of earshot, he looked over at Nathan and smirked. "Touchy. Touchy."

Nathan narrowed his eyes and contorted his face into a scowl.

Captain Marx stood at the podium to talk about the case. "'Blue-Eyed Doll Killer'. Coined the name from his MO for victims: all females in their early twenties; all with jet black hair; bright, blue eyes; and pale, white skin."

A porcelain doll, Nathan thought to himself as he crossed his arms in front of him.

"So far, there have been seven victims, all taken from different parts of the country and all dumped in Sitka and the surrounding area. The victims were murdered differently each time, but after their deaths, the psychopath took the time to clean them up, dress them in a white, lace dress, and position their bodies. Each girl had been positioned in a different location with no apparent pattern."

Marx addressed the fact that the precinct still had no definitive connections between the victims besides their appearance. There was no understanding of why this was happening, only that the killer was getting bolder. The last victim was taken in broad daylight. Every lead was a dead end. This guy's end game was thought out. He was clever, and he knew how to cover any trace of evidence.

As they sat in the room listening to Marx finish up, they heard a loud commotion outside, bringing the debriefing to a grinding halt. They quickly filed out of the room. In the middle of the lobby stood a young girl in her early twenties with jet-black hair, bright, blue eyes, pale skin, dressed in a white gown that was steadily growing red around her stomach region. Facing all of them with wide, mystified eyes, she collapsed to the ground.

Nathan was the first to run to her side. He gently lifted her head from the ground and cradled her body in his lap. He tried getting her to speak, so he could ask what happened. She was fiercely trying to get her voice to cooperate, but her body was traitorous, and when she finally opened her mouth to speak, red liquid oozed from the side of her lips. He looked down and saw her stomach and been sliced open, and there wasn't much time before she would ultimately bleed to death. He tried to comfort her in these last moments as the EMT trained officers rushed to her side. They quickly worked to stop the bleeding, but Nathan knew it was no use. In her final breaths he wanted to soothe her so she wouldn't be scared of what was about to happen. As he continued to cradle her head, he noticed something. Pinned to her dress was a small note. Written in a jumbo, red sharpie was a message for them:

Have you found her yet?

Nathan stood by his desk. He stared down for a minute and then, in a fit of uncontrollable anger, he shoved everything off his desk. He threw papers and office material to the ground and kicked his chair back.

Tommy rushed over. "Nate, Nate. Calm down. Go home."

Nathan felt his body shaking and quivering, radiating with anger. He looked at Tommy and then glanced around to see everyone balking at him. He nodded his head in agreement and left the building.

When he got home, he stood in front of the kitchen sink for a long time. He stared down at the bloodstains on his hands. He felt so helpless—again. Why was it becoming routine to watch someone die and not be able to do anything about it?

"Dad?"

Nathan swirled around and saw Parker, Henley, and his father all staring at him wide-eyed, fixated on the red that stained his hands and shirt.

Jack was the first to speak, "Parker, take your sister upstairs."

After the kids left the kitchen, Jack walked over to Nathan and grabbed his face in his hands. He examined Nathan's face before finally asking, "Are you alright?"

Nathan pulled his face away. "I'm fine. I just didn't get a chance to clean up." Nathan walked out and bounded up the stairs two at a time.

He showered hoping to wash off the day. As hard as it was to leave behind what had happened earlier, he knew he had to focus on his family. He had made such a mess of things, and it was his responsibility to clean it up. He had to make it up to Parker—to Tess. He let her down by letting their son down, and that was unforgivable. His son didn't deserve a father like this. His son deserved so much more, and Tess, wherever she was, she deserved to know her children were being taken care of and that they were happy and loved.

He got cleaned up and went to set up the backyard. When he was done, he came back inside and yelled up to the kids to come out back. When they walked outside, they saw the campfire he had set up for them on the deck with pillows surrounding it like chairs. On the far side of the deck, he had set up a s'mores station complete with chocolate bars, graham crackers, and marshmallows. When Parker stepped towards Nathan, he handed him a marshmallow stick.

Nathan bowed his head and cleared his throat. "Normally I'd wake up and make waffles, and your mom—well she always knew how to make a day special." He hesitated slightly, choking on the bittersweet memories. "When you'd come home at the end of the day, she would have baked your favorite chocolate cake. I already messed up the first part of today, and well to be honest, I don't know that I could bake even if I tried."

"It's okay Dad. I don't really care about my birthday anyway." Parker shuffled his feet as he spoke.

"Thank you, Parker, but it's really not okay. I know this isn't much, and I know this isn't how it should be, but I was thinking we could just make this year different entirely. Just this once. Just this once we'll do birthdays differently, and I was thinking this year we'd do s'mores like we do when we go camping?"

Parker stared up at his dad and it was Henley who was the first to speak, "So does that mean Parker gets to eat eleven s'mores?"

Nathan couldn't help but laugh genuinely for the first time in ages. He crouched down and picked Henley up in his arms, hugging her closely. With Henley in his arms, he looked over at Parker. "Well? What do you say?"

Parker looked up at his sister and his dad and smiled as he nodded yes. The three of them sat around

the fire eating s'mores and laughing like they hadn't in a
long time.

Chapter Twenty-Four

"Suppan. Cofax. In my office." Marx yelled out from his office doorway.

Tommy and Nathan looked at each other once before they got up and headed into the captain's office.

"Close the door behind you."

"Captain?" Nathan eyed Marx as he sat there behind his desk rubbing his forehead.

"Sometimes I really hate this job. There really is no such thing as not taking your work home with you."

"Sir, why exactly have we been called in here?" Tommy asked, his interest obviously piqued.

Marx looked up and stared back at them as he huffed, "Because we've been given another message from the 'Blue Eyed Doll Killer'."

"Great, but what does that really have to do with us. Brady and Culter are the leads on the case." Nathan spoke petulantly. He had poured over those case files and was pissed when Marx assigned it to them.

"Not anymore." Marx grumbled as he slammed a file down on the desk in front of him. He thumbed through the file until he grabbed a surveillance photo and placed it in front of Nathan.

The photo was taken inside of the precinct; it was a photo of Nathan holding the last victim in his arms. His face had been circled with a jumbo, red sharpie. Nathan looked up at Marx quizzically. Marx nodded and motioned for him to turn it over.

On the back, in the same red sharpie, was a note:

I speak with Suppan and only Suppan

"What the hell is this?"

"Best guess? Maybe he picked you because you were the one to help the vic. But the thick of it is, we have absolutely no clue why he picked you or where he wants this to go."

Tommy spoke up with mutinous intent, "And you really want to play into his hand? Is that really the best idea?"

Marx grunted at Tommy's audacity. "Of course it's not a good idea, but we have eight bodies on our hands. The time for 'good ideas' passed long ago."

Nathan tossed the picture back towards Marx. "What do you want me to do?"

Tommy rocked back in his seat and rubbed his chin. Marx leaned forward and folded his hands on the desk.

"Keep working the case. Try to find a connection or find this girl he's talking about. And maybe he'll reach out to you, or maybe he won't."

As Tommy and Nathan left his office Tommy turned to Nathan. "Nate, man, do you really think this is a good idea?"

"No, but like Marx said, do you really have any better ones?"

"Dude, I'm just saying, think about the position this puts you in; how reckless it is."

Nathan felt his temperature begin to rise; there was that word again. The word Tess used so many times before, so many times when she waited each day for him to come home to her.

"Let it go Tommy." He spoke through clenched teeth trying to fight the onslaught of memories.

Tommy stared at Nathan's back as he watched him walk towards his desk, under his breath he muttered, "Man, if Tess could see you now."

Nathan could barely hear Tommy, but he was just loud enough. Nathan rushed at Tommy grabbing him by his shirt and pushed him against the wall. With his left arm he pinned Tommy's chest to the wall holding him there.

He put his face in close with Tommy's and spoke through gritted teeth, "Don't you *ever* fucking bring her up like that again."

Tommy stared back at Nathan with his mouth shut and his lips in a firm hard line. After a second of a stare off between them, Tommy pushed back and shoved Nathan away from him.

"Screw you Nate. Tess was my family too." Tommy pointed at himself in aggravated movements. "And those kids of yours are like my own flesh and blood. When Tess died who the hell do you think she left in charge to take care of you?"

Nathan waved a dismissive arm at Tommy.

Tommy exhaled deeply before continuing, "She left me in charge of watching out for you cause you're too damn stupid to do it yourself."

"Watch it Tommy, I'm warning you." Nathan pointed at Tommy. His eyes glared with irrefutable rage.

Tommy raised his arms out wide. "Go ahead Nate. Give me your best shot if it will make you feel better. Actually, if you could, I'd prefer it if you knock me out cold. That way at least I'll know that when Tess starts haunting my ass, I'll have an excuse as to why I wasn't watching your back."

Nathan stood facing Tommy with his fists clenched at his side and he breathed heavily trying to control his anger. Nathan couldn't form the words and as much as he would have loved to beat the crap out of someone, it shouldn't be Tommy. He took a look around him at all of the shocked faces with their eyes locked on the two of them. He exhaled deeply as he stalked out of the precinct without another word to Tommy.

•••••

Parker answered the door. "Hi, Uncle Tommy."

"Hey, my main man!" Tommy held out his hand for Parker to slap. "Look buddy, is your dad here?"

"What are you doing here Tommy?" Nathan ambled towards the front door with his arms crossed.

Tommy looked down at Parker and then back up at Nathan. Nathan shifted his weight. "Parker, can you give us a minute?"

Parker looked from Nathan to Tommy and just shook his head as he left the room.

"Look Tommy, I get what you're—"

"Nathan, I'm not here for you. Quite frankly, you deserve to get your ass handed to you, but I made a promise to Tess that I would always have your back no matter what. And, I guess in some ways I made a promise to your kids that I would make sure you always came home to them. So, if you decide you're going to be a one-way radio with this guy, then I have no choice but to help you. But, don't think for a second—I'm doing this for *you*."

Nathan bowed his head slightly as he shoved his hands into the pockets of his jeans. After a few seconds of standing in perpetual silence he shrugged his shoulders and gestured for Tommy to follow him into the garage. He knew there wasn't anything he could say. He knew he was wrong, but that didn't really matter. Truthfully, he wanted nothing more than to find this son of a bitch, and he knew that meant losing sight of self-preservation. And yet, somehow, Tess—even after death, found a way to humble him and keep him in check. Her hold over him, and over Tommy, was impenetrable. It would have pissed him off if he hadn't found it to be so damn like her.

Nathan flipped on the light and led Tommy over to his investigation board. Tommy took a moment to examine it and then leaned back and looked over at Nathan. "Is this everything?"

Nathan nodded yes as he took a seat. Tommy scratched his chin and hopped up on the tool bench. "Any theories?"

Nathan sighed as he leaned back. "Not really, but I'm thinking he's trying to get a story or a scene just right. I mean look at the time he takes to clean up the vics and positions them and everything. I would have initially thought it was repentance, but after sending in the last vic like he did—he's trying to tell us he has a story to tell."

"What kind of story?"

"I don't know. I didn't say it was a solid theory."

They both chuckled softly. Nathan scratched his head and looked over at Tommy. "When did you make Tess that promise?"

Tommy eyed Nathan with scrutiny before he spoke, "Well, I guess we always had an unspoken promise that I'd watch out for you, but clearly I wasn't doing a bang-up job, so Tess felt like she needed to spell it out for me."

Nathan laughed. "Yeah, that sounds like Tess."

Tommy smiled. "Yeah." He chuckled before continuing, "Anyway, it was after you two got back from North Carolina. She cornered me one night."

"Thomas Elliot Cofax." Tess spoke directly as she walked over and took a seat next to Tommy at the bar.

"How the hell do you know my middle name?"

She laughed freely and nudged him slightly. "I know a lot about a lot of things."

Tommy nudged her back. "You're gonna have to teach me that trick someday."

She widened her eyes playfully and tilted her head coquettishly. "What, and give away all my secrets?"

Tommy chuckled as he took a swig of his drink. He took a moment and then looked over at Tess. "Thank you for coming back."

Tess took a moment to consider it before she lightly patted Tommy's hand. "You two needed me. I couldn't leave you out in the cold." She winked at him.

"Always taking in strays?"

She shrugged and gave him an enigmatic smile. "So, Tommy," she cleared her throat slightly before continuing, "did Nathan tell you about what happened in North Carolina?"

"You mean the part about you being a swing dancing fool or him kicking your ex's ass to Timbuktu?"

Her eyes widened before they fell to her hands on the bar as she flushed slightly. She smiled to herself and chuckled lightly.

He scoffed into his drink. "Yeah, I heard, and I have to say, that's the one fight I wouldn't have tried to stop Nathan from getting in."

Tess looked over at Tommy with a puzzled expression.

"Are you really that surprised? The idea of someone hurting you pisses me off just as much as it pisses off Nate."

"Aw, Tommy." She wrapped her arm around him and pulled him into her giving him a soft hug.

"Yeah, yeah." He gently waved her off. "Well Tess, I know you didn't come here just to give me a hard time."

She eyed her hands folded on the bar in front of her. "I can't get anything passed you, can I?"

Tommy smiled genially and looked over at Tess waiting for whatever it was she came there to say.

Tess swallowed hard. "Truth is Tommy, Nathan means more to me than I thought possible. It's more than love, because aside from being the love of my life, he's given me a home—a family." She gently nudged Tommy indicating she meant him. "But most of all he's made me feel safe. Like I've finally been saved from everything bad in my life, and he was the one to do it. I can't let that go, Tommy."

Tommy sighed slightly. "What do you need me to do?" He asked as he turned and looked her in the eyes intently.

She looked up at him and smiled faintly. "Promise me you'll always watch out for him; that you'll always have his back? I need him to come home to me each night."

"I swear it."

Tess smiled and tried to hide the tears in her eyes as she quickly stood up and hugged Tommy tightly. She gave him a kiss on the cheek and squeezed his hand. "Thank you, Tommy."

He nodded his head and gave her a closed lip smile as she left the bar.

Tommy shook the memory away. "Truth is Nate, she needed you just as much as you needed her. She made me promise to watch out for you and make you sure you came home to her each night. As much as that last part kills me to say, I intend to keep my promise to her because that's what she deserves."

Nathan nodded that he understood. "Tess definitely had a way of making people see things her way, didn't she?"

Tommy laughed. "Sure did, but I dunno, I guess it was part of her charm and why we loved her so damn much."

Nathan squeezed his eyes shut forcing the tears to stay back. He groaned slightly. "Tommy, I miss her. I really miss her."

Tommy stood up and squeezed Nathan's shoulder. "I know Nate. I know. And as much as I would love to say differently, the truth is I can't imagine the day that you won't."

—•◦●◦•—

"Alright Tommy, I'll see you tomorrow." Nathan clapped Tommy's back as he started to open the front door for him to leave.

Tommy cocked his head to the right as he looked down at the floor mat in front of the door. He reached down and picked up a photograph left on the front porch.

Nathan watched as all the blood from Tommy's face depleted. "Tommy?"

Tommy handed the photo to Nathan with a shaky hand. Nathan looked down at the photo in his hand: it was a picture of Parker holding Henley's hand as he walked her into school. When Nathan flipped it over in red sharpie there was another message:

Have you found her yet? You know deputy that daughter of yours has the right blue eyes and white lovely skin. All she would need is some hair dye.

Nathan bolted back into the house dropping the photo as he ran. He bounded up the stairs and into Henley's room but it was empty.

"Henley!" Nathan screamed at the top of his lungs.

Parker and Henley popped their heads out from Parker's room at the sound of his voice. "Dad, what's wrong?"

Nathan fell down at their feet and grabbed Henley and squeezed her tight. The little girl giggled but Parker stared nonplussed at his father.

"Dad?"

Nathan shook his head and grabbed Parker and pulled him in for a hug. He sat there in the hallway holding onto them for a moment before he finally pulled away. With a hand on each of their faces he looked back and forth between the two of them. "I need you both to pack a bag. You're going to go visit Grandpa Dawson for a few days."

"Dad, what's going on?" Parker begged.

"Parker, I need you to do this, please. Help your sister as soon as you're done. Do not let her out of your sight, do you hear me?"

Parker stared unblinking at his father. Nathan quickly grabbed Parker by the shoulders. "Do you hear me?"

Parker seemed to shake out of his shock and nodded that he understood and he led Henley back into his room and quickly started packing.

Nathan ran back downstairs and grabbed his phone. As he was dialing he looked over at Tommy who answered his unspoken question, "I already called it in to dispatch. They're sending a unit over here and they're going to send another to take the kids to airport."

Nathan nodded a thank you as the phone connected. "Dad, I need you to get here as soon as you can and pack a bag."

"Nathan, I don't understand, how long do you want us to stay away for?" Jack asked as they stood out on the front porch.

Nathan rubbed his face. "I don't know Pops, as long as he's still out there? I don't know, all I know is he threatened my baby girl."

Jack shrugged his shoulders in quiet defeat. "Okay. Does Henry know we're coming?"

"Yeah, he'll be waiting for you at the airport when you arrive. I already gave him your arrival times and everything."

"What about you? What are you going to do?"

Nathan crossed his arms. "I'm going to catch the son of a bitch but I can't do that if I'm worrying about

Henley. I need both of my kids to be safe, and I need them to be far, far away from here."

"I get it son, and I'll do whatever you need me to do." He stuck his hand out for Nathan to shake and then he pulled him into a hug.

"A squad car is going to drive you to the airport, it's safer that way. And just give me a call every chance you get, especially to let me know you got in okay."

Jack nodded in agreement as Parker and Henley walked out front. Nathan leaned down and fixed Henley's coat. He looked back and forth between Parker and Henley. "Do you have everything?"

They both nodded a yes. Nathan hugged Henley tightly and then turned and hugged Parker. After finally letting go he breathed heavily as he spoke, "You two are gonna go with Grandpa Jack and you're gonna go visit Grandpa Dawson in North Carolina. You two will do exactly as Grandpa Jack says, and Parker, I'm counting on you to watch after your sister."

Parker nodded and reached his hand down to hold Henley's. "I will Dad."

Nathan ruffled Parker's hair. "You're a good kid, you know that? I love you both so much and I want a phone call every day." He pointed down at both of them and gave them one last small smile before he nodded to his father for them to leave.

Nathan watched as they drove off in the back of the squad car. Tommy walked up and clapped Nathan's shoulder.

Nathan immediately turned and strode back towards the garage with renewed purpose. "Let's end this."

Chapter Twenty-Five

"So, I'm thinking you were on the right track."

"What do you mean?"

Tommy scratched his head. "Both times he's asked if we've found her, so I'm thinking maybe you were right. Maybe he is trying to get a scene right, but he hasn't found the right girl yet."

"Is he blowing through these girls looking for one that finally fits, or is he finding ones that match the girl he's after?" They both knew the answer to that question revealed an even bigger question—it defined the murderer: serial killer or psychopath?

Tommy put his hands on the workbench and stared at the investigation board. "I don't know."

"Okay, well what do we know? We know that the vics are taken from all corners of the US, but they're all brought back here. So, is here ground zero? Home maybe?"

Tommy turned to look at Nathan. Something wasn't making sense to him. "Why hasn't this become a federal case?"

Nathan erected himself from his leaning position. He grabbed his phone and dialed Marx.

"Captain. It's Suppan. Not only has he crossed state lines, but we also know he's capable of hacking our systems, so why isn't Sitka crawling with feds?"

'Feds aren't coming boys. The bastard has been rerouting all of our messages to the bureau. We can't send anything out, so we're on our own.'

"If he's got that kind of Intel are we thinking he's one of our own?"

'It's something that's crossed my mind a few times, but truth is we only know what he wants us to know.'

Nathan clenched the phone in his hand after he hung up.

Tommy shook his head. "This case just gets uglier by the second, don't it?"

"I think he grew up here. I mean why else would he continuously bring the girls back here?"

"Okay, so, if he grew up here, you're thinking what? Look at anyone with law or military experience under their belt?"

"It's a start."

"Yeah, but Nate, that's also our whole force, not to mention countless others in this town."

Nathan took a moment to look up at the board. He stared intently at it, and then he quickly shuffled through loose papers on the workbench.

"What are you looking for?"

"This." Nathan pulled out a map of Sitka and a black sharpie. He looked up at the board as he spoke, "I want to map out the locations of each vic." After he finished, each location was erratic with seemingly no pattern.

Nathan was staring down at the map when the phone rang. Without tearing his eyes away from the map, he answered absentmindedly, "Yeah?"

'Deputy Suppan, pleasure to meet you.'

Nathan stood up quickly and stiffened. "Who is this?"

'I think you know.'

The voice was scrambled, but he knew it was their guy. He signaled to Tommy to trace the call.

'I'll take your silence as a yes.'

"You threatened my daughter." Nathan's voice was barely louder than a whisper, but was laced with deadly intent.

'No Deputy, I think you have me all wrong. That wasn't a threat, merely an observation.'

Nathan hissed into the phone, "If anyone that I love so much as gets a paper cut, I will burn your world down to the ground."

'Yes, I see. Tell me Deputy, have you found her yet?' He mused obviously unphased by Nathan's threat.

"It's not like you've given me much to go on."

'Well, that's just not true, is it? I'd say you're getting somewhere with that map of yours.'

Nathan's eyes darted around his garage and over to the security camera he had installed years ago and saw that it was blinking with a red light. Nathan walked towards it looking up at it.

'*You should have guessed by now that I see all.*'

"I'm starting to get that." Nathan spoke as he reached up and yanked the camera from the wall.

The man snickered.

"Why me? Why even contact us?"

'*In due time Deputy, you may be useful to me. As for you personally, why not?*'

Nathan felt his jaw tighten and his body became rigid.

He heard the man on the other end laugh. '*Well, I'll let you get back to your work, but Deputy, if I were you—I'd start with one.*'

Nathan heard the phone click and turned around to look at Tommy who was staring at him with an exasperated look and his hands in the air. The call wasn't long enough to make the trace.

"He said I was on to something with my map and then he said if he were me, he'd start with one."

"With one? What the hell does that mean? Victim number one?"

Nathan rushed back over to the workbench. "Location number one." He pointed at the University of Alaska Southeast's campus. "There. That's location number one."

"Okay, so what? We have no leads, no witnesses, nothing."

"Maybe he was enrolled there."

"Nate, we're grasping at straws."

Nathan put his hands up over his head. "I know, but I am out of ideas."

•◦◆◦•

It was a little after two-thirty in the morning by the time he walked into his bedroom. He and Tommy had gone over every piece of evidence repeatedly, but they were still coming up empty. He wiped his face from exhaustion as he slowly sauntered in towards the bed. He jumped slightly when he noticed her. Tess was sitting on the edge of the bed basking in the rays of the moonlight seeping in from their window.

"Tess?"

She turned and smiled warmly. "Hi handsome."

He shuffled over to the chair by the bed and sat down staring back at her. "Tess, you came back."

She shrugged her shoulders lightly as if it was obvious she would come back. "You needed my help."

He shook his head. "Tess, I've needed your help for a long time now." He eyed her carefully and his expression changed. "This is about the case, isn't it?"

She stared emotionlessly back at him in silence.

He nodded. "It is. Look Tess, I got the kids out of here. They're safe. They're staying with my dad and yours in North Carolina."

She smiled softly. "That's not why I'm here. I trust you to keep them safe."

"Then why?" He wanted to eat his words as soon as they left his mouth. He was more than thrilled to see her, he didn't mean for what he said to sound so rough.

She cocked her head slightly and sighed. "Because you aren't seeing it yet."

"What Tess? What am I not seeing?" His tone was pleading.

"What all the locations have in common."

He shook his head. "There isn't anything in common. All of them are random dead-end places."

"Places like you used to take me?"

His head shot up at her remark. "What?"

She gracefully stood up from the bed and walked over to the window and stared out. She stood quietly for a moment and then turned to look at him, a light dancing in her eyes. "Remember when you took me to see that truly horrible Hitchcock film?"

He chuckled. "The Birds. I remember. You were terrified of anything with wings for an entire week after that."

She laughed with him. "Or, remember that time I dragged you to see the New Archangel dancers at Harrigan Centennial Hall?"

He smiled to himself remembering the memories flooding back from his first few months dating Tess.

"Or, what about when you took me to Ludvig's Bistro or when we went kayaking or hiking?"

"The locations are all dates, aren't they?" Nathan scratched his head and stood up. "They're all places he went to with *this* girl. The girl he's trying to find was his girlfriend, wasn't she?"

Nathan looked up at Tess; she gave him the faint trace of a smile.

"But, he told me to look at location one. It's a college. I don't think taking you to a college would have been much of a date."

"What would our location one be?"

"The carnival." He said without hesitation.

She shrugged in response. "I would have said the parking lot of the Spar."

His brow furrowed. "We didn't have a date there." She stayed silent as he processed. "But, that is where we met for the first time."

He smiled widely up at her. "Tess, you are a genius."

She shrugged her shoulders and smiled modestly. Nathan could feel his muscles tensing. It would have been natural to walk right over to Tess and plant one on her. His excitement was short lived when he realized he could never do that again.

"Will you stay tonight?"

"I don't know if that's such a good idea."

"Please, stay." He looked up at her under hooded eyes.

She exhaled. "Okay, Nathan. I'll stay."

He gently laid her limp body on the cold, wet pavement. When he looked down at her, her wild hair lay out around her; her peach colored dress was now stained brown in spots and clung tightly to her like a second skin. He looked at her hands. They looked so frail and cold, and he could see that her wedding band looked loose around her finger. She was so cold. Her lips had turned blue and her once luminous white skin was now pale and bleak. He gently brushed the hair away from her face and noticed a red clump that slowly leaked down the side of her temple. As if woken from a trance, he abruptly sprang into action trying to save her.

He tilted her head back slightly as he breathed into her. He then began doing chest compressions. "Come on baby, come back to me."

After the first set of compressions, he leaned forward again breathing into her. He rocked back on his heels and began the compressions again. "Don't do this Tess, don't leave me. Come on baby, come back!"

After countless tries, when he knew there was nothing he could do, he fell forward with his head on her chest, and he cried. With his left hand, he gently squeezed her shoulder. "Baby. Please. Come back. Please don't leave."

He continued to lean with his head against her chest listening to the rain pound down on the pavement around them. It wasn't fair; none of this was fair. He sat up assertively and began to pump her chest again. He couldn't give up—not yet.

"One, two, three, four. Breathe baby, just breathe."

Nathan woke up panting. Tess walked over from the window and took a seat next to him on the bed.

"Another nightmare?"

Nathan rubbed his eyes as he sat up in bed. "A variation of the same."

She looked at him with pain in her eyes.

"Tess?"

"I don't understand why you can't see or feel it."

"Feel what?"

"Feel in your heart that I am okay?" She held her hand against her chest as she spoke.

"Tess I—"

"No, Nathan—I don't understand. There are some things in this world the brain cannot understand but the heart *feels*. Your brain cannot process that I am okay, but your heart—you should be able to see that I am okay, *feel* that I am happy." Her voice shook and he could see just how distraught this made her.

He sighed heavily. "Do you want to know the truth? I mean the real truth, the deep dark secrets?"

She looked up at him and stared into his eyes. "You know why your heart won't accept it?"

He exhaled sadly as he gathered courage to speak, "Did you know Henley has me tell her your bedtime story about angels almost nightly?"

"Nathan, what does that have to do with anything?" A look of confusion flashed across her face.

He shifted in the bed pulling his knees up and resting his arms on them.

"Tess, I want to be selfish with you. I want you to stay here every moment of forever. I never want you to leave my side—dead or alive. But the truth is, you're still here."

"Nathan, I don't understand?"

He sat frozen in place, a grieving effigy. He then tilted his face so their eyes could meet as he spoke, and she could see the anguish in them. "Tess, why hasn't your angel wrapped you in its wings and flown you into heaven?"

That was it. This is what it had always been about. For as much as he missed her, for as happy as he was to see her, he thought seeing her meant she couldn't get into heaven. That she was incapable of moving on because of him.

Her eyes widened and she sighed softly finally understanding. "Maybe I told my angel I wasn't ready. Maybe all I am is a figment of your imagination, something your mind conjured up to help you heal. Maybe all I am is a ghost. Or maybe—I'm *your* angel."

"Tess, what are you saying?"

"I'm saying I can't explain it to you yet, but regardless of the 'how'—there is a reason why I'm here and it's not because I'm shut out of heaven."

Chapter Twenty-Six

"Are we really saying this is our guy?" Tommy crossed his arms as he stared at a photo on their investigation board at the station.

Nathan sauntered up next to Tommy. "It fits. Witnesses confirm seeing a girl matching our descriptions with this guy at every one of the locations."

"Right, but when we traced this girl's cards, she's a legal blonde and always has been."

Nathan held up a finger as he walked around the desk and picked up a file. "April Marie Young, 5'5'', 24 years old, blue eyes, Caucasian, black hair."

"Where did you find that?"

Nathan handed over the file. "When she first enrolled into the university that was her profile. Since then, she's gone back through and updated all of her information including DMV records to match her blonde hair. Oh, and did I mention she started going by her middle name now?"

"Marie? I'll be damned. You did good Nate."

"Actually, I did even better."

Tommy looked up from the file to see Nathan smiling.

"So, Tess made me think—"

"I'm sorry, did you just say Tess?" Tommy cut Nathan off mid-sentence.

Nathan waved Tommy off. "That's not the point. Point is I found a theme with their dates. Each date, no matter how remote, had something to do with art and culture."

"So?"

Nathan exhaled subtly, thankful that Tommy had already forgotten what he heard Nathan say about Tess.

"So, April, or Marie, I guess—studied ancient languages and cultures. She was particularly interested in Tlingit."

"Nate, you're gonna have to dumb this down for me."

"Exactly eight months ago, April Young up and took off on a sabbatical to Siberia where she was studying the paths of the first Russian settlers of Baranof. Same time she changed her hair color and started using her middle name."

Tommy stared blankly at Nathan.

Nathan huffed, "Dude, seven months ago the first vic popped up and he's killed a victim once a month since then. That's in addition to this guy being way good with the tech stuff. His major was in Technical Engineering, and he was at the top of his class."

"Right, but what about a military or law background? He doesn't exactly have that."

"Actually—he does. I had to dig for it, but he did go through basic at Fort Benning. Right after, he worked in a cyber terrorism unit for about six months before being dishonorably discharged. After he was discharged, he came back home and enrolled at UAS."

"Discharged for what?"

Nathan shrugged in irritation. "Couldn't get any further, his files are considered classified. Honestly, I'm impressed I found out as much as I did, almost feels too easy, like he wanted me to know."

Tommy crossed his arms over his chest. "Okay, say I'm on board with this, say this really is our guy, how are we gonna prove it?"

"Get April Young to come in."

"I thought you just said she was on sabbatical?"

"And that, my friend, is why I am so good. April Young just flew in and as of twelve minutes ago, is now in our interrogation room."

"That's awesome, except one problem."

Nathan looked over at Tommy. "Oh yeah, and what's that?"

"Psycho killer made you his one-way radio. He's hacked our system, and not to mention is probably capable of hacking every video feed within the city. Bringing April in, don't you think he's going to notice? We will have literally delivered her on a silver platter."

Nathan loosely shook a finger at Tommy. "I thought about that, but here's the thing. He didn't know where she was which is why he contacted us. The only reason I even know is because I noticed the theme to their dates and happened to stumble across the *one* professor at UAS who knew about April's involvement in this research project. But, figuring he may have realized my game plan, I decided to call an audible. April flew into Sitka Rocky Gutierrez Airport, or so all of her plane information says, but really, a private third party flew her in. All paper trails lead to her coming in by commercial, but I have her coming in the back door."

Tommy stared dumbly at Nathan who was beaming with pride and maybe a little arrogance as Marx walked up to them.

"Well, you boys ready?"

"Ms. Young, thank you for coming." Nathan spoke as he calmly sat down across from April while Tommy leaned up against the wall.

She nodded. "I don't really see how I had a choice. I mean I was rushed out of a plane and into a prop plane and flown here. Care to fill in the blanks?" She responded acidly.

"Ms. Young, are you aware of the 'Blue Eyed Doll Killer'?"

"Is that some kind of band?" She asked sarcastically.

Nathan chuckled lightly; the girl was shrewd, he'd give her that. "I wish. Truth is, Sitka has been plagued by a sick, twisted son of a bitch who's playing God."

That got her attention. She looked across at Nathan and stared intently at him, her demeanor obviously more contrite.

"In the past seven months there have been eight murders. Our killer is smart and calculated. He's covered every trace of himself. He takes risks and has become bolder and bolder."

"What does that have to do with me?" Her tone more sincere now.

Nathan sighed heavily before continuing, "Each victim was a female, mid-twenties, jet black hair, blue eyes, and pale, white skin."

The color immediately drained from her face.

"You think I'm next?"

Nathan looked over at Tommy and then back at April. "No April. The truth is, we think all of these killings, well we believe it has to do with you."

"Brooks."

Tommy leaned forward perceptibly intrigued. "Now, why would you say that name?"

"He's my ex. He's the reason I ran off to Siberia—literally," she huffed the irony not lost on her, "but this—you think it's him, don't you?"

"This murderer, he put his victims on display, for a lack of a better word, but he put them on display in locations that you have been to."

"What do you mean?"

Nathan sighed again. He knew he was breaking this girl. To put this kind of burden on her was unfair, but he had to do everything within his power to catch him. Unfortunately, in a situation like this, truth was his deadliest weapon and his most powerful ally.

"Each of the locations has been confirmed as places you went to while dating him."

She put a hand over her mouth trying to stifle a cry. Nathan and Tommy stayed silent to give her a moment.

"What do you want to know?" She collected herself and looked up at Nathan with her brow furrowed in remorseful determination.

Nathan smiled intrinsically; he admired her bravery and resolution to do the right thing.

"What can you tell us about him? About your relationship with him?" Nathan folded his hands on the table in front of him and leaned forward.

April exhaled deeply. "We met at UAS. We ran with the same crowd and were friends, and then eventually started dating. I was with him for a little over two years."

"What happened?" Tommy asked her.

She looked up at him from her seat. "Well, the truth is, it started off as us wanting different things, and we just approached things on different levels."

"Like fundamentals such as religion or marriage?" Nathan tried to piece together the muddled picture.

"Like, I always wanted to explore the world. He wanted to stay here. I had dreams and goals, but with him, it was so damn hard to get him to do anything other than exactly what he wanted. He could never think outside of himself."

She looked up at them and chuckled to herself. "Sounds really lame when you say it out loud, but the point was, we never saw eye to eye on anything, and because of it, we fought constantly. He believed my duty was to stand by his side. I was never allowed an opinion of my own and I continuously found myself giving up certain dreams or goals so I could be there for him."

"So, you left him and decided to give yourself a full makeover?"

"Not exactly. I stayed with him; I think out of fear that maybe he was all I was ever going to get." She played with her hands as she spoke, "I don't know. I think I had finally resolved myself that this was going to be my life."

"But then something happened." Nathan eyed her carefully, the way she stared down at her fingertips, it was exactly like Tess. When Tess finally told Nathan about Bobby, he remembered watching her so intently. The way she kept her eyes glued to her hands, so ashamed of her past, so afraid to look him in the eye as she spoke. Maybe it was because she didn't want his pity, but he thought it was more for the fact that she wanted more than anything for it to not be her truth.

"It wasn't as if it was one incident, more just like things kept piling one on top of another until I finally felt like the walls were collapsing down on me. He was always controlling, but it became incessant. I mean, he hacked into all of my accounts: bank records, phone bills, social media, email—you name it, and he hacked it. He censored every inch of my tech life. But, it didn't stop there; his reach far extended that. He got me kicked out of my apartment so I had no choice but to move in with him."

"You didn't have family you could stay with?"

"Honestly, I think that may be why I stayed as long as I did. My parents died when I was young, so I grew up in the system, bouncing from foster home to foster home. I never had a family, not until Brooks anyway. With Brooks I was finally a part of something special, and it really had nothing to do with him and had everything to do with his family. His family welcomed me with open arms and treated me as one of their own. For over two years I had a mother, a father, two brothers, and a sister. The idea of ever letting that go became my justification for staying."

Tommy took a step forward. "Ms. Young, April, or Marie, or whoever you are, I know it's difficult, but you need to tell us what happened."

She looked up at Tommy with a steely resolve glinting in her eyes. "He hit me. He hit me, and I broke up with him and stayed with a friend. Within hours, he found me and dragged me back home. He apologized profusely and I'm ashamed to say it, but I believed him." She paused as she looked back down at her hands on the table. "So, I stayed with him. The arguments continued. His possession over me worsened—I found out he hacked the GPS in my phone and my car, and he even went so far as to put surveillance cameras in our apartment. He literally watched my every move. Do you know what that's like? To be monitored, and studied, and watched, twenty-four seven?"

Nathan cleared his throat. "I can imagine."

April looked up at him with vehement candor. "No, you really can't."

Nathan bowed his head in concession and remained silent.

"I found out I had been accepted as a research assistant to travel to Siberia for further research of the Russian influence and heritage of Baranof. I had forgotten I even applied. I applied eighteen months prior, and that was on a whim. When I found out, I just left. While he was in class one day I packed a bag, liquidated all of my accounts, and paid cash for everything. Brooks can't leave the country due to his military discharge conditions, so I knew I would be safe to re-identify myself in Russia. By the time I reached Petropavlovsk-Kamchatsky, I bought hair bleach and with the help of a few tech savvy research peers, I changed my name to Marie and effectively wiped every other trace of me off the planet. I kept my school records and everything, but as far as email, banks, social media—April Young no longer existed."

"And you've stayed hidden ever since?"

"Yes and no. I stayed in Siberia because I truly loved my job, and an experience like that, it doesn't happen often. But really, I decided to stay there not just because of Brooks, but also because I couldn't bear to face his family. For as much as I wanted away from him, I loved that family and the thought of me hurting them by abandoning them, the guilt I felt—the guilt I still feel was more than I could bear."

Tommy shifted where he stood. "So why come back now?"

"The professor I was assisting was presenting his findings and as terrified as I was to come here, I needed to see this project through. Wait, how did you know when I was coming?" Fear flashed across her face.

"Actually, most of that was luck. We only just suspected Brooks and you. I only found about your arrival in the US because a professor at UAS told me about the project you were presenting in a week."

She nodded, and then she cleared her throat. "Why is he doing this?"

Tommy leaned back against the wall and shoved his hands in his pockets before nodding to Nathan to fill her in.

"We don't know necessarily. At first, we believed it was as if he was trying to play out a scene that he couldn't get right. Most likely because he couldn't get the girl right. But then, a couple weeks ago, he delivered a message asking if we had 'found her yet'. My best guess, he's looking for you and had been trying to get your attention. When he didn't get that, he turned to us for forced help."

"What are you going to do?" She looked up under hooded eyes.

Nathan leaned forward. "We have enough reason to bring him in, and I'm hoping with your help, we can do that."

She looked over at Tommy and then to Nathan as she shook her head yes.

Chapter Twenty-Seven

Nathan looked over at Tommy as they stood on opposite sides of the door. Tommy steadied the gun in his hand and nodded to Nathan that he was ready.

Nathan took a deep breath before he quickly turned and kicked the door in.

"Sitka Police!" Nathan and Tommy declared in unison.

Nathan's eyes darted around the room as Tommy and two officers stepped inside and began sweeping the place. He couldn't help but shake the feeling that something was wrong. From what April said, this place was his fortress. He rented an office space in the basement of his apartment complex; an office that, as April described, should be lined with a number of computers and hard drive systems. The place should be radioactive with technology, but, from the looks of it, there was nothing there. The walls were barren. There was one wooden chair in the corner, two wires hung loose on the ground, but that was it.

"Nate." Tommy pulled Nathan's attention to the far end of the room. Tommy opened what was originally assumed a closet. When he opened it, both he and Nathan walked into a second room. In the room there was a small folding table in the center of the room with a single computer monitor on it.

Nathan holstered his gun as he approached the screen. The screen was a live video feed of them entering the room. Nathan looked up to the upper right hand of the room and saw a small camera blinking with a red light. He clenched his fists as he looked back at the screen. Taped to the middle of the screen was a small piece of paper with a note written in red sharpie:

Did you really think it would be that easy?

———•••◆•◆••———

"Ms. Young is there any other place you can think of?" Nathan took a seat on the corner of the table.

"I wish I could, but, truthfully, when he wasn't with me or in class, he stayed locked away in that place."

Nathan sighed. "Alright. Well, listen, if his end game really is to find you, then we absolutely have to keep your presence here a secret. No phone calls, no nothing. You are on lockdown, but it's for your own protection, I promise."

She folded her hands and kept her eyes down. "I understand."

When Nathan pulled into the driveway, he watched as the headlights washed across the front porch. More than anything he wished she were sitting there waiting for him. She had this uncanny ability to know exactly when he needed her most. Tonight, would have been one of those nights.

He sighed heavily before slowly crawling out of the car. He kept his head down as he walked to the front door. Fumbling with his keys, he finally looked up. There she was, smiling gently with the tilt of her head in puzzlement as he laughed quietly.

"I shouldn't be surprised, should I?"

She shrugged her shoulders before she said the same thing she told him all those years ago, "I just didn't think you should be alone tonight."

He smiled as he walked up and took a seat on the porch swing. She waited a moment before taking a seat next to him. She looked over and waited for him to tell her about his day.

He leaned forward putting his elbows on his thighs and resting his chin on his fists. "I told a girl it was basically her fault for all these killings. I told her that so I could catch the bastard, thinking that would make up for it. If I caught him, maybe me telling her those things would somehow make it justifiable. But, it turns out, he's always one step ahead."

Tess sat patiently by his side in silence. She knew that what he really needed was for her to just listen.

Nathan peered up at her. "Tess, what if I can't find him? What if I ruined that poor girl's life for no reason? What if—what if I can't bring our children home?"

"I admire you, you know that?"

"Why?" Her question disarmed him completely; that was the furthest thing he ever expected her to say.

She sighed lightly as she rubbed her knees. "Because you have the ability and the strength to make the hard decisions when it's crucial. What you did by telling that girl the truth was neither good nor evil, it was necessary."

"How can you be so sure?"

"Because no matter how hard you beat yourself up for your short comings, you have always been and will always continue to be the good guy."

"Nathan."

He groggily opened his eyes at the sound of her voice. "Tess? What is it?"

He rubbed his eyes to try to wake himself. Tess stood at the foot of the bed in the early morning light. He looked up at her and smiled. She was so beautiful. She smiled back at him and then disappeared.

"Tess?" Nathan jolted up in bed. He didn't understand why she would appear and then just leave.

He tried to shake it off as he got dressed. Something felt wrong, but he knew he had to focus on finding Brooks. He owed it to April. He owed it to all those girls. He owed it to his children. And, he owed it to Tess. He would find this guy and he would be the good guy. He would be the man she believed him to be.

When he opened the front door to leave, something on the welcome mat caught his eyes. As he looked down at the cell phone sitting there, it rang. Nathan felt his body tense. He knew it was him. He quickly bent down to retrieve it, but he held it in his hand for a moment trying to muster the strength to answer it.

"Brooks." Nathan hissed out.

'Deputy, it's so good to hear from you.'

"Wish I could say the same." Nathan's eyes scanned the street looking for any signs of Brooks.

'Aw, now you're hurting my feelings.'

"Kiss my ass."

'Wow, language. Did you kiss your wife with that mouth?'

"Listen you son of a bitch—"

'Deputy, I've been playing nice so far, it's you who is playing dirty.'

"What?"

'You have something of mine. Give her to me and I will leave you alone.'

"You know that's not gonna happen." He spoke through gritted teeth. He knew it was a real possibility that Brooks knew they had April, but he hoped he had more time to create a plan.

'Do you know why I picked you, Deputy?'

Nathan stayed silent as he mentally cursed himself for not trusting his gut that there had always been a purpose as to why he was chosen.

'I picked you because I know that you know what it feels like to lose someone. To have someone ripped from your world and to never be seen again.'

"Don't you dare talk about my wife." He yelled into the phone as his temperature began to rise.

'But Tess was such a beautiful woman. I understand how much you must miss her. To not be able to hold her, to kiss her—to not have her there to help raise those two kids of yours.'

Nathan swallowed hard trying to fight back both the anger and the tears building behind his eyes.

'See, you and I have more in common than you know. I too, lost someone I love. All I want is to have her back.'

"You disgust me."

'Fine Nathan, if you don't want to admit it, that's fine. You're only lying to yourself. Anyway, it doesn't really matter. You will give me April or I will kill someone every twenty-four hours until you do so. Who knows, maybe next time it'll be a lovely woman with red hair and green eyes, or maybe a boy, eleven or twelve years old, or maybe I'll just kill a little girl with big, blue eyes, just like your daughter.'

Nathan moved the phone away from his mouth trying to get his breathing under control before he replied. "Where should I meet you?"

'I'll be in touch—'

Chapter Twenty-Eight

Nathan sat on the hood of the Impala as he stared down at the water below him. The wind howled through the marina, rattling the boats against the docks like a warning whispered in the dark. His mind wandered in and out of the flood of memories tied to the marina and he felt a fire deep in the pit of his gut. Anger flared through him that Brooks took his town from him. Darkness had fallen on Sitka when he lost Tess, but not like this. The darkness without Tess was in absence of her light—but the darkness here now, was a shroud of evil. He took a steadying breath as he made his resolve to end this once and for all.

Nathan raced through town trying to get to the station. He was in the process of dialing Tommy when he saw her in his rearview mirror. He slammed on the breaks bringing the Impala to a screeching stop. He looked back over his shoulder and saw her standing there.

Tess stood at the crossroad staring intently at Nathan. The peach-colored dress she wore on their anniversary waved gently in the cool breeze. Her wild, reddish-brown curls danced across her face as she watched him looking at her. She stood patiently for a moment and then turned and started walking down the road away from Nathan.

As he watched her walk away, she slowly began to fade away until she was gone completely. He whipped back around in his seat facing forward and gripped the steering wheel tightly. He tried to calm his aggravated breathing and swallow the lump that formed in his throat. As he sat there panting, he slowly wiped the cold sweat from his forehead. He understood everything now.

"Nate, what do you mean you know where Brooks is? How do you know?" Tommy questioned Nathan as he walked through the station towards the captain's office.

"He knows about Tess. That's why he chose me."

Tommy stopped dead in his tracks. Nathan slowly stopped walking. He turned around to face Tommy.

He took a deep breath with his brow furrowed in pain. "He chose me because he says I understand what it's like to lose someone that you love."

"Nate—" Tommy's voice was strained.

"It doesn't matter why he picked me, all that matters is that I know where he is."

"Where?"

"If he knows about Tess, then he knows everything."

Tommy looked at Nathan with a slight scowl on his face. "What does that mean?"

Nathan shrugged his shoulders despondently. "It means he's hiding in the one place he knows I would never go."

Tommy looked at Nathan questioningly.

Nathan dropped his head as he spoke, "The bridge, Tommy."

Tommy bowed his head as soon as Nathan said it. Truth was, even after nearly a year of her being gone, he would find himself taking any route that didn't involve crossing that bridge.

"You haven't gone there?"

Nathan closed his mouth in a firm line and shook his head. "I couldn't. I couldn't go back there. It was too much, too painful, I just—"

"You're sure he's there?" Tommy cut him off so Nathan wouldn't have to finish that thought.

Nathan nodded. "I know he is. There's an abandoned bunker on the north side, military or something, but yeah, I know he's there."

"But, how do you know? Did he tell you?"

"No, the opposite in fact. He made some pretty convincing threats this morning, and I agreed to meet him and give him April."

"You did what now?" Tommy's eyes grew wide in bewilderment.

Nathan waved him off. "I'm not that stupid Tommy. I was just trying to buy myself some time, and then I figured it out on the way over here."

"How?"

"Tommy, I need you just to trust me and know that I will explain some day, but that day isn't today."

Tommy eyed him carefully for a moment before responding, "Okay Nate. I have your back."

Nathan nodded a silent thank you as they walked into Marx's office.

———————•••••———————

Nathan took lead as they slowly approached the entrance to the bunker. It was quiet out. The woods behind the bunker were dense and a cool gust of wind rattled and shook the branches of the trees. Nathan breathed heavily watching his breath curl up like smoke around him. He glanced back over his shoulder at the truss bridge. When he looked over he saw her standing there watching over him. Her dress swayed in the wind and snow began to gently drift down around her. He tried to fight back tears; this was the first time he had been to the bridge since the accident. He saw it nightly in his dreams, in his nightmares, where Tess died over and over again. But now, as he watched her standing on the bridge looking down over him, something felt different, and he had no clue why.

He turned back to focus on the door in front of him. With his gun held out in his hands, he quietly crept closer to the door before silently signaling S.W.A.T. to enter behind him.

Nathan quietly snuck in through a loose panel on the door. When he entered, he walked out onto a small platform at the top of a staircase. Water dripped from the ceiling and from the broken pipes lining the concrete walls. Nearly everything metal was covered in a layer of rust.

He quickly scanned the bunker around him and then looked back at Tommy to motion for him to follow him down the stairs.

Once he reached the bottom, he realized he was in what looked like an electrical tunnel. Wires and pipes ran along the concrete walls and ceilings. The metal hissed and vibrated, and the ground was covered in a layer of water from a sprung leak. Nathan clicked on his flashlight and followed the cables. He could hear them humming and realized they were powering something. Nathan and Tommy quietly made their way down the corridor. Nathan noticed a door with a shaft of light under it. He motioned for Tommy to look. Tommy saw it and nodded to Nathan.

Nathan silently counted to three as he slowly turned the doorknob and pushed the door open. As they entered, they were faced with a front room that connected to others. They saw six computer monitors all pulled up to surveillance cameras in Sitka. There were cameras angled on the department, at UAS campus, on Nathan's street corner—he realized this was how Brooks was monitoring them and staying one step ahead of them at every turn. His lips turned upward into a twisted smile when he noticed the loop he had their surveillance team play for the camera on the precinct. No way did Brooks know their team was coming, at least not until it was too late.

As Nathan stepped closer, he noticed that next to a computer there was a half empty cup of still steaming coffee. He quickly turned and signaled to Tommy to keep moving.

As Nathan rounded the next open door he caught movement out of the corner of his eye. He saw Brooks make a run for it through the kitchen. Nathan holstered his gun and took off running after him. Brooks was quick, but so was Nathan. Nathan cut him off and had him confined to the kitchen with nowhere to go, unless it was through Nathan.

As Nathan stood in the kitchen entrance he smiled with a sinister sneer at Brooks. Brooks glared at him as Nathan took in his image. He was a decently sized man, maybe a little smaller than Nathan and without his athletic build. With snarled lips, brown eyes looking black in the light, Brooks glowered at Nathan. His short beard and the bags under his eyes made him look wild and desperate.

Nathan gleamed to himself knowing Brooks was finished and would rot in prison for the rest of his life. Before Nathan had time to react, Brooks charged at Nathan taking him down to the ground. He was slammed against the cold concrete, but he quickly recovered using his feet to shove Brooks off. Nathan's thrust was hard enough to throw Brooks back into the oven. He smiled when he heard Brooks fall against the oven's edge and let out a gurgled moan.

Brooks lost his balance momentarily but easily stood back up.

"Really Nathan? From your past I thought I would be more impressed with your fighting, but truthfully, it's a little lacking." Brooks spoke with a disdainfully nonchalant voice.

Nathan grinned menacingly and shook his head slightly taunting him forward. Brooks lunged forward connecting hard with Nathan's jaw. The blow made Nathan stumble backwards. He had to give it to Brooks; at least he was smart enough to go for the jaw rather than his gut, which was protected by Kevlar.

When he gained his footing, Nathan rubbed his jaw in time to defend Brooks' next lunge. Thinking quickly, he grabbed a towel from the counter next to him and wrapped it around Brooks' outstretched arm. Twisting it, he was able to pull Brooks' arm around him. With Brooks off balance, he lifted the towel and wrapped it around his throat. Nathan yanked hard making him stumble. As Brooks tried to get his feet beneath him, Nathan let go of the towel and shoved Brooks into the wall with a kick to the gut.

Brooks doubled over. As Nathan advanced, Brooks corrected himself and met Nathan face on. They locked onto each other's shoulders and Brooks gained momentum. He threw Nathan onto the kitchen table and was pinning him down as Nathan swatted his left arm away, breaking Brooks' hold on him. Nathan used both hands to grab Brooks' right arm and twisted it turning Brooks away from him. Brooks fumbled forward. Grunting heavily, he turned around to attack Nathan but froze in his tracks.

Four red dots appeared on his chest. He slowly raised his hands over his head. Nathan swiveled around on the table and looked up at the kitchen entrance. Tommy and four S.W.A.T. officers were facing Brooks with their guns locked in position.

As a S.W.A.T. member cuffed Brooks, Nathan sauntered over and leaned forward towards his ear. "You and I are nothing alike. Because unlike you, I never had to hunt to find the woman who I loved and lost—and she actually loved me back." He whispered quietly before Brooks was led out of the room.

Chapter Twenty-Nine

Nathan leaned against his desk silently waiting for April to speak. Even after he told her that Brooks was in custody, that she was safe and all of this was over, she still stayed silent. He couldn't blame her. What could be said in this kind of situation?

His attention was drawn to another deputy who walked up to him. "Suppan, there's somebody here you might want to talk to."

Nathan motioned to April that he would be back and he followed the deputy out to the lobby. Standing in the lobby with his arms crossed was a man in his late twenties with similar features to Brooks.

Nathan eyed him carefully as he approached him. "I'm Nathan Suppan. How can I help you—?"

He paused waiting for the disheveled man to introduce himself.

"Uh Daniel, Daniel Warren."

Nathan nodded his head. His intuition was right. "What can I do for you Mr. Warren?"

"My brother, he was the 'Blue Eye Doll Killer'—wasn't he?" His voice shook subtly with acquiesced resistance.

Nathan put his hands in his pocket and peered over at Daniel.

"Oh my god, he really is, isn't he?" Daniel put his hands over his head and tried to control his breathing.

"Mr. Warren, I understand this must be difficult to hear, but I need to know, how did you find out? We haven't released his name to any media outlets."

Daniel brought his arms back down to the side. "Truth is, when I started hearing about this killer and his victims, the thought crossed my mind. The girls sounded so much like his ex, but I don't know, I couldn't believe it. He's my brother. I never wanted this to be true."

Nathan nodded in understanding of his apprehension.

"I really wasn't sure, but a buddy of mine says he swore he saw April Young come in here. He said she was blonde, but he could've sworn it was her. When I heard that—I knew it was true then. My brother is a *murderer*." Disgust masked as sadness crossed his face as he ushered the last word.

"Daniel?"

Nathan swiveled around to see April standing behind him staring at Brooks' brother.

Daniel eyed her carefully before nodding for her to come forward. She ran to him and he embraced her in his arms. Nathan could hear her sobbing into Daniel's chest.

"I don't understand Daniel. How could Brooks do something so—"

"Insidious?" He finished for her.

Nathan stood leaning against his desk listening to Daniel and April. Nathan watched the two of them. He couldn't imagine being either of them. He had his fair share of guilt, but what they must be feeling was beyond that. None of this was their fault, but to know someone capable of murder was a burden no one should have to bear.

April stared at Daniel with tears in her eyes waiting for him to speak.

"April, he loved you in his own sick way. I truly believe under it all, he missed you. But the truth is, this was about betrayal. *We* loved you. You were a part of our family, and then you left. *His* family loved you too much, and when you left him, you destroyed his world and took all his aspirations with you. You emasculated him, took his own family from him. We were so busy mourning over you that we didn't comfort him in the way he thought we should. In his eyes, our—our loyalty lied with you, not him, and that made him feel weak and powerless. This, this was his way—"

"Of showing that he still had control." Nathan interjected as he walked closer to them.

Nathan sighed heavily as he looked April in the eyes. How do you tell two people who loved Brooks, that the darkness in his soul was always there. That it took root long before he met April. "You will never understand why he did the things he did. Brooks was angry and hateful, and he never learned one of the most important lessons, that hate corrodes the container it's carried in."

Nathan pulled the Impala over on the shoulder of the road. He sat there for a moment and then quickly climbed out of the car slamming the door behind him. He walked forward, took a deep breath, and then took a seat on the hood.

"Tess, if you can hear me—"

"I'm here Nathan."

He turned at the sound of her voice; she was walking towards him from the back of the vehicle. She wore her simple, lavender dress and her hair hung loose at her shoulders. Even after countless conversations with her, he still felt his heart skip a beat whenever she appeared. She was staggering in life and now, in death, she was heartbreakingly beautiful.

She walked slowly and gently hopped up on the hood of the Impala next to him. He smiled over at her and together they leaned back on the hood and stared up into the night sky.

After what must have been a half an hour or so, Nathan cleared his throat. "I miss this."

She turned her head to face him. He kept his head straight still staring up at the stars. "Star gazing?" She asked.

At that, he turned to face her. "No. I miss this. Lying here with you."

"Me too." She murmured softly.

Nathan returned his gaze back up at the stars. "It's moments like these that I remember finding a stillness and a bravery within myself that I didn't know was possible to have until I had you. But now—"

"You're worried you won't feel that way again?"

"It's more that I already don't feel that way."

Tess pulled herself up to a sitting position and waited as Nathan did the same.

"The truth is Tess, there's no threat anymore, yet I can't help but feel like those kids are better off without me."

"Nathan, how could you think that?"

"Because Tess, I have never felt more incapable of taking care of someone in my life."

Chapter Thirty

They sat alone in the living room not saying a single word to each other letting the silence fill the distance between them. A cool breeze drifted in through the window, and the sun shone brightly outside. Tess always loved days like these; days sitting in the sun's rays and soaking them in. He sat in his chair with his elbows on his knees and his hands on his head and then he slowly looked up at her.

She was so beautiful sitting there on the couch. The sun from the windows danced along her arm and glimmered brilliantly on her hair that cascaded down her shoulders, and those beautiful, green eyes were gleaming at him with a fire that reached down into his soul. There were days he hated her for how beautiful she was. No matter how angry he was, he would still get lost in her, completely spellbound. She weaved some pretty powerful magic that left his heart aching in its wake.

Overwhelmed by her presence and her immensity in his life, his voice disrupted the silence. "I worked hard to be the kind of man you deserved, be the kind of man that our children deserved; and along the way I started to believe in my dreams again. I started to believe that people just go through things, challenges that make them stronger, and then, you were gone. I waited for you there at the bridge, and you never came. You never came back to me. And I realized that we're not invincible. Dreams die. And so did you."

His breathing trembled from his speech. He had been so sad for so long, and finally saying it out loud—he didn't realize the anger he had been masking. He had kept her gaze throughout his speech, and he noticed how perfectly still she stayed. She didn't flinch nor move. She just sat there and listened deeply.

Seconds ticked by slowly, and then he watched as Tess shifted her weight on the couch and leaned forward. Her eyes now piercing his vision. How was this possible? Why did she still come to him? He wasn't dreaming; she was there. She invaded his life even after her death. It wasn't fair to see her and not be with her, to not be able to hold and touch her.

"So now what are you going to do? Sit on this couch and watch ball, afraid to live? That's what you're going to do? That really pisses me off. You know why? Cause you have a second chance. You get to be with our children, watch them grow—love them. But I never will." Her voice was stern and commanding, but that didn't surprise Nathan. Tess's presence alone always commanded the attention of anyone near her.

She stood up and softly walked over to where he was sitting. She kneeled down next to him, exhaled softly, and looked into his eyes. With an uncompromising yet gentle voice she said, "So damn it, you can't sit here and let those beautiful kids grow up without a father too."

———— •••◆•◆•• ————

"How are they Pops?" Nathan spoke softly in the dim lights of the hallway as he peered into Parker's room.

Parker was fast asleep with his arm wrapped tightly around Henley who slept easily in his arms. Nathan couldn't help the sudden pang of guilt that he felt when he thought about the fact that he considered not bringing his kids home. The thought now of not having them here with him seemed cruel and devastating.

Jack scratched the rough stubble on his chin and smiled a soft genial grin at Nathan. "Better now that they're home."

———— •••◆•◆•• ————

Nathan smiled an all-teeth-showing smile when he heard the sounds of little feet coming down the staircase.

"Good morning, pumpkin." He bent down to Henley's level and stretched his arms out wide for her to run to. She beamed up at him with a radiant, cheerful grin and leapt into his arms.

Nathan laughed softly as he stood up with her in his arms hugging her close.

"Oh, I missed you, baby girl."

"I missed you too, Daddy."

He gently set her down on the kitchen counter and smoothed away her wild hair from covering her eye. He laughed to himself; she was so much like her mother in every way.

"Want to help stir the batter?" He presented a wooden spoon to her and pushed the large bowl towards her on the counter.

Henley's bright, blue eyes widened in undiluted joy, and she gave him a face-splitting grin. "Waffles?!"

Nathan couldn't contain his elation. He hadn't seen Henley so happy in such a long time. He didn't realize until that very moment just how much he had missed this, or just how healing it could be for the both of them.

He bent forward and rubbed his nose against hers making her giggle as he whispered, "It is Sunday last I checked."

She gushed with excitement and quickly got to work mixing the batter. Nathan bit his lip trying to stifle the laughter as he watched his daughter. She quickly tucked a piece of hair behind her ears and furrowed her brows in determined concentration and her tongue poking out of the side of her mouth as she worked.

After Nathan poured a round of batter into the machine, he walked over to the high shelf in the kitchen and lightly tapped on the small, black boom box. He stood there silently for a moment and smiled a sad, bittersweet smile as the music slowly kicked on.

Finding a hidden strength and courage in himself, he spun around to face Henley. He grinned widely at her as he stepped closer and held his palms up in front of her. She smiled and slapped her little hands down onto his, and he lifted her off the counter and onto the ground.

"Ready?"

She nodded in exaggerated movements and smiled as the two of them danced around the kitchen with each other. Nathan laughed and smiled as he watched Henley twirl around the kitchen to the beat of *'Do You Love Me?'*. She giggled and held tightly to Nathan's out-stretched hand as he attempted to teach her how to do the twist.

When Nathan looked up, his laughter faded out as he straightened himself. Parker was standing at the kitchen entrance gawking at the two of them dancing in the kitchen. Nathan shrugged light-heartedly and gave Parker an apologetic smile. Parker shook his head in quiet laughter.

"Parker! Come dance with us!" Henley screamed in shrill laughter as she held out her hand for Parker to take.

Nathan hesitated, looking from Parker to Henley, but he couldn't control the unbelievably large smile that spread across his face as he watched Parker sigh in defeat. Parker lunged forward grabbing Henley's hand and twirled her around the kitchen. Henley's contagious giggle erupted as she and Parker danced in circles around the kitchen.

Nathan's head fell back in pure, unbridled laughter. The kind of laughter that started from somewhere deep in the pit of his stomach and continued its assault relentlessly.

He joined Parker and Henley as they danced around the kitchen. Once Nathan got in front of them, he threw his arms out wide like Tess used to and motioned for them to follow suit. With their arms out wide, they leaned and tilted their arms like wings as they glided around the kitchen.

As the song was nearing the end, something caught Nathan's attention and his head snapped up. Standing at the kitchen entrance was Tess.

She was wearing a floral print, summer dress, her hair hung loose around her face, and she was smiling. She clapped her hands silently in front of her and he watched her laugh and smile the most beautiful, joyous smile he had ever seen. Tess swayed to the music subtly and beamed over at her family as she watched them dance in the kitchen like she used to do with Nathan.

It was the first moment since she appeared to him that Nathan finally understood what she meant when she said she was happy. And now, he truly felt like his family would be okay.

Chapter Thirty-One

Nathan squinted his eyes against the radiant, warm light. He drew his hand up to block out the sun as his eyes adjusted to his surroundings.

Something felt foreign about this place, and yet he felt as though his mind, body, and soul were at peace. He glanced down at himself and frowned slightly at his clothes; he didn't remember changing into them.

He wore a soft linen, button-up, white shirt undone at the top, khaki pants, and was barefoot. He stared down at his feet confused at the grass beneath them.

After momentarily examining himself, he raised his eyes. It was a warm, summer day and the sun shone down on him. He was standing in a garden. The grass was a brilliant, raging green; ahead of him was the mythical Angel Oak Tree looming up around him. He shook his head in puzzlement. He recognized the tree from pictures of Tess's vacations in South Carolina, but this tree wasn't as it was in pictures; its surroundings were different.

He looked at the base of the tree and tilted his head slightly to the left. Hundreds of Casablanca lilies poured out and around the tree. If he couldn't plainly see the shapes of the flowers, he would have assumed it was a running spring of white trickling out from the hollows of the tree. The flowers pooled out around the trunk stretching at least fifty feet around.

He gaped wildly at his surroundings stunned by the beauty and serenity in front of him. He had never seen something so fiercely beautiful—that is until she emerged.

With her hand lightly trailing along the trunk of the tree, she stepped around from behind and waded through the flowers towards him.

His breath hitched as he watched her slowly weave her way towards him. She wore a long, white gown with a ruched neckline and front slit accent that made her long leg glimmer in the sunlight as she moved. She bowed her head lightly in shyness, and he watched as her long, riotous, red hair fell softly down in front of her. Even with her hair pinned up on one side, he could see it still billowed out around her completely untamed and unchecked, just as it always had. Her green eyes gazed out from under thick, dark lashes against her fair skin.

He stood immobilized with his eyes locked on her and with bated breath waited for her to approach him. She dipped her head ever so slightly and then tilted it at the last moment just enough to let her eyes meet his as she placed her hands on his chest.

Nathan had to force himself to keep upright as he felt his legs wobble beneath him. He gaped down at her delicate hands on his chest, and he felt his heart begin to beat frantically against the feel of her hands on him. He stared at her completely beguiled. Her hands were warm on his chest, and he felt all the air escape his lips as he sucked in precious breath.

"Breathe, Nathan." She implored in a low whisper.

"Tess?" He struggled with her name.

She smiled timidly up at him as she stretched up on her toes and let her hands wind up and wrap around his neck. She gently pulled him close to her as her arms tightened around him, and he felt the steady beat of her heart thrumming against his chest.

"Tess?" He stuttered out once more as he let himself wrap his arms around her.

He breathed in the scent of her hair as he buried his face in her neck and squeezed her body into his. He didn't understand how or why it was possible, but to feel his wife, to hold her in his arms for the first time in nearly a year was everything he had ever dreamed of.

Tess didn't say a word. She stood wrapped in his embrace and gently caressed his head as he leaned into her. She smiled to herself letting the sensation of his touch wash over her.

"Tess, how is this possible?" He finally breathed against her neck.

"You've dreamed of me before."

Nathan pulled back slightly to face her without letting go. "Not like this Tess. This is different. This feels so *real*."

With one hand, she gently cupped his face and smiled as she watched him close his eyes and lean into her touch. When he opened his eyes, she could see the longing in his smoky, grey eyes and she whispered, "For now, maybe it is."

She pulled her hand back and wrapped it around his shoulder and pressed her face into his chest. "Will you dance with me?" She murmured against him as she puckered her lips and gently kissed the bare v of his chest.

He smiled as he kissed the top of her head and tightened his grip on her. "Anything for you."

Together they swayed gently spinning slow circles around the garden of lilies. Nathan quickly looked up as small, white petals drifted down all around them. A sense of warmth and peace washed over him as they clung tightly to each other embracing and savoring the feel of their bodies. The chance to remember what this felt like was more than Nathan could have ever hoped for, and he wanted nothing more than to have this moment last forever. With Tess's uncanny ability to read his mind, she pressed herself closer to him in an unspoken gesture that she too felt the same.

"This is goodbye, isn't it?" Nathan resistibly broke the shared silence with a voice no louder than a murmur.

She gently pressed her lips into his chest once before turning and leaning her cheek against him. "I'll never be far from you."

He stroked her hair softly with his hand. "Tess, I don't want to say goodbye."

She leaned back to look him in his warm, steel-grey eyes. "Then don't."

He stared down at her quizzically. "What do you mean?"

She cocked her head to the side and sighed lovingly. "Just because you won't be able to see me doesn't mean I won't be there. And on days that you just really can't stand the distance, you'll know where to find me."

"I don't understand?"

"I will always be there for you, and Parker and Henley, but on days that you just can't seem to feel me—look for me at the bridge. I'll always be there when you need me."

His chest tightened, and he pulled her in close to him once more. "You brave, beautiful girl, what am I going to do without you?"

She chuckled softly to herself. "You're going to watch our children grow up, and you are going to share hundreds of laughs and dances with them. In those moments, I will be there, I promise."

"You promise?"

She leaned back momentarily to give him her signature smile. "I wouldn't miss it for the world."

Before she could lean forward into his chest, he brought his hand up and rested it on her cheek with his fingers around the nape of her neck. He held her there and gazed amorously into her green eyes. He took a deep breath and leaned forward pressing his lips to hers. He forced himself to memorize every second of this last, passionate kiss with her. He needed to remember how his lips fit so perfectly against hers, how her breath curled in his mouth, and how her lips were always so warm and soft.

He pulled back ruefully as they caught their breaths. He pressed his forehead against hers and whispered, "I will continue to love you for every moment of forever, until kingdom come."

He gently kissed her forehead and watched as she closed her eyes savoring his touch, and she whispered, "'til kingdom come."

Chapter Thirty-Two

"Life vests on?" Nathan asked Parker and Henley from the dock as he, Tommy, and Jack started untying the sloop.

"Yep." They responded in unison.

Nathan took one last glance at the sloop, which finally had its new name adorned on the back: TESS. He smiled to himself before he hopped on board.

"Okay, good. Hold on tight and don't stand up." He ordered as the sloop lurched into motion making its way out of the marina.

As the sloop slowly sputtered out of the marina, Nathan took a deep breath looking back at the shore.

"See that diner up there?" He pointed to the Spar just on the edge of the marina.

"That's where Mom used to work, isn't it?" Parker piped up.

"Sure is. That's where I met her." He smiled fondly as they trolled through the water.

"Daddy, it's dark out here." Henley said peering around as they made their way into open water.

"It won't be too much longer, pumpkin." He cut the engine not far from shore and waited as other boats took their positions out on the water.

"What are they all doing?" Parker asked.

"I'm going to tell you the same thing I told your mom, they're waiting."

"What are they waiting for?" Henley asked.

Nathan squatted down low to face them towards the shore.

"Look up over there. Do you see it?" He asked quietly.

She gasped, "Fireflies. Millions and millions of fireflies!"

Parker cocked his head a little to the left. "Those are too big to be fireflies. What are they?"

Nathan reached into one of the cupboards and pulled out two mini, sky lanterns. He held them out before his kids.

"These are sky lanterns. You light them and send them up into the sky with your biggest wish and let the heavens sort them out." He smiled as he remembered the night he brought Tess here all those years ago.

"Your mommy is in heaven right now watching us. I'm sure she is dying to know your wishes, so she can help make them come true."

"Really?" Their eyes were wide with fascination.

"Really. Okay, now come on, hold out your hands." He showed them how to hold onto the lanterns as he lit them.

Tommy and Jack watched from behind them with faint traces of smiles on their faces.

"Okay, did you think of a wish?" He watched as Henley squished her eyes tightly together thinking of the perfect wish.

"I have mine." She exclaimed.

Nathan nodded and looked to Parker. "Me too," he said.

"Okay, on the count of three, you're gonna push them up into the sky like the rest of the lights out there. Ready? One, two, three."

He watched as both kids pushed the lanterns into the sky and stared in amazement as they took flight and joined the hundreds of other lights lining the night sky.

Watching their joy, he knew they needed this night. He knew he needed this night to finally say goodbye.

"Are you ready for this, Nate?" Jack clapped Nathan softly on the shoulder after having watched the lanterns in silence for a while.

"They need this. I need this." He confessed.

Jack shrugged his shoulders in agreement and made his way towards Tommy who was working on quietly tying up ropes on the bough of the sloop.

Nathan sighed heavily in abandoned longing as he gazed down at Parker and Henley who were sitting on the portside bench. He picked up an extra jacket and made his way back over to the kids and crouched down to their level once more.

"Here baby, put this on." Nathan helped Henley get into the larger coat.

Nathan looked back and forth between the kids as they both stared innocently at him.

"Did you know I took your mom out here on our second date together?"

They both shook their heads and Nathan smiled contritely.

"It was our second date, and your mom was the most beautiful girl I had ever seen in the entire world."

"I miss her." Parker stared down at his knotted fingers as he muttered under his breath.

Nathan reached his hand up and clasped Parker's hands under his. "I know buddy. Me too."

Nathan took a deep breath and exhaled softly before lifting a small wooden raft from under the bench. He held it out in front of him and placed three, solid white candles on it.

"There's a candle for each of us. Each candle represents your mother and the thing we miss most about her. We'll take turns lighting them and then we'll send this out to sea to join the others."

"The others?" Henley cocked her head slightly as she looked at Nathan.

He nodded for her to look behind her. Parker and Henley turned around immediately. Smiles spread across their faces as they watched the water light up with thousands of small candles on floating rafts. Parker was the first to turn back around to face Nathan. "What do I do?"

Nathan pulled a lighter from his pocket and handed it to Parker. "Close your eyes. Think really hard. What do you miss most about Mom?"

Parker obediently closed his eyes and let out a heady sigh. "I miss the way she used to tuck me in and sing me lullabies or tell me stories of faraway places. That's what I miss most."

Nathan's throat constricted as he helped Parker light his candle. He cleared his throat slightly and turned to Henley.

"Pumpkin?"

Henley looked up at him with her big, blue eyes and smiled. "I miss her hugs."

Parker dashed hastily at a fallen tear with the back of his hand as he murmured quietly, "She gave the best hugs."

Nathan tightened his lips to quiet an unbidden sob from escaping. He reached forward taking the lighter from Parker and lit Henley's candle. Nathan tried to take a steadying breath, but was disrupted when Jack and Tommy stepped closer.

Tommy shoved his hands in his pockets and bowed his head. "I miss her humor. She always knew how to make me laugh, especially when I didn't want to." He chuckled fondly as Nathan grinned up at him.

Jack cleared his throat. "I miss her cooking. Haven't had a good home cooked meal in ages." He snickered playfully as everyone laughed quietly with him.

Nathan shrugged his shoulders apologetically. "Sorry."

Jack smiled warmly. "No, what I truly miss most is the way she provided comfort like no other. She knew what to say and how to say it, making you feel like you were something special."

Nathan and Tommy shared a quick look and nodded. They knew better than anyone that Tess's ability to console them was one of her most loved qualities.

Nathan took a deep breath and held the lighter over the last candle. "It's hard to pick the one thing I miss most about your mom because there are so many things to miss. But, what I miss most is her faith and love in me. Your mom believed in me and loved me more than I thought possible—more than I deserved. I will miss that," his voice quieted to a whisper as he ushered out, "'til kingdom come." His hand shook slightly as he lit the last candle.

They stared in silence watching the gentle flicker of the flames in reverential commiseration. After a long moment, Nathan looked up at Parker and nodded to him. Parker carefully took the raft from Nathan's hands and walked over to the edge of the sloop. He leaned down over the bough and gently pushed the raft out onto the water.

They watched silently as the raft made its way to join the others. The gentle glow of flickering lights danced across the glassy water leaving a sense of peace in its wake.

⸻ ••◆◆•• ⸻

"Beer?" Nathan held out a beer to Tommy as he hopped up on the hood of the Impala in the garage.

"Thanks. Kids asleep?" Tommy asked as he took a seat next to Nathan.

"Yeah, they knocked out pretty quickly. I think tonight's festivities drained them."

Tommy cleared his throat lightly. "Yeah, but it was good for them, Nate. It was good for all of us."

Nathan took a sip of his beer and nodded with an impassive expression as he stared out into the night.

"Can I ask you something?"

"Sure." Nathan quickly glanced over at Tommy warily.

"Maybe this isn't the right time, but I guess I'd rather talk about something."

"What, you don't want to go home?" Nathan teased playfully.

Tommy chuckled. "No, I guess I don't. Like Parker said, it gets quiet."

Nathan immediately quieted and looked down at his hands. "I know what you mean." He sighed, "What was your question?"

"How did you know where Brooks was?"

Nathan almost spit out his beer as he looked over at Tommy. "Jeez, how long have you been holding onto that one?"

Tommy shrugged. "It's always nagged at me, but I dunno, I thought I'd wait for you to spill, but you never did."

Nathan let out a shallow breath as he turned his gaze avoiding Tommy's perplexed look. "Tess told me."

"That's the second time you've said something like that. What do you mean Nate?"

"It started about three months after she passed. Truthfully, I thought I had finally lost my mind with grief."

Tommy tried to catch Nathan's gaze with the most deadpan expression he could muster.

Nathan's shoulders heaved slightly. "Tess came to me, Tommy. She moved in and out of my dreams. She visited me when I needed her most."

"Nate, I'm really trying to understand here but I don't—" His voice cracked and withered as it faded out.

"I saw my dead wife, Tommy."

Tommy shook his head in disbelief. "So, what then? She was a ghost?"

"Or an angel." Nathan muttered inaudibly.

"Nate."

"There was a time, Tommy, where I thought knowing the answer to that question was important. But, the truth is, how I got to see her doesn't matter. All that matters is that I did and that she helped me in ways I will never begin to understand."

Tommy's rational self wanted to immediately refute the possibility, but his heart, his gut, told him Nathan was telling the truth. The 'how' wasn't important, like Nathan said. All that mattered was the 'why', and he knew the answer to that. She came to him because Tess was the one person in this world to make Nathan see straight. And, she was the one person in life who had enough magic in her soul to make seeing her possible in the after-life.

After a brief respite, Tommy shrugged his shoulders as he lifted the beer bottle to his lips. "I'm hurt she didn't haunt me at least once."

Nathan's eyes grew large with bemusement. "You believe me?" He ushered in an incredulous whisper.

Tommy turned to look Nathan dead on. "Nate, if it had been anyone else I would have taken you to the hospital to get your head examined, but we're not talking about just anyone. We're talking about Tess."

Nathan couldn't help the small chuckle that bubbled its way to the surface. He grinned widely at Tommy. "No, I guess you're right."

"How does Brooks fit into this though?"

Nathan clenched his teeth, although Brooks was safely behind bars, a small part of him still wished him dead after all he had put his entire world through.

"I'm mad at myself for not figuring it out the moment we knew it was him. Hell, a part of me is a little mad at Tess for not being more direct with me, but maybe there was a lesson in there, somewhere."

Tommy eyed him wearily as he waited for him to continue.

"Brooks toyed with me, he only gave me little hints as to why he chose me, but it was much deeper than that. He chose me because he *knew* Tess."

"Personally? You're telling me Brooks knew Tess, *personally*?" He gave a bewildered look as he tried desperately to process this information.

Nathan huffed roughly. "I told you about Tess's ex tracking her down in Canada, right?"

"Yeah, why—" he paused briefly as his mind filled in the gaps. "No fucking way. You're joking right?"

"Joke seemed to be on me, Tommy. I should have known the moment I saw where he did basic."

Tommy clenched his fist hard at his side. "I knew this guy was deranged, but his madness went that deep and that far back?"

Nathan chuckled softly to himself. Tess would be smiling down on Tommy, seeing how much he loved her too. "I'm pissed I didn't figure it out sooner, Brooks had the jump on me for that. I didn't fully understand until the moment I saw Tess standing there. She was standing by the bridge turn off and it was like this horrible, ugly truth just came slamming into focus."

Tommy let out a low deep breath as he absorbed this information. He shook his head to himself as he realized something that Nathan definitely hadn't. Tess would be so damn proud. For the first time in maybe ever, Nathan didn't *just* react. Even though Nathan learned of Brooks' involvement in Tess's hurt, he didn't let that blind him. He did things by the books. He wasn't reckless. He chuckled softly. Tess had really done it. She had really changed the man next to him, even after death.

Nathan eyed Tommy cautiously, unsure if he should break the silence.

Tommy straightened his expression once more. "So, tonight then?"

Nathan knew what Tommy was trying to ask. "Tonight, was my way of saying goodbye for the first time."

"She's not coming back?"

Nathan shook his head. "Not in that way. No."

Tommy's brow furrowed in question. "What do you mean?"

"I got to have conversations with my dead wife off and on for close to a year. I saw visions of her, dreams of her, and I was with her. That's more than anyone could ever ask for. But she knew, and deep down I knew—she couldn't stay forever."

Tommy nodded and patiently waited for Nathan to continue.

"She came to me in a dream last night to say goodbye. She let me know she would always be here with me and the kids, but I wouldn't be able to see her anymore."

"Are you okay?" Tommy's voice was so small it betrayed him.

"Yes and no. The thought of not seeing her anymore cuts me to the quick, but I think Tess knew that so she gave me a back door."

"What do you mean?"

Nathan smiled down at his hands that were tearing at his beer label. "She knew there would be times that I just needed to know she was here, so she told me where I could find her when I needed her most."

Tommy stared blankly at Nathan and watched as Nathan grinned softly. "She's waiting at the bridge, Tommy. Anytime I really need to know she's still with me, I can go there, and she'll be waiting for me."

"So, you *can* see her?"

"Not exactly. I woke up from my dream about three in the morning and decided to go to the bridge, and I finally understood."

Tommy looked at Nathan with a look that said, 'Yeah. Okay. And?'.

Nathan would never be able to fully articulate what Tess had taught him, but through her, he did learn that the weight of grief was not something you could set down—it was something you learned to carry.

"It was dark out when I got to the bridge. I waited maybe five minutes and then I saw it. Dancing over the water was a flickering light and I knew. I can't explain, but I knew it was her. She was there, just as she said she would be."

"Dad?"

Nathan stopped in his tracks in the dim hallway. He pushed the cracked door open further and peered into the darkness of Parker's room.

"You okay buddy? It's late. I thought you were asleep."

Nathan's eyes were having a hard time adjusting to the light, but he could still make out Parker sitting up in bed staring at him.

"I just wanted to let you know that I know what your wish was tonight."

"Parker?" He said his name again unsure of what to say in its place.

"I just wanted you to know that seeing her again was my wish too, but I'll keep it a secret so that maybe it'll come true for one of us at least."

Chapter Thirty-Three

"You, and you—in the back." Nathan teased in a gruff voice to the kids to get in the Impala.

"Where are we going Daddy?" Henley's little voice asked over the sound of the engine.

"We're going to see something very special." He said looking in his rearview mirror.

As the Impala slowed down along the asphalt, Nathan took a deep satisfying breath as he put the car in park. He turned around in his seat to face the kids. He looked at Parker whose face was ashen.

"Parker, you okay bud?"

Parker shook his head. "I don't want to be here."

Nathan pursed his lips and nodded his head. "Buddy, I wouldn't bring you here if I didn't think it would help. Trust me Parker, I was just as scared and angry as you when I considered coming here for the first time since—well, since your mom passed away."

Parker locked his eyes on his father's. "Then why bring us here?"

"Because there's something you need to see."

Parker shrugged his shoulders in solemn consent.

Nathan carried Henley in his arms and walked side by side with Parker as they made their way across the truss bridge. He stopped once they reached the center and motioned for Parker to look out over the water.

He cleared his throat. "Your mom is with us every, single day. Even if you can't see her, she's here. But, sometimes, it's hard to go on faith."

Parker's eyes darted up at Nathan, and he looked at him questioningly.

Nathan gave Parker a faint lopsided smile. "On days that you just can't feel your mom, or you just don't believe she's there with you, you can come here."

"Daddy?" Henley whispered.

He tightened his grip on her and nodded for her and Parker to look back out on the water.

"On days when you really miss her, come to this bridge and look out over the water and she'll be there."

"Dad what do you—"

"Is that Mommy?" Henley cut Parker off mid-sentence as she gaped out at the water in front of her.

Nathan smiled widely as he looked out at the flickering light dancing above the water in the dusky sky.

"That's her, baby."

Parker stared with his mouth open and tears in his eyes. After staring for a few quiet moments, he looked up at his father and whispered, "She's really here?"

Nathan tried to fight back his own tears. "Anytime you need to see her come to the bridge and look for the lights."

THE END

ACKNOWLEDGEMENTS

How can I even begin to express my gratitude to those that have supported me or given me the courage to publish this story?

I will start with someone that I never could have imagined the relationship I have now when I first met her. The day I met her, I went home and cried because I wasn't sure how I could spend every workday with someone who was so bubbly and charismatic, when I myself was not that way. Little did I know the love that absolutely grew, and now I hold her in my heart as one of the greatest friends and aunt to my daughter that I could have ever hoped for. Not only has she supported and encouraged me in everything I do, she worked tirelessly behind the scenes on this story. She proved herself to be a trusted advisor and editor that I owe so much to. The greatest gift of all was the time spent together working on this novel. Thank you Asemina Georgiadis, I will forever be grateful.

To my daughter, Bellamy Catherine: you may be little when this is published, but your impact on this project is profound. You have taught me to be courageous and tenacious and wildly unapologetic for pursing my dreams. No matter where this leads me, I hope you can look back and say, "My mom was brave, and that means I can be too."

To my parents, whose unwavering support and cheerleading taught me to continue on, even when my own self-doubt clouded my judgment.